A Right Royal Wedding

By Jayne Hecate

&

Ian Housby

Contents

Dedication...5

Chapter 1...7

Chapter 2...47

Chapter 3...85

Chapter 4...115

Chapter 4 and a bit more.................................153

Chapter 5...165

Chapter 6...195

Chapter 6 ½...213

Chapter 7...223

Chapter 8...253

Chapter 9...285

Chapter 10...319

About the Authors.................................341

Also available by the authors.................................343

The Cast 347

Bye then..349

Dedication

This year has seen us go on many adventures and also have some moments where the love and support of our friends has really got us through. So this book is dedicated to you all, our friends. Without you all, life would be harder than it already is.

PS. The Tories are still cunts!

Chapter 1

The table was laid out for a grand meal, twenty four places, with gold plated cutlery, bone china side plates and crystal glasses. The Butler had carefully filled an antique crystal decanter that was shaped like a royal swan about to take flight (a tasteless thing that had been a gift decades before from the British royal family, but which Queen Linda seemed to like!). He had then left the wine to breathe for exactly twenty four minutes before replacing the crystal glass stopper. The dining room was immaculate, every place setting had been measured by the Butler using his silver plated set square to ensure that each item was the exact same distance from the edge of the table and from each guest. The meal was set for a quarter past Hedgehog throttling time, or for those more used to a military clock rather than the archaic Faerie clock, thirteen fifteen hours. The guests had gathered in the room formerly known as the smoking room, which was no longer used for smoking since the King had outlawed smoking on all royal grounds. The Butler had shaken his head sadly at that piece of news as he had been ordered to put the smoking apparatus into the deepest, darkest part of the palace basements, including his favourite Elvish Silver Hookah. This metallic eyesore had been made in the shape of the famous singer from the human Elvis. Elvis (it rather surprisingly!), turned out to have been half Fae, who had faked his own demise in the human world when he had grown tired of the fame he had accrued there. So it was that he returned to Faerie Realm with his favourite guitar and moved on to a small cabin in the wildwood where he chose to live out his final days singing for the trees. Unfortunately, he had been crushed to death by a sentient oak that had asked him three times to shut up while it recovered from a particularly petulant hangover.

When King Bobney arrived in the dining room, he was dressed in the pale green lightweight trousers, green high wicking t-shirt and black plimsolls of the Special Faerie Service sports training kit. The Colonel of the Special Faerie Service was dressed almost identically to the King, but wore a dusky green beret and walked a step behind the King, while laughing with the General. The General was dressed in her smart green daily uniform and she wore the special cap badge that showed that she had previously served with the Special Faerie Service. Walking with a highly polished cane and on the arm of a friend, came Felicity Hopeforthebest. Her friend whose arm she held was that of the retired Colonel and current Lighthouse Keeper and intelligence officer, Mr Olajlámpás. Next to enter the room came the city Wizard, Professor Brianco Oxx, who was engrossed in conversation with the Chancellor of the University, Professor Sophie Daphodils. He was dressed in the dark purple robes of his magical office, which clashed abominably with the bright white training shoes he had purchased on last trip to the human world. The Chancellor was dressed in her University Gown, over the top of her suit trousers and a purple silk top, with black low heeled shoes. The final two guests were Queen Linda, who was happily chatting with the city Mayor, Wuffles.

The Butler directed the guests to their seats at the table of the King, rising in rank to the King's chair at the head of the table and opposite the King's throne for him to retire to once the meal was finished. Bobney gave the Butler a subtle look of concern and strode down the length of the dining room and took a seat next to his friend, Colonel

Thrashgood. The Butler dropped his head sadly and tried not to let his disappointment show as the King pushed the plates and glasses aside so that he could lay out a large plan map of the city, using some of the heavier cutlery and glassware to hold down the thick old paper maps that wanted to curl back up.

"Right, now that we are all here, I want you all to look at this because we have a serious problem in this area." He pointed to an area of Winscombe that had had been carefully outlined in red ink. It was the part of the city that had over the decades become a filthy slum, the streets ran with sewage, the housing was awful and when the great plague had entered the city, the poor folk who resided there had suffered the worst of all of the city residents.

"As King, I cannot in good conscience allow these people to live here in such filth." He pressed his forefinger onto the page and tapped it hard. "This place is bloody revolting and the poor people living there are forced into abject squalor."

Queen Linda leant across the table and whispered to her son. "Darling, you cannot simply bulldoze people's homes just because you are King."

King Bobney gave his Mother a look, that had it been directed at anyone else, they would have wet them or withered up with shame. When he spoke, his voice was carefully controlled. "Mother, these bloody people need our help, not our ignorance. We must make this area suitable for the families that live there, so that they can live peaceful happy lives that do not include having to wade through liquid shit every time it rains for more than an hour."

Queen Linda smiled, it was a smile of pure pleasure and great pride. "Bobney, I could not be more proud of how much you care about your people." Her face became stony. "But, those people chose to live there, it is not our place to tell them how to live."

Bobney stood back up and then leaned forwards across the table towards her and with a barely controlled snarl of anger spoke again. "It is my duty as King to ensure that they can live, work and thrive in a clean, safe environment."

Wuffles, seeing that the air was growing hostile, interrupted with a small whine, which caused the King and his mother to turn away from each other and face the hound. Wuffles wagged his tail twice, gave a short yap, dropped his left ear and growled slightly, before raising his paw up high and seeming to kick it in the air twice.

"See, Wuffles agrees with me." Said King Bobney quietly, a dark smile on his face. "He knows that those people need our help."

Queen Linda took a deep breath. "OK, that maybe so and our new Mayor has made a very good point." She looked towards the Chancellor of the University. "However, Chancellor Daphodils has asked that we consider her plan for extending the university and building a new halls of residence. Maybe we could relocate the people to the edge of the city and build the new halls there?"

King Bobney turned to face the Chancellor. Her face had the look of someone who had asked for a penny, but had been given a dollar, albeit, buried in a pile of convulsing shit. "Is this something that you would consider as viable Chancellor?"

"Actually," said the Chancellor tactfully. "I have brought some first draft plans with me that would extend the university out towards the back of our land, with maybe a possible purchase of some of the King's land to build the halls on?" She pointed to a small area of green parkland on the map that showed where previous Kings had cultivated flowers, trees and hunting lands exclusively for royal use.

"I can answer that right now Chancellor. Go ahead. You can dig up the whole fucking travesty and put it to some actual use." Said King Bobney jovially.

"Actually dear," interrupted Queen Linda again,

"that is where Craig and I take our evening walks."
The King gave his mother a hard look. "Yes I am aware Mother, Craig has told me that he hates the place and only goes there to keep you quiet!"
Queen Linda blushed a deep shade of purple. "I would have you know that it was in that park that Craig and I held hands for the first time, on our first walk together after we were engaged." There was a small murmur of hushed whispers from around the table and the Queen continued. "That park is one of the few places where we can be private together."
The King blinked slowly. "Mother, you have ample lands for taking private walks in the palace and I hardly think that you and Craig should be copulating in the park, it sets a bad precedent!"
Despite his best efforts, Colonel Thrashgood did not manage to stifle his laugh and Queen Linda shot him an eyeful of daggers before she turned back to the King. "I shall ignore your tone, however, we do not copulate in the park. We are hardly rutting animals!"
Professor Sophie Daphodils cleared her throat before speaking quietly, but firmly. "As chancellor of the university, I can assure you that have we have no desire to upset the royal household. I am sure that we can find another site."

King Bobney looked at her and grinned. "Thank you Professor for your act of diplomacy. However, you can start work on that site right away."

Queen Linda stood up and was about to walk away when she felt a small damp nose in her hand. Wuffles sat in front of her and dropped an ear and looked at her quizzically. He whined slightly and let out a sudden yip and then wagged his tail furiously.

The King clapped his hands. "Thank you Mister Mayor, that is an excellent suggestion. The people will love it if Queen Linda, the royal Mother, was to take up their cause and ask them to work with her redeveloping the inner city slum area."

Queen Linda's shoulders slumped slightly and she returned to her seat. "Don't think that I will forgive you for taking away my park my boy. I love that park."

The Professor spoke up again. "Excuse me Queen Linda, would you do us the honour of becoming our patron figurehead and adviser to the designer of the new building?" She passed a small copy of the plans to Linda. "Perhaps if you have a quick look at these plans, you will see that it was always our aim to keep the beauty of the area and to actually erect a building that is considerably more ecologically considerate of the surrounding parklands."

"Thank you Professor." Said the King firmly, while giving his mother a dark look. "Turning to other business now." He sat down and turned his face to The General of the armed forces, the seemingly taciturn looking Gladys Meuchelmorder. When he spoke, his voice had softened and was somehow more appreciative of his guest having been there. "May I ask how the troops are settling into their new accommodations?" As he waited for her reply he found himself gazing at her. She was a magnificent woman, no one could realistically call her beautiful as she sat in her stern military uniform, yet she carried herself with such grace and elegance that the King found his eyes drawn to her across any room she entered.

Queen Linda stared at her son mystified at his sudden and apparent change in mood and when she turned her head to follow his gaze, she found that it ended at Gladys. It was at that precise moment that she knew that her son was profoundly and utterly devotedly in love with the woman, even if he was not yet ready to admit it to himself. She looked across the table to where a quiet and thoughtful Felicity Hopeforthebest was sat reading a report and after two seconds of hard staring, Felicity looked up to Linda, who flicked her eyebrows meaningfully at

Felicity, towards King Bobney. Felicity looked at the King for the first time during the meeting and suddenly her face broke into a happy beaming smile. She turned back to Linda and nodded her head, silently laughing. "It's so beautiful," she mouthed silently to Linda.

General Meuchelmorder cleared her Throat. "Your Majesty," As she spoke, she gently bowed her head. "The troops are honoured to have taken over the royal summer residence. As we speak, all ranks are working hard, converting the grounds to include extra living shared quarters for those without dependant families, with a small housing development being built to house the families of married soldiers."

"That is wonderful to hear, General." The King purred, his voice soft, happy and respectful of the woman before him. "Please carry on with your report, General Meuchelmorder."

Gladys smiled at the King, it was the sort of smile that fills the person's face with happy radiance, the purity of her spirit shining through to the love in her heart.

Queen Linda let out a sudden high pitched squeak as she contained her gleeful laughter. She felt a sudden gentle kick against her shin and looked up at her attacker, Colonel Thrashgood, who was sat opposite her. He was rapidly swiping at his throat with the flat of his hand, trying to get her to kill her laughter, which only made her snigger more loudly, which in turn forced her to pretend to cough and reach for a glass of water. Thrashgood turned to Felicity and she smiled as she gently shook her head. Neither the King nor the General noticed any of the tiny fuss around the table, for as far as they were concerned, no one else in the entire universe existed for those few brief seconds that they filled each other's gaze.

The room fell silent and finally realising that he had other duties to attend to that did not include gazing at the General, the King broke his gaze and turned back to the other members of the meeting. "So we are looking to redevelop parts of the capital city, but what of the city's outlying regions and our trade with our allies in other parts of the Realm?"

Wuffles yipped and whined, waggled an ear and raised his lip in a slight snarl, before letting out a long slow whine of unhappiness.

The King nodded his head and let out a sad sigh too. "So what can we do?"

Felicity Hopeforthebest spoke up. "Sadly our esteemed Mayor has hit the nail on the head, we simply do not have enough water to sustain the inner city let alone the suburbs and the reservoirs are already dangerously low." She shuffled through the papers in front of her and then found the pages she needed, before continuing. "Construction of a new reservoir is a possibility, but we will need a feasibility study to look for a suitable location." She turned to the Chancellor of the university, "Professor Daphodils has a team working on the problem, so if I may ask her for her input on this matter?"

The Chancellor nodded politely to Felicity, "my learned friend is correct in all aspects of this matter. The University currently has a team from the very best among the environmental department and they are working on the problem, with input from the Fae representative of Mother Nature." She paused as she handed out some sheets of paper. "If you look at the sites chosen, you will see that which ever site we choose, we are looking at major development and some compulsory purchase orders to buy up the land. All of which will cause some significant short term disruption"

"How much land are we talking about?" Asked the King, his voice filled with concern.

The Chancellor turned to Felicity with a half smile

and Felicity gave her friend a nod of encouragement. The Chancellor took a deep breath and spoke with brevity. "We need at least three square kilometres for the reservoir and dam." She looked around the room, but no one was disagreeing with her. "We have also developed a plan where we could put in place a hydro power plant, during building, with catch pools on the lower level to store drinking water."

"Excuse me asking, but why do we need this hydro power plant?" Asked Queen Linda, her voice full of concern.

"We fully expect to outstrip the current electricity demand levels within the next thirty years." Stated Felicity. "This would be a case of pre-empting the increased demand by building in future proofing expansion. By the time the hydro dam is ready, we should be able to shut down all of the current power plants and be able to rely upon the entirely sustainable renewable energy generation systems."

"If I may add something to the conversation at this point?" Said the Wizard politely. "I have been working with both Ms Hopeforthebest, and the Chancellor and her energy studies researchers on this project." He nodded to the Chancellor and she smiled back at him, her eyes glittering. His face reddened slightly, but he continued with his input. "We have found that because the energy used and the energy supplied are not exactly the same, there are peak times when energy is in greater demand and slump times when we are looking at over production."

"I see," said the King nodding his understanding.

"So," continued the Magician. "I have been leading a team made up of the University researchers and some practitioners of the arcane, to develop a system of energy capture and safe storage."

"How has this been developing?" Asked the King.

"Thus far, not great." Said the Chancellor. "Storing energy in the raw state requires being able to effectively hold lightning in a jar, which as I am sure you can imagine, is extremely dangerous. We have already had some minor accidents that have required some of our team to require medical treatment for minor burns and exposure to huge EM fields."

"How is this safe?" Queen Linda demanded to know, her voice shrill with concern. "We cannot put the lives of those involved at risk."

"Absolutely," stated the Chancellor firmly. "However, some areas of this research have led to unexpected results, which we have now accounted for, ensuring that extra safety protocols have been put in place."

"So," said the King, "what would you say is the expected time line for developing this energy storage system?"

"I fully expect that the systems will be perfected by the time the dam is ready for start up." Stated the Chancellor.

She nodded to Felicity who continued. "However, that is going to take roughly seven years of construction, once the site has been approved and all land purchase orders have been carried out and then all forms of sentient life have been relocated."

Wuffles let out a sad whine and put his paw on the table and gave it a couple of firm taps and dropped his ears down low.

"I acknowledge your distress, Mayor," said the King sadly. "There is indeed both a long term and a short term problem facing our great city. However, we shall have to make do with the current infrastructure until the new dam can be built." The King turned to Mr Olajlámpás. "Now if I may I ask the chief of our underground network, how things are going within our city?"

"My quiet investigations and work with both General Meuchelmorder and Colonel Thrashgood have thus far revealed that the city folk are, in general terms, reasonably supportive of the new administration under Mayor Wuffles." He let out a small chuckle, "Let's all face a hard truth here, Mayor Wuffles is the first Mayor in many years to take the civic responsibility of the role seriously and some of the internal systems have required a major rethink."

Wuffles yipped brightly and wagged his tail twice more, with his head up and his ears fully forwards.

Mr Olajlámpás nodded to Wuffles. "Mr Mayor, you are indeed kind with your words, however, this is your doing not mine. I am simply reporting the word from the streets."

Queen Linda leaned forwards and let out a hiss of annoyance. "I am not sure I approve of these secret Police operatives, spying within the city. When did Winscombe become a Police State?"

Mr Olajlámpás shook his head, "Madam, I suspect that you have me at crossed purposes."

"How so?" She said archly, her eyebrows showing her inclination not to believe the elderly Fae.

He smiled as he spoke. "The operatives I refer to are not any kind of police force, but we are enablers, simply listening to the people."

The Queen folded her arms across her chest.

"Surely, we should listen to the people in a public forum, instead of using spies on the streets?"

The General coughed quietly and spoke with a gentle reserve. "If I may your Highness, the people we speak to are the very same ones who approach us with their concerns. We find that these days, the older style of public forums are not trusted by the very people they are for. The word from the street is that public forums are usually overrun by loud-mouthed, overly opinionated, under educated or ignorantly misinformed individuals."

"As always, General," the King's voice was wistful and seemed unusually light. "You have your finger on the pulse of the city."

The General smiled at the King, her face seemed to glow when she looked at him and likewise the King smiled at her, with his eyes seemingly filled with wonder.

"Well, I am not happy about this." Said Queen Linda tersely, "I am old enough to remember the Stasi, in East Germany."

Realising that the King and the General were still gazing at each other, Colonel Thrashgood spoke up. "I give you my word Ma'am, we are not using any methods that are in any way impacting on the civil liberties of the people."

Mayor Wuffles whined and shook his head, before adding a small yip of approval.

"Thank you Sir," said Colonel Thrashgood in reply to Wuffles. "The armed services are here for the people, we are proud to work with your office and as you have confirmed, we do not spy on any individual."

The King suddenly realised that conversation was continuing while he was drowning in the eyes of a beautiful woman. He looked up as if waking from a pleasant dream. "Well, thank you for your reports, all of you, they were most enlightening." He looked around the room and noticed that Queen Linda was staring at him with an unreadable look on her face, Felicity and Colonel Thrashgood were quietly whispering to each other and the Chancellor and the Wizard were both writing small notes on the pieces of paper that they were examining.

"Do we have any last business to discuss before I call a close to this meeting?"

"I can think of a couple of things." Said Queen Linda to herself.

"I beg your pardon Mother?" Said King Bobney, giving her a sideways look.

"Ah um..." Queen Linda suddenly reddened. "Well actually, yes. I have some news from the human world."

"I dread to think what that could be, but go ahead, you have the floor so to speak." Replied the King unenthusiastically, his face suddenly dark.

Queen Linda sat up and spoke with a hint of sadness in her voice. "As some of you will be aware, last year we lost a member of our distant family, when our dear Queen Elizabeth passed away. We sent a representative of the Faerie Realm in the form of myself and my companion, Craig, to the funeral."

"I am aware Mother, thank you for your service to the Realm."

The Queen shot the King an acid look. "It was somewhat more than service to the Realm my dear boy, we are family, albeit distant." Her face showed her anger, but it quickly mellowed and she continued. "However, her oldest son is to be crowned King and we should again have a representation at the coronation."

The King nodded his head. "I shall inform Craig myself, that he is to accompany you to the service. I for one am not keen to show my face at the event, the new King is a little too partial to his shotguns and bird shoots for my liking. He has had rather more 'accidental' Fae casualties that I am comfortable with."

"Now you show some respect you little bast..." Queen Linda hissed and she suddenly felt all of the eyes in the room on her and none of them seemed friendly. She nodded her head politely. "I am sorry, I meant no offence to the room or to my son the King."

"Thank you Mother." Said Bobney, his eyes narrow, knowing full well that when they were in their more informal quarters, she would no doubt give him an earful.

"So I was thinking that maybe, The Faerie King himself, with maybe a beautiful Fae woman as his companion should be in attendance." Queen Linda said gently.

"Thank you for your invite Mother, but I shall prefer to send Craig in my place."

Queen Linda smiled, it was a backhanded compliment, but she took it none the less. "Well actually, I was thinking it would maybe make more of a statement if you were to attend, and maybe you could take the delightful and dedicated General Meuchelmorder as your companion?"

The King let out a small chuckle. "Mother, I am sure that the head of the armed forced for the entire Faerie Realm, has significantly more important things to attend to, than to accompany me to some damnable event in the human Realm." He turned to the General, "would you not say General Meuchelmorder?"

Gladys smiled kindly at the King. "Being your personal Guard at such occasions is a position that I would consider to be one of my most important duties, your Highness. We wish only to serve the Kingdom and the people who reside within it."

Queen Linda shook her head and let out an exasperated laugh. Neither of the two idiots were getting the hints. She rolled her eyes and turned to look at Colonel Thrashgood who was silently laughing.

"Well, if that is all of today's business," said the King jovially, "Shall we have lunch?" He waved over to the waiting Butler. "Would you care to join us too, it seems only fair that you should since you put it all out for us?"

The Butler felt a small part of himself wither inside as he gently declined the King's offer, especially when the King poured a glass of sparking wine and offered it to him.

After lunch the King gave his friends a broad smile as he stood up and spoke calmly, "well my friends, you will have to excuse us, Thrashgood and I have some recruits to run around the field."

The Butler shook his head, it was not right for a King to enjoy getting muddy, while playing with the troops, especially during a time of peace. He stood quietly at the back of the room, waiting for the royal attendees to leave, so that he could tidy the room, have the dishes taken away for washing and then reset the dining room. Alone with his thoughts, he had not noticed that the King had padded across the room towards him.

"I am terribly sorry, but I don't know your name, I only know you as Butler."

"As it should be, Sire." Said the Butler sagely, gently bowing his head as he spoke.

The King frowned, "well Butler, would you be so kind as to gather all of the staff for me, at evening meal this evening please? I would like to have a meeting with them, yourself included."

"It is not usual for the King to meet the palace Staff Sire, we are here to serve, silently and without complaint. If you have any complaints or new demands, I am here to pass your wants or concerns on to them."

The King remained calm. "Think of it as a royal order, if that is more comfortable for you."

"Yes Sire, thank you." Said the Butler. "It shall be

done."

"Jolly good old bean, well don't let me hold you up, I am sure that it must be time for your own lunch. Off you go old chap."

The Butler tried to stifle his gasp, to be dismissed from his duty by the King was unheard of. His eyes wildly searched the King's face looking for signs of disappointment and when he found none, finally he turned to Queen Linda who was stood nearby and silently appealed to her. Seeing his distress, Queen Linda wandered over and quietly spoke to her son, in a voice only he could hear.

The King snorted and let out a harsh exclamation. "Utter nonsense. This is exactly the sort of thing that I want to change." He turned back to the Butler, "I beg your pardon, Sir. You are free to go about your duties."

The Butler fled the room, his heart pounding, his mind almost wild, his eyes dripping with tears.

The other guests had left, along with Queen Linda, only Colonel Thrashgood remained and he was flicking through some important messages from his staff on his phone as the King wandered back. He looked up at the King and flashed him a grin, "You ready to go and beast some new recruits?"

Bobney nodded his head, "more than you can imagine. This place is driving me fucking nuts with all of the customs and deference. They are fucking people, not slaves to my whims."

Thrashgood nodded his understanding and gave the King an understanding smile. "Think of it in terms of military law, they are simply showing respect to a higher rank." Replied Thrashgood good naturedly.

"That's as maybe, but I'm sick of it. I didn't ask to be King, in some cases these people are better educated and have lived more useful lives than I have and they treat me like I'm special and know shit that they don't." Said Bobney as they wandered through the doors from the dining room and out into the hallway.

"To be fair, the previous King was a bit of a cu..." Thrashgood suddenly stopped, his face turned crimson. "I'm so sorry, your Highness."

"Don't you bloody well start too!" Said Bobney chuckling. "Listen, first and foremost, we are friends. Our jobs come second."

Thrashgood grinned, it was good natured and looked mischievous on the warrior's face. "It is just a bit harder when your best mate is also the King."

Bobney stopped and faced Thrashgood. "Did you just call me your best mate?"

Thrashgood grinned. "Well, to be fair, we do hang out a lot. So yeah."

Bobney looked happy and then crestfallen. "Do I stop you hanging around your other friends? What about your other half?"

Thrashgood put a hand firmly on the King's shoulder. "Listen, Bobney. Strictly between us as friends." He paused for a moment and Bobney leaned in closer. "You're being a silly twat."

Bobney roared with laughter. When he finally managed to speak, he had only kind words for his friend. "Do you know, that is exactly what I needed to hear?" He patted the Colonel on the back, "You are a damn fine officer Thrashgood, the service should be proud to have you."

"Go easy on them though," said Thrashgood sagely. "They have endured too many years of service to some guy who thought that he was all but a god." He gave the King a broad grin. "Now they have a King who wants to be one of the lads with them. You need to respect them, as much as they respect you. They are not showing deference to a belief they don't want. This is a good job for them." He leaned in close again to the King. "You should check out the war record of that old war horse you have for a Butler, by the way. That guy would give his life saving yours and do so with a smile on his face. Not because of you per-say, but for the office you represent."

The King nodded. "Thank you, I hadn't thought of it like that."

Thrashgood grinned again, "I know, come on we have some recruits to beast and I heard that the Princess is back from mission, so they are about to meet a Royal dragon for the first time."

The King grinned, the first time the recruits ran past the Princess always brought a smile to his face. She was a graceful, elegant creature, her scales often buffed to a high shine when she was on parade, her medals pinned to a sash she proudly wore as a representative of the Dragon royal families. However on the filthy damp field runs, she was often heavily disguised in mud, with just the narrow slits of her bright orange eyes visible as she lay in wait to ambush them. Then as the recruits trotted past unaware of the danger they had wandered into, she would rise from the mud and roar, a jet of blue flame, hotter than a welding torch scorching the ground. For some, the encounter was terrifying and quickly put them off of the idea of joining the elite unit known as the Special Faerie Service. Those who made it past the Princess without losing the contents of their bowels into their military issue under garments, were moved onto the next level of training. It was for this reason that the drop out rate was so high and the number of applicants finally accepted into the SFS was so low.

The Butler was sat in his room and polishing his medals. There were six of them in total and all had been awarded for feats of incredible bravery. In his three hundred years of life, he had fought in several wars and each one had left him sickened by the violence and death of battle and with feelings of despair that the old ways would never change. When it came for his time to retire from the Army, with all of the pomp and ceremony that went with the event, he took on the job as Butler to the old King. When the old King died, it had been the Butler who had prepared his remains and informed the royal household. He had lowered the standards that hung on the walls above the palace and insisted that all staff wear a black armband for the period of mourning that he considered the old King deserved. The Old King had not been a good King and he had made a lot of very poor decisions, many of which had a negative impact on the Faerie Realm and its people, but the Butler had stood by his duties, dealing with the violent mood swings and maniacal outbursts that the old King was so well known for. The new King, King Bobney, was something else. He spoke to the staff respectfully, he did not expect them to bow to him or act like he was somehow just born better than them, he made decisions that were based entirely on making the Realm a better and safer place to live. Yet despite this, he caused disquiet among the palace staff because the old traditions were being eroded by his actions. The huge state banquets happened less and less frequently. The gaudy and extravagant balls thrown by the old King so that he could entrap young female Fae for his own amusement had been replaced by charity events and acts of sacrifice made by the King, purely for the good of the people. The Butler spat on his polish rag once more to give a little damp to the drying polish as he brooded. He had seen how the new King spent far too much time in the company of the Colonel of the Special Faerie Service, a proud Military man of no doubt, but who lacked the manners and brevity of a royal advisor. But what really upset the Butler was the fact that the King treated him like an equal, speaking politely and had even asked his opinion on some matters of state once or twice. It was unheard of, Kings were not supposed to be like this and they were not supposed to hang around the army, while also failing to choose a wife to sire the royal heir with. The Butler suddenly noticed that he had been polishing his medals so hard, that he was at risk of wearing away the fine moulding around the edge of his most prestigious medal. He stopped and put away the polishing kit and pinned the medal bar to his black long coat and checked his reflection in the mirror. Black shoes, highly polished, black trousers with a razor like crease ironed into them, white shirt that almost appeared to be made of a rigid cloth, it was so well pressed and then came his black, long coat, the jacket style worn by previous Butlers for as long as the palace had existed. He stood up facing the door of his spartan room and stepped into the corridor. The Head Chef was waiting outside, leaned against the wall, chewing the end of a cocktail stick, having been all but forced to quit smoking his foul-smelling cigars. "So, Brian, what is this meeting about?"

The Butler looked bleak. "Probably wants to sack us all because we are all equals and don't deserve to live in a palace." He snorted, his voice full of contempt. "I ask you, what are these youngsters coming to?"

The Head Chef also snorted. "The fucking cheek of it, six generations of my family have served this fucking family and now this poxy little squirt wants to sack us all." He pulled the well chewed cocktail stick from his mouth and spat the woody fragments into a tissue, which he dropped into a nearby waste bin. "Well, I can't say I will be sorry. The miserable fucker won't even let me put a good hearty dressing on all of the fucking salads, the miserable bastard orders me to make." He shook his head sadly, "it sets a bad precedent when the King won't demand a feast every week. The staff get lazy, I caught three of the kitchen boys playing cards in the palace larder two days ago. Could I give them a whipping? No chance, the King does not allow the staff to be disciplined anymore." He shook his head again, "it's all about understanding and empathy... It's fucking shameful."

The Butler nodded. "I caught two of the serving maids gossiping recently, not one of them had had the King force himself on them and they seemed quite happy about it!"

The Head Chef narrowed his eyes and gave the Butler a sideways look. "Steady on Bri, the old King was a shitbag, but he wasn't a rapist."

The Butler snorted out a bitter laugh. "Wasn't he?"

The staff were all assembled in the main dining room and the King was laughing and joking with some of the younger members when the Butler and Head Chef entered the room, the King looked up and then wandered across to meet the two men. "I'm so glad that you could make it." He held out his hand first to the Head Chef and then to the Butler. Both men shook the royal hand, if somewhat reluctantly. The King faced the Butler, "if you would be so good as to bring the meeting to order?" The Butler stared at the King for a second or two and then seemed to jump into action. He clapped his hands twice and gave a command that all staff were to sit down and prepare to listen to the King. The King smiled and patted him on the back. "I can spot a military man when I see one. Jolly Hockey sticks old bean."

The Butler could not help himself. "Jolly hockey sticks, Sir... I mean Sire." His face reddened, but the King did not seem to notice, instead he walked to the front of the room and spoke up, his voice loud but friendly.

"I would like to thank you all for coming to this meeting today, I am aware that asking you to attend here now will interfere with your duties, for which I am very sorry."

"That's all right Sire," chirped up a young voice, "I was only folding your sheets." The King looked at the young speaker and gave the young Fae a broad grin, before speaking again.

"I am very aware that there are traditions and ways of running the palace that I am not familiar with, I am also aware that if I should create little transgressions by breaking with those traditions, it can cause some upset among the staff, for which I am again, very sorry." He beamed another smile, "however, just because something is traditional, it does not mean that it is the right thing to keep doing. So, working together, we are going to make some changes around here for the better and I hope that you will be able to work together with me to make them?" There was a small smattering of applause from the younger staff members, while many of the older ones watched the King with cautious curiosity. The King addressed the waiting staff with a polite and restrained solemnity. "When I was born, I was in the human world, where I was kept hidden by my Mother, who believed that the old King would try to hunt me down, to prevent my succession to the throne. As such, I did not have the correct royal education that many of you would have liked me to have had." He paused and smiled again. "Instead, I was educated in a rough inner-city school, where I learned how to survive in the tough human life, never knowing who or what I was." He seemed to sag a little, as if some inner pain was rushing forward in his mind. "When I did find out who I was, I was a terrible excuse of a Fae and I even killed a proud Faerie Warrior in a cruel and dishonourable way." He reached into a pocket and pulled out a hanky and wiped his eyes. "After that incident and once I had been brought into this proud Realm, I vowed that I would do the very best job that I could do for all of the people in this Realm and those realms connected to our own." He paused and allowed his words to sink in before continuing. "I will do my absolute best to be a voice for reason, for peace and for respect for all Fae, yourselves included." Again there was a small smattering of applause and even a couple of cheers from the junior staff members who had already liked the new King even before the meeting.

The Butler loudly cleared his throat and called for decorum while the King spoke, which made the King bow slightly to the Butler, before he spoke again. "Thank you, Head Butler, advisor to the King's ear, Master of the household and organiser of Palace duties. I am indebted to you Sir."

It was rare that anyone used the full title of the Butler's position within the palace and more rare that a King would even know it. A small smile ached across his stiff upper lip.

The King turned back to his audience. "First of all and probably of most importance to all staff here. I want to assure you that I will not be sacking any of you, your jobs are secure for as long as you live, as is your housing within the palace. However, I want to introduce schooling for your children, so that they do not feel that they are born into royal servitude, or trained from birth to perform a specific duty within the palace." He looked around the room and could see some worried faces. "I know that some of you here are from generations of palace staff who have given the royal family, your dedication and devotion for hundreds of years." He saw the startled looks and the worry among the staff, particularly the older staff members growing more intense, but he knew that he needed to press on. "We need to bring the palace in line with current environmental understanding." He pointed to head bed maker, a non-gendered Fae of middle age, with greying hair and smart black and white dress uniform. "How many times a week do we change the bedding and have it washed?"

They looked up and gave the King a fragile smile. "All bedding is changed once per day, as soon as the King and his family and guests are risen and at breakfast."

The King nodded before pointing to the Head Chef. "Head Chef, how much food is prepared and then thrown away each day?"

The Head Chef suddenly alarmed to have been called out, stammered and tried to find his words. "Well, um... It's hard to say Your Highness, the kitchen scraps are given to the palace pigs, there is not much waste so to speak."

Again the King nodded and he pointed to head Cleaner, a severe looking female Fae of advanced years and with bright gem stone eyes. "How much cleaning materials do we get through each month?"

The elderly Fae stood up with great dignity and bowed her head to the King before standing up straight again. "Your Highness, all of the gilt-work and ornaments are polished once per day, to prevent tarnish and the accumulation of dust."

"I see," said the King. "How much of the polish that we use comes from pressurised single use, spray bottles that are simply thrown away when they are used up?"

Again the old woman bowed her head before answering. "Your Highness, we have a special supply delivered each month, the empty cans are disposed of with the palace waste in the incinerators."

The King bowed his own head, "thank you head cleaner, you have been most helpful." He turned back to the staff as a whole. "It all sounds like we have an awful lot of busywork and an awful lot of waste produced at an almost industrial level. This has to change, not just for our benefit, but for the benefit of future generations." He smiled again because he could see the discomfort that his new ideas were causing among the staff. "I hope that you will work with me to introduce these changes and to make the palace not only more sustainable, but a healthier place to be?" Finally he turned to the Butler. "Sir, I would ask that you accompany me tomorrow morning on a full tour of the palace staff accommodations. I want to ensure that all of you have the facilities appropriate for such a dedicated and hard-working team of people."

The Butler gave a cold smile, he had been cornered, he was going to have to help make the palace into a hippy friendly, eco-palace, that no good King or warrior chieftain would ever care to call home. "It would be my honour, Sire. I am here only to serve you." He answered coldly.

The King grinned again. "No actually, that is not what you are here for." He approached the Butler and stood in front of the man. "Your duty is to serve the palace, not me. I am just a humble visitor, the palace is ancient and will stand for hundreds of centuries more than I, but to do so, she needs you to make her better so that she can make that thousands of centuries more."

The Butler rocked on his feet, he saw clearly for the first time, the King fully understood the Butler's role, possibly even better than he did. He bowed his head to the King, his eyes closed, but prickled with tears. "The palace thanks you for your care, Sire."

"You changed your tune rather quickly!" Hissed the Head Chef under his breath to no one in particular, but giving the Butler a cold stare of mistrust.

The meeting came to an end and as the staff filtered out of the room through the main door, the King stopped each member and thanked them for their service and their dedication. Finally, it came to the Butler and he approached the King with caution. The King stood up straight and saluted the Butler, with a stiff military salute. The Butler suddenly stood rod straight, clicked his heels together and raised his own hand. The King spoke, "Butler. Brian, if I may use your given name? I need your help, I really do." The Butler nodded unthinking, but agreeing as the King continued. "I know barely anything about royal protocol while I am resident in the palace, other than what I have picked up from the staff already." He gave the man an uncertain smile, "but I want all of you to know how much I value you all, for the work you have all done here. The palace could not stand as proud as it does without you, and no one more so than you."

"I am aware of my duty, Sire. It is to the staff and the palace and then it is to you."

The King gave the old man a firm smile. "Would you care to join me for a regimental brandy old bean?"

The Butler nodded his head once, "it would be my honour Sire." He smiled, a rigid and uncertain smile, but a genuine one more or less. "I have heard that the SFS have a rather fine regimental brandy, Sire."

"Indeed they do, Brian, indeed they do, and I am sure that a glass or two of that fine drink will do us both the world of good." The King turned towards the door and as they began to walk to the King's private office, he began to hum a quiet pop song from the human world, he turned to the Butler suddenly. "I also need your help with another matter, my Mother seems to think that I need a wife. Is there any chance that you can help distract her from this fact while we deal with everything happening here?"

The Butler smiled again, "the previous King was also without a wife Sire, but I suspect that this was for far different reasons to your own." He gave the King a conspiratorial smile, "I am sure that I can do something to assist you in this matter, with the Good Lady, Sire."

The King nodded his thanks and grinned again. "Good man Butler, I knew that I could trust you."

Chapter 2

The days fled by like a river after a deluge, King Bobney attended meetings, organised his social diary to fit in every envoy who came to Winscombe and every delegation who wished for an appeal to the King. He spoke with lowland farmers facing hardships due to polluted rivers and the owners of companies that were found guilty of causing the pollution, with little or no regard for those affected. He issued several decrees and just when he thought that he was on top of the modern environmental issues facing the faerie Realm, another crisis came along. Someone was strip mining vast areas of the Realm and doing so without consultation with anyone or approval of any kind. The mines would appear, almost overnight, as if some giant creature was biting chunks out of the firmament and eating all of the precious goodness from the soil, leaving only spoil and mess as a sign of their passing. The areas mined were always remote, but the actions of the miners were felt across the Realm and in his private office, the King was incandescent with fury. One such mine had been discovered by Wuffles, the Mayor of Winscombe, while he was undertaking a spiritual journey he referred to simply as walkies. Wuffles had seen first hand the damage that the mine had caused and the poisonous filth that drained into nearby river, a sample of which Wuffles had collected and presented to the King upon his return to Winscombe. The diagnosis was that toxic metals were being extracted from the ground, but by whom remained a mystery.

Finally, the King consulted a young woman, of slight frame and gentle features, known among her friends as Deborah, but to the Faerie world at large, as the reincarnation of the spirit of Mother Nature. Deborah said that she could feel the pain of the Realm and would notify the King as soon as she felt a new mine open. The first time that she reported the feeling, the King immediately dispatched a survey group to locate and discover who was mining, but word had obviously got out to the miners and when the site was located, it had already been abandoned and the damage had once again been devastating. The hole left behind in the hillside was in the scale of such things small, but the chemicals used to extract the metals from the crushed rock had badly contaminated the area and the clean up was likely going to take decades.

Angered once again, the King did what he could to

catch the miners, but his small team of environmental experts were unable to mobilise fast enough to then catch the miners in the act of despoiling the landscape. The answer came during one of his morning runs with Colonel Thrashgood and the small regiment of elite warriors known as the Special Faerie Service.

The morning had started out cool, the sun still low in the sky, which was a deep blue, warming to a gentle orange where the sun hid below the horizon. Colonel Thrashgood was stood outside the small barracks that housed the SFS, where he was gently stretching, warming up his limbs and getting ready to run the assault course with his soldiers, when the King skipped across the field towards him. "Good Morning Thrashy," the King greeted him, but the King's usual joviality was damped by the dark thoughts that plagued him, both night and day.

"Good morning to you too, my friend." The Colonel replied, seeing that the King looked troubled. "You look like you've already had a rough day and it hasn't even started yet."

The King nodded despondently. "Those fucking miners have struck another patch, three days ago. By the time our investigators got there, they had once again already moved on and left the place in a filthy fucking mess."

"The bastards." Hissed Thrashgood angrily, "you should let me and the team here take them down. The SFS will gladly beat some sense into the blighters."

The King laughed and patted his friend on the shoulder. "I am so stupid, why didn't I think of that?"

Thrashgood gave the King an understanding nod. "Probably because you wanted to use your team of scientists and advisers to catch these scumbags, rather than make this into a military action, where we have no expertise in what damage is being actually done." Replied Thrashgood, his tone concerned.

The King gave him a look of understanding and then nodded his head, "are we going to run this thing or not?"

Thrashgood grinned, "I was almost ready, I will muster the troops, they are getting suited and booted as we speak."

Almost like a gust of smoke on a still night, the troops of the SFS had appeared and were stood at attention behind Thrashgood and the King. The King turned around and grinned. "That never ceases to amaze me, I have no idea how they do that so quietly that I don't even hear them come."

One of the SFS troops let out a small titter, which caused Thrashgood to turn around and face them. "Something amusing?"

"Just a rude joke, Sir."

"I see," replied Thrashgood. "Shall we add an extra set of aerobics after our morning run, given that we have the energy to be rude before the sun has fully risen to the sky?"

The King chuckled and turned to Thrashgood, "well now, it would be rude not to, don't you think, old man?"

"Jolly hockey sticks Sire." Replied Thrashgood as he set off at a fast run. The King fell in beside him, followed by the SFS who remained in formation and kept easy pace with the two leaders.

At the end of the exercise field, was the gateway that led to the assault course, a series of wooden beams, climbing nets, rope swings and monkey bars that led to first a set of water filled tubes, five metres in length that the troops quickly passed through as the King and Thrashgood stood above them, supervising. After the water tubes came the swamp, a patch of thick mud, covered over by a strong low net that the troops had to scramble under to come face to face with the Princess, a Royal dragon who was seconded from her family to serve with the SFS, a duty she took the utmost of pride in. As the troops emerged from the swamp net, the Princess was already taking a huge breath and then she released a jet of pale blue flame. The soaked and muddy troops rolled below the flame and set about approaching the Princess, with the aim of each one of them placing a muddy hand print on her shoulder. She was careful with her flame, not to actually burn any of the troops, but at the same time, she made sure that their task was not easy to achieve. When training recruits, this was often the part of the SFS selection process that intimidated the most of them away from pursuing a career with the SFS.

The troops dodged and weaved through the flame until each of them had placed their hand on the Princess's shoulder. With the task complete, the Princess bowed her head to the King and he in turn saluted her back.

"Good morning to you, your Highness." Said King Bobney politely.

"It is as always my pleasure to greet you, King Bobney." She replied, her voice a soft purr. She turned to Colonel Thrashgood. "Jolly hockey sticks Colonel, aye what?"

"Indeed Major, jolly hockey sticks." Thrashgood replied, his voice filled with jovial friendliness.

The King stepped forwards and addressed the troops. "If I may take up a moment of your time, I have something to put to you all." He turned to the Princess, "yourself included if I may, Ma'am?" The royal dragon bowed her head and stepped forwards to stand with the rest of the regiment of eleven Fae and herself. The King smiled and then spoke. "As you know, the Realm is facing a problem with rogue miners causing havoc with the ecosystem and despite the best efforts of my team of geological experts, we have thus far been unable to arrest either them or their efforts."

"Sir, yes sir." barked the squad, the anger among them was palpable.

"So it was suggested to me by Colonel Thrashgood that maybe you all would have better luck." The Squad cheered and when they fell silent, the King continued. "Can I ask you, the best of the best, the elite among all warriors to hunt down and capture these illegal miners before they unleash some unholy evil upon us all?"

All eleven of the troops and the Princess stood as

one and raised a clenched fist above their heads. "Aye Sir!" They barked as one.

"What about you Thrashgood?" Asked the King, "is this a task that you believe the SFS can and should undertake?"

Thrashgood was silent for a moment, his face concerned. Finally he spoke. "I feel that as a military force, we can indeed take on this challenge, however." his voice was serious. "I feel that we shall need an expert in the science field, a scientist who can work with a military unit. Who can guide us when we need guidance, stand back when we need to take action."

The King grinned. "Do I need to say her name or have you already discussed this matter with her?"

Thrashgood grinned. "She is a canny warrior Sir, I imagine that she was already preparing for this campaign before either you or I thought of it, Sir."

The King nodded his head in agreement. "Then I shall speak with the Royal Science Advisor myself this afternoon." The King turned back to the troops. "Thank you, the hopes of the Realm will rest upon your shoulders, but I have every faith in you. He turned back to Thrashgood. "Now about those extra aerobics you mentioned?"

Thrashgood grinned and nodded to the Princess.

"Your Highness, would you care to start the music?"

Much to the amusement of the King, the Princess let out a delighted giggle and quickly dashed into her small cavern dwelling. A few seconds later the crackle of a record player could be heard from the large speakers in the entrance of the cave and then the music started, a fast and hard dance music opening beat. Thrashgood led the troops in side steps first one way, then the other, before he led into star jumps and squats.

Queen Linda sat nursing her morning coffee, behind her and stood at a small kitchen range with a frying pan in his hand was her husband, the royal advisor Craig. He broke two eggs into the pan and then whisked them up until they began to solidify. He then added some finely cut slivers of pre-ccoked bacon and stirred it into the egg, before grinding some pepper over the top. Finally he lifted the pan and began to serve out the scrambled egg onto a slice of toast that sat on the each of the two plates warming on the range.

"Breakfast is served my Lady." He said as he flourished a tea towel across his arm and placed one of the plates in front of the Queen.

Queen Linda smiled and then kissed him as he leant in towards her. "My maestro, my master chef, my muse and my husband, you spoil me." She purred, her eyes sparkling with love.

Craig sat down opposite her at the small kitchen table. "As if I could spoil you, you are and always have been perfect." He winked at her and took a mouthful of his breakfast. He chewed, swallowed and then spoke again. "I think that this needs some Tommy K, maybe a dash of salt. What do you think?"

Linda took a mouthful and felt the flavours wash across her tongue. What she tasted was rich, but light. Full of flavour, but not overwhelming. "No, I don't think so. I think that ketchup will detract from what you have done."

Craig rocked his head from side to side. "Perhaps, but for a man of such a delicate palate as myself, I am conscious of every delicate flavour, as I search to fulfil every desire"

"You certainly fulfilled my every desire last night, you were a wild and mighty stallion." She licked a crumb from her lip, allowing him to see the movement as a slow deliberate enticement.

"My lady, when one burns with such passion, it is only because one's heart is filled with such love," he bowed his head slowly, "in this case it is for you, my sensual, goddess of light."

Linda stood up, leaving her breakfast and approached the tall, handsome Fae and gently brushed her hand across his face, delicately stroking one of his ears. "Oh Sir, you flatter me. I am but an innocent, delicate milking wench."

Craig pulled her to his lap and embraced her comely form. "Well, a milking wench should be taught how to treat a man!" He stood up and she wrapped her legs around him as he carried her towards the door.

"Oh, you must teach me Sir, teach me!" She whispered breathily into his ear as she nibbled upon his smooth fleshy lobe. "For sir, I have a hunger deep in my loins that only you can satisfy!"

The Kitchen door swung closed, the breakfast plates left on the table, the food barely eaten. There came the sound of the happy couple kissing as Craig climbed the stairs, then the bounce as he deposited the queen upon her bed, there were gasps, moans and grunts, hisses of breath and then the rhythmic compression of bed springs, that began to speed up to a climax of cries of delight from the two occupants.

As the morning air filled their bed chamber, waving

away the aroma of their love making, Craig gazed at the woman laying next to him, her eyes watching him back, were filled with stars of light. "You are the most magnificent woman I have ever met." He said, his voice a deep timbre of adoration. "A true beauty, a warrior maiden and a ferocious lover. The Old Gods must have blessed me many, many times for me to have you in my life."

"Oh, you sweet boy." The Queen purred, "You make my loins burn for your touch, my heart ache for your love, my soul demand your presence both with me and within me." She reached her hand to his face and pressed his nose once. "Boop!"

Craig couldn't help himself, he started to laugh and the bed shook as he did so. The Queen sat up and reached for a cloth. "Look what you have done to me, you wicked boy!" She teased as she leaned her head against his shoulder. "Will you do it to me again later?"

The afternoon sun was poking out from behind the grey clouds and the royal garden glistened with the moisture of a recent rain fall. Queen Linda was knelt in the short grass, weeding her flower bed, an activity that she found was great for helping her focus her mind as she considered the problem of her son and his wilful lack of a wife. Craig had gone into his office in the palace where he was making enquiries into the problems of the university and the new buildings that Linda was to publicly support with her name, despite her not wanting it built. It was obvious to all around the King, to his closest friends and even to the rest of the palace staff, that the King often lost himself dreaming of love, in the eyes of the highest ranked General of the entire armed forces of the Faerie Realm. But to Linda's mind, there were problems with her as a royal bride. She was pretty enough once she was properly dressed, away from those drab and austere military uniforms she was so keen upon, but she was not the radiant beauty that a Queen should be. For a start she had rather too many battle scars in some visible places, including on her gentle face. Then, if Queen Linda was being very critical of the woman of her son's desires, the General was rather too muscular to be considered a gentle Faerie girl. Another concern of Linda's was that with the General being of a military background, she wondered if the girl was as pure as a royal bride needed to be. Especially thought Linda, with all of those dirty young soldiers, panting and grunting in their tight military uniforms as they worked their powerful, fit young bodies... Linda suddenly found herself aching for her husband, Craig. With a smile on her face, she knew that he would be home by sunset and then she would pounce on him with her womanly guile, riding him until he exploded within her loins once more that day. She had wondered if they should be using birth control, given that as a Fae in only her middle sixties, she was still plenty fertile enough to sire another child. But the thought of using hormone tablets or the cervical cap, sponge or whatever other vile contraptions the human world had given to her over the decades of her life there, really made her stomach turn. So, if she sired another child, so be it. She would raise the child with all of the love in her heart, just as she had with Bobney, albeit in the safer, happier world of the Faerie Realm.

Another thought struck her mind with the force of a steam hammer on a glowing rod of iron in a foundry, what would a child sired by her and Craig be like? If it was a male child, it would no doubt resemble it's father and be almost unbearably handsome, with a mind as sharp a chef's best knife. If she birthed a female child, it would be heartbreakingly beautiful, with a voice and mind of perfect clarity. A perfect Princess for her to raise as her best friend and... "Oh fuck." She suddenly whispered. Not that there was anyone else in the garden to hear her. "I'm fucking pregnant!"

Bobney sat at his computer and read the latest report on the illegal mining that had just been found in a distant region of the Realm. An entire hillside had been scooped up, sifted and all of the mineral goodness had been extracted, leaving only dead soil and a filthy slurry pond of poisonous waste that was overflowing into the nearby river, made worse by every rainstorm that continued to fill it. He closed the report and then forwarded it to both Colonel Thrashgood and his science advisor Felicity Hopeforthebest and then as a respectful gesture onto General Meuchelmorder. The General had been busy on the new Barracks, training a new team of officers in how she wanted the modern military to be run. She was creating change, making the military less about warfare and more about keeping peace and acting as humanitarian aid in areas hit by natural disasters. The King realised that it had been several days since he had seen the General and with that realisation came the feeling that he was actually rather fond of the General and that he very much missed having her to talk to. She was to his mind terribly brave, tactically brilliant and a fearsome warrior on the hand-to-hand combat practice arena. He let out a long sad sigh and wondered when he would get to practice with her again. As much as he loved doing the more sporting events with his best friend Thrashgood, the General was fun in an entirely different way. Suddenly startling him from his moment of reflection, the mobile telephone that he kept in the drawer of his desk when he was working, began the shrieking siren song of a phone call from his mother. He rolled his eyes and wondered what the old woman wanted this time? He could not face yet more discussions about his lack of a love life with her, but she was his Mother and she had given up so much of her life as she protected him for four decades from his evil uncle, who would have had him killed. So reluctantly he had answered the call and spoke to her respectfully. "Hello Mother, how are you and Craig on this beautiful day?"

"Oh my lovely boy, you sound so regal, you really are settling into this King business very well." Queen Linda sounded unusually shrill, even for her.

"What can I do for you Mother, I am afraid that I am terribly busy at the moment, we have found another illegal mine and they have left the area in a terrible state."

"Well," said Queen Linda. "I was, well more like Craig and I were... No hang on, I haven't told him yet. Bugger it!" She fell silent for a moment. "Something has happened!" She suddenly blurted out.

Bobney sat up in his chair, alarm filling his every cell. "Mother are you safe? Are you in danger? Do I need to call the army out for you?" His voice was urgent. "Are you OK Mummy?" He said reverting to the childlike concern for his Mother.

She started to chuckle and then started to cry. "Oh, I'm fine, wonderful in fact. I'm just so happy..." She started to cry again and then sniffed. "Craig and I need to get properly married and very soon as in the next nine months! I love him so much and he is a wonderful step father for you..."

Bobney let out a strained breath. "Mother, you know that I am indeed very fond of Craig, he is indeed an excellent Fae, a wise Fae and an honourable Fae. I shall speak with him and ask him as to his intentions regarding the Royal Mother."

Linda made a decision. "Bobney my dear son, please would you come to breakfast with Craig and I one day this week so that we can discuss another urgent piece of news with you?" She paused for a second or two, "well, once I have told him anyway." There was another pause. "Oh my God, what if he doesn't want it? What will I do?"

Bobney smiled, it amused him that even at his mother's age, she was still unsure if her husband would actually have the official state marriage that convention said that they needed to have. "Mother, I am sure that Craig will hardly refuse to marry you, I shall speak to him myself if you are concerned?"

"For fucks sake," she suddenly hissed, "I'm not talking about marriage, you silly boy!" Bobney was puzzled, his Mother was being even more peculiar than even he was used to. Finally she spoke again. "Come for breakfast the day after tomorrow, I really need to talk to you both, well once I have taken care of a few things." She said firmly.

"Oh shit, please do not do anything drastic. You absolutely must not track down any of his ex-girlfriends and have them murdered!" But Queen Linda had already hung up the call, even though Bobney had not noticed. "Mother, are you still there?" The screen of his phone went black as he pulled away from his face and he struggled to locate the unlock button, but then it refused to recognise his finger print and in frustration he started to rant at it, calling it foul and filthy insults, in a loud and angry voice.

Outside of the royal office, the Butler stood waiting, ready to knock on the door. Stood next to him was an official from another dignified family in the Faerie Realm. The Butler took a deep breath and tried to ignore the foul language, finally he was forced to speak. "I can assure you that the King does indeed hold his mother in very high esteem."

The waiting guest nodded silently, a troubled look on his face. Finally the door burst open and the King strode through it and threw the mobile phone into a distant waste bin in a fit of disgust. Suddenly aware that he was not alone, he turned at once and came face to face with the waiting guest. Startled by the appearance of a stranger in the palace, the King turned again and came to face the Butler.

The Butler smiled calmly, it was clearly going to be one of those days. "Sire, as per the royal diary, we have a guest here to petition the King on behalf of the farmers of the lowland families. Those that have been informed of the future building of a new dam."

"Oh shit, is that now?" Spluttered Bobney, before he slapped a hand over his mouth in mortified shock. He took a deep breath and then let it out slowly and released his mouth. "I am so terribly sorry." He said turning back to the guest. "I have just had a rather traumatic telephone call from the Royal Mother." He turned back to the Butler. "I am terribly sorry to ask this of you, I am aware that this is not a part of your duties, but would you ask my step father to visit me this evening, as a matter of great urgency?"

"Of course, Sire." Said the Butler as he bowed slightly, "it will be my pleasure to do so."

"Thank you so much, Butler," said Bobney as he turned back to the guest. "Please come into my office, I can order us both a coffee and then we can have a proper talk."

The man nodded doubtfully as the King turned away from him and walked back into his office. Looking to the Butler for permission, who nodded to him politely, the man followed the King into his private office and took a seat where he was directed. The Butler closed the door carefully, wandered across to the vibrating bin, where the King's phone was now silently ringing and retrieved the device from the bottom of the clean liner. As he picked it up, the screen went dark and the vibrating stopped. "Typical, I wonder who it was who has the King's personal number?" He said as he smiled, "I am sure that they will phone back." He slid the device into his pocket before returning to his own office in order to contact the Queen's consort and then order the kitchen staff deliver a tray of coffee for the King to share with his guest.

The King took his seat and settled down comfortably, trying to put the last few moments of events to the back of his mind. Opposite him, and looking sick with nerves was the man who had come to petition him about the plans to build a dam in the Realm. There was a quiet knock at the door and a servant came in with a tray of coffee from the kitchen, along with a plate of biscuits and two small cakes. The servant placed the tray on the King's desk, smiled at the guest and then wandered away, as the King called out his thanks. The door closed again and the room was silent once more. The guest felt his mouth go dry as he realised that he now had no escape, it was just him and the King. The King finally spoke, "My friend, what can I do for you today?"
With eyes like a frightened rabbit caught in headlights, the man leaned forwards and began to speak, his voice a near quiet squeak that Bobney could barely understand or hear. "I'm terribly sorry," replied the King, but you will have speak

up, I am am afraid that I have had my mother squealing down the telephone at me and I seem to have developed tinnitus!" He pointed to the tray and spoke again. "Can I offer you a coffee, with maybe a biscuit and a cake, perhaps that will help?" "Yes Please, Highness. That would be delightful, Sire." The man replied glad of the distraction, even if only for a few seconds.

The King poured out two cups of rich black coffee and passed one cup over to the man. "Would you like cream and sugar?" He asked.

"No thank you Sire,"

Bobney lifted the plate of biscuits, "go on, have one of these. The Chef bakes them himself and gets terribly upset because I cannot dare eat one, in case I put on weight again." He smiled at his guest, "as my mother is often heard saying, a moment on the lips means a life time on the hips!"

Hesitantly the man took a biscuit and then he nibbled at it nervously. He well remembered what the old King had been like and despite the seeming hospitality that he was being shown, he was dreading having to explain his issues, fearing that once he had said his piece, he would not make it out of the palace alive. Bobney watched the man eat his biscuit and smiled gratefully. "Thank you, trust me, if none of them get eaten, the Chef will have my head!" Said Bobney jovially. He sipped his scalding hot coffee and settled in his chair. "So, what is this urgent matter that you need to discuss with me?"

"Your Highness, we have been visited by a royal inspector, who has stated that our lands, which have been in our family for generations, are to be bought by the palace and flooded to make a royal lake." His face looked glum and he put down the biscuit he had been nibbling. "I am here to petition that you please, do not take our land or our family plots away from us."

Bobney let out a deep sigh, it was filled with sadness and concern for the man and his family. "Are you alone with this petition?" He asked.

The man shook his head. "No Sire, I represent a community of twenty farms, all of them small, all of them poor."

"I see." Said the King, "so even if you are all paid market value for your land, you will have no chance of paying for new land elsewhere?"

"That is so, Highness, farming is hard labour and we earn little, despite it being essential to the Realm. It is a hard truth that we Farmers are a dying breed."

The King nodded again, "If I were to show you a

map, would you be able to show me where the farms that you are speak of, are located?"

"Your Highness, I can do that."

The King stood up. "Please, come with me?" He smiled, "bring your coffee with you, I am spoilt for time, but this time is precious for you. So drink while we discuss this urgent matter."

The man picked up his cup and saucer and brought it with him to the large table that the King led him to. Laid out on the table was a map of the valley that the dam was going to flood. "This is the area of the proposed dam." He pointed to the general area before speaking again. "Now where are we talking about?" He picked up a pen and passed it to the man who took it and bent over the table to draw on first his farm.

"This area here, Highness, is my farm."

The King sighed sadly, the man's farm was located in the centre of the valley, next to the river. The man continued to draw the other farms onto the map and pretty soon it became obvious that every farm he was petitioning for was going to be lost for good beneath the waters of the new reservoir.

Bobney let out a deep breath and then spoke. "I am terribly sorry. But would you mind if I called in my advisers who are involved in the planning of this venture? I want them to understand your point of view as we discuss this very difficult decision."

The man bowed his head. "No Highness, I am humbled that you would listen to me."

The King shook his head, there were days when he hated being King and this was one of them. No matter where they put the dam, someone was going to lose their land and their livelihood. He took a small, dark blue telephone from his pocket and scrolled through a list of contacts, until he found the one he wanted. The call went through and started to ring. It clicked and a voice spoke from the other end. "Hello your Highness, Wizard Oxx here."

"There has been a development with the dam project, can you come down to the palace?" His voice was quiet. "Also, can you bring the University Chancellor with you too?"

Hearing the serious tone in the King's voice, the Wizard agreed at once and ended the phone call. The King looked up, "I shall just be another minute, I have another couple of people to call." The Man nodded and waited politely. He had expected to be brushed off, he had not expected the King to take him seriously, or to call his advisers so that they could hear what the man had to say.

"Hey, I am really sorry to bother you Felicity, I

need your input and can you bring Deborah too please?"

"Is everything all right?" Felicity asked quietly.

"No, sadly not. I have to make a very difficult decision that may affect the lives of twenty farms and the families that run them. I want to make sure that I am making the most informed decision that I can make."

"Understood Sir, I will bring Debs, she is here working at the recovery centre anyway."

"Thank you Felicity, you are a gem." He closed the conversation and returned the tiny phone back to his pocket. My best team are on their way, I want them to show me why they chose your area and why nowhere else is suitable. Would you do me the honour of staying to consult with them please?"

The man staggered slightly. "Sire, the honour is mine." He knelt down, "My King, I did not expect you to hear my plea."

The King wandered over to the man. "What is your name Sir?"

The man looked up, "I am Waldo Klemp, Sire, of Klemp Farm."

"Well Master Klemp, I rather suspect that we are going to detain you for a while."

"But I have done nothing wrong Sire!" Waldo

exclaimed, shocked.

"Oh my word no, I am so sorry for the misunderstanding Mr Klemp, I meant that we are going to be taking up a lot of your time for the duration of the meeting, please forgive me." He smiled at the man, but inside felt rather sick at the thought of what the previous King must have been like for the people to have such fear about speaking with him. He took a breath and spoke again. "Mr Klemp, as a consultant to the King in this matter, may I offer you some food and a comfortable bed for the night? Well, once we have finished our meeting."

"Thank you Sire, that is appreciated." Waldo said, more curious than relieved.

"May I ask how you travelled here today?" Bobney asked.

"I am afraid that I came by myself Sire."

"You walked!?" Asked Bobney, incredulous. "I shall insist that you return home with a member of my office to save you such an arduous journey home.

"Do you think that you will allow me to keep my home, Sire?" Waldo asked quietly.

The King gave him a serious look. "If I am to take your home away from you, I want you to understand why and I want to look you in the eye if I do. I am not going to allow a faceless bureaucrat to do that dirty job for me." The King looked down at his shoes for a moment and then back at Waldo. "I know that this is of little comfort to you, but I want you to see that if we must go ahead with this project, then I made the best decision that I could make, in the interest of all of the people of the Faerie Realm."

"I understand Sire," Waldo said, his voice was uncertain, but he was at least being heard by the King.

The meeting was long and arduous. The discussion went into deep science and discussed the geology of the land to be flooded, the safety of the rocky substrate that would allow the dam to be built as strong as possible, but the hardest part of the discussion was as always, the impact that the dam would have on the people who lived upon the land and it was here that Waldo was able to speak about his family history and the rights of the other families to live where they did. Deborah listened, tears dripping down her face, as Waldo spoke, but he knew that by the end of the meeting and despite his best efforts, he was going to lose his land and his income.

Finally the King spoke, his voice a rich timbre, filled with the heaviness of what he was about to do. "Mr Klemp, it is with a heavy heart that I agree with you about the value of the lost land, not just for the farming, but for the culture of the people who live there. However, in terms of the whole Realm, I must make a decision that will be of greater impact." He paused for a moment as he chose his words carefully. "At the moment, we rely heavily upon human technology to deliver our energy needs and this is having a very negative, if not suicidal impact on our drinking water and the greater Realm environment. You have heard here today all of the argument and reason as to why this dam will remove our reliance on fossil fuels or the other more toxic human methods of energy generation and also provide us with as much clean drinking water as we need." He paused again and looked the man in the face. "I am most dreadfully sorry, I must allow this dam to go ahead."

Waldo seemed to visibly deflate. "My whole family history is linked to that land."

"The King is aware of that Mr Klemp," said Felicity kindly. "I know that he would not have wasted your time in making this decision, nor was it a decision that he made easily."

"I am going to lose everything, including my way of making a living."

The King stood up. "No, I will not allow that." He turned to Deborah. "Is there anywhere, any place where I can put these people where they can continue their lives and livelihoods?"

Deborah shook her head. "Sire, to displace twenty families from one place and move them to another place, will displace many others. The cycle goes on."

The King walked around his office, pausing at his desk for a moment. Then he pushed a button on his desk systems. "Butler, May I ask you to step into my office please?"

"At once Sire," Came the curt reply.

The Butler entered, his uniform and shoes immaculate and the King smiled when he saw the man. "Butler, please would you show Mr Klemp to a room, I would also ask that he is provided with every comfort and is given the opportunity to contact his family if possible?"

The Butler bowed slightly. "At once Sire." He turned to Mr Klemp and gave him a convivial look. "If you will follow me to the guest suite please Sir?" Waldo stood up and followed the Butler from the room as the King watched on. A few moments later the Butler returned. "Sire, Mr Klemp has retired to a room in the East Wing. He has been provided with a meal of his choice and has been given access to a telephone. He was speaking with his daughter when I left his room."

"Thank you Butler, you have made a horribly difficult job, a little easier." Said King Bobney gratefully.

"As is my duty Sire." Said the Butler, after which he turned on the spot and marched from the room.

Bobney turned to his friends in the room. "This fucking sucks, to use an Americanism from the human world." He sat down and put his head in his hands for a moment and then an idea struck him and he reached into his pocket and pulled out his phone again and called his Mother. "Hey Mum, is Craig there please? Yeah, can I speak to him? Yes, I will be quick!" He waited for a moment and then began to speak animatedly. "Listen Craig, I know that you are supposed to be having a meeting with me this evening, but could I ask you to come sooner, it's just that I have a problem and it is ripping my guts out. I have just displaced twenty families to allow building of a dam that is going to supply Winscombe with energy and drinking water." He went silent for a moment as he listened and then spoke again. "Yeah, the shitty part of being King is that I always make someone unhappy. Anyway, have we got any land, suitable for farming that we can relocate twenty families onto that they can begin again when the new season starts?" He listened for a few seconds. "No, as fast as you can, the man is returning to his family tomorrow morning and I want him to go home with some hope." The King waited for a few more seconds. "Yes, I will be up and in my office. I am happy to sign the forms as soon as you can generate them, even if we are going to be awake until dawn." He stopped again and listened. "No, that's not the way things work, I am here for the people, I cannot ask them to work while I sleep." There was an audible sigh from the other end of the phone call and then the King spoke again. "Thank you Craig, please apologise to Mum for me, I hope that I have not ruined your evening.

When Craig arrived he was carrying an armful of maps and with him came Queen Linda, who carried an extra load for him too. She looked around the room and smiled at her friends and then walked up to Bobney and stood in front of him. "Are you going to make such a fuss about every difficult decision you must make?"

"Mother, the man spoke to me, to all of us. If that was the hard way to make a difficult decision, then yes, I will do exactly the same again." He stood firm, resolute and proud before his Mother.

Her face softened. "Then I raised you to be a good King," she said quietly. "Which the people of the Faerie Realm have not had for far too long." She reached up and put her arms around her son's neck. "I am very proud of you, Bobney." She looked over to Craig and held out her hand to him. "By the way, while you have everyone here, I have some news and I, or rather we would like you all to know first." Deborah stood up and looked at Linda, a strange look on her face and then she broke into a huge beaming smile and walked up to Linda and spoke quietly in her ear, "go on, tell them."

Linda turned to Bobney. "You might be about to have a younger brother."

Bobney stared at his mother, uncertain as to what he should say. His Mother looked suddenly worried and then he spoke. "My dear Mother, that is wonderful news." He embraced Linda and then reached out to Craig and embraced them both

79

together. When he finally let them go, Deborah approached Linda, her gentle smile was sweet, but her eyes were jet black pools of darkness that sucked in light in a way that was truly startling to see. "Would you like to know what your baby is?" She held out her hands to Linda, who took them hesitantly before looking to Bobney.

Bobney smiled, "Don't worry Mother, you have met Mother Nature before."

Linda smiled at the young woman, who seemed to suddenly be as old as the world and then back to a young woman again. "Can you see my baby, my dear?" She waited and Deborah nodded her head silently. Linda spoke again. "Is my baby safe?" Again, Deborah nodded silently. Finally Linda asked the question. "Is my baby a little boy?"

Deborah grinned and wrinkled her nose slightly, "oh no, she is going to be something else entirely." She reached out her hand towards Linda's tummy. "May I sense her?" Linda took the young woman's hand and pressed it against her gently and Deborah closed her eyes for a few seconds. When she opened them again, her eyes were pale green and almost back to normal Fae eyes. "Your daughter will be great, she will be kind and most of all, she will defend the rights of the people against anyone who would cause them harm. She and her brother are going to make the Faerie Realm a place of peace and Fae magyk once again, for the next thousand years." She beamed at the King. "Balance is important and we will find it again very soon."

Craig smiled as the King pressed a hand to his shoulder and spoke. "Stepfather, thank you and my Mother for my sister."

Suddenly uncomfortable, Craig started to chuckle. "Well, it took a lot of effort!"

"Craig!" Shrieked Queen Linda horrified.

Changing the subject quickly, King Bobney called the meeting to order. "Now if I may, I have twenty families that I need to find a home for."

Craig laid out a large map that showed a part of the Kingdom some distance away and then pointed to a large section of it. "This area of land was taken by a King of the Realm about four thousand years ago. No one living has any connection to it and it was used for exercising Royal Camels, prior to their retirement from the palace."

The King nodded his understanding. "So it is safe to say that we can re-home the people there?"

"It is not the lowland easily flooded land that they currently have, but they can produce hardier crops, graze livestock and raise families. In short, they can make their living there, especially if we help them out." He turned to Linda and held out his hand to her. "Queen Linda has told me that the royal money box has not been emptied for hundreds of years, rather the pile of gold has instead gathered dust as it grew larger. A tiny amount of it from our point of view will set those families up for the next ten years, until they are self sustaining, by which time, the dam will be producing enough energy that we can shut down all forms of unsustainable energy production, making greater savings for the Realm as a whole."

"We can build them state of the art, modern homes that are energy efficient and ecologically sustainable, with little impact on the surrounding landscape, at a tiny cost to us and then gift them to the families for perpetuity." Added Queen Linda gently. "The change will be hard for them at first, but with our support and with our love, they can make it work."

"No." Said Bobney firmly. "We are not making the decision for them, we ask Mr Klemp for his grace tomorrow morning." Stated Bobney firmly.

At breakfast Mr Klemp was greeted by the Butler who led him from the luxurious room in which he had spent the night, to the small private apartment where the King was cooking breakfast for himself and his friend Colonel Thrashgood. Thrashgood was reading the plans that the King had spend most of the night going through and was nodding his head as he read. He looked up at the King and spoke, his voice deep and respectful. "You have got some strong points, but it's still going to be hard for them." He suddenly turned to the doorway as Mr Klemp came through. The Butler bowed to the King, hiding his disapproving look at the monarch as he cooked food for the two waiting men. Thrashgood reached out his hand to shake and greeted the man. "You must be the man who kept our King awake all night."

Mr Klemp looked like he was about to fall into a trap and hesitantly shook Thrashgood's hand. "I rather hope that I have not caused our King such worry."

Thrashgood laughed and pushed the man gently towards the small table and chairs. "Fuck him, he's a King, they rarely do any real work!"

"I heard that, you bastard!" Called Bobney from the cooker, where he was unloading some fried eggs to the three plates, that already contained sausages, beans, hash browns and tomatoes. He carefully carried the plates to the table and invited Mr Klemp to sit down, before sitting himself.

"A good brekky there Bobney, cheers." Said Thrashgood enthusiastically. He turned to Mr Klemp, dig in or it will get cold. Confused, Mr Klemp did as he was asked and began to eat the meal cooked for him by a tired looking King Bobney.

Bobney spoke between mouthfuls. "Ignore this old warhorse, we have a plan and I want your opinion before I present it to your collective of families."

Thrashgood grinned at Mr Klemp. "Don't worry, it's not as bad as you think."

"Well, maybe." Said King Bobney, I might have a job for you, if you are interested, it will mean spending some time at the palace from time to time?"

Mr Klemp sat bewildered as the King and Colonel Thrashgood joked and chatted as they ate. It took a short while, but finally, Mr Klemp began to relax, he had a strange feeling that his life was about to get a whole lot stranger.

Chapter 3

With the extending of the days into the warmth of long summer evenings, the Kingdom was starting to bloom as the unusually light April rains washed the winter from the trees and the skies. However, with the warming came a threat, a threat that the weather was just too warm, the rains were too little and landscape was already thirsty after a unseasonably dry winter. The dam project had started, with preliminary ground work starting and the removal of all sentient life from the area to be flooded when the river was finally dammed. The families had been unsure about moving, until the King had given them a chance to make new lives, with the certainty of extra support if it was needed. The valleys and hillsides were empty, all that remained were the flies, bugs and the ever-present mycelium network that connected all of the realms and all of the worlds to that of the Fae. Before the work could commence, Mother Nature in the form of a young Deborah, visited and blessed the site, asking all life and spirits to move aside and allow the waters to rise. The landscape let out a sound that only Mother Nature could hear and slowly, the streams that flowed from all of the valleys settled into the final valley river where the dam was under construction. The main river had been redirected slightly and the river bank had been reinforced to allow the waters to be channelled and thus pass safely through the workings, without causing any damage to the construction site. The Mother Goddess' blessing of the landscape and of the many streams that fed into the valley had another purpose too and that was to cleanse the landscape and wash away the sadness of those families who had been forced to move away, leaving behind untended pasture and abandoned crops.

Florence Grim, a troll of good standing, stood at her desk in the office of the construction site and stared hard at the architectural plans and next to them the schedule for the works to be done. Phase one was complete, but phase two was already three days late and with each day that passed, it grew later. She had spoken with the King who had made a flying visit on the back of Princess Rupertina, so that he could inspect the site of the dam and she had been happy that the visit had gone well. The King had been pleased with progress that the project was making and the team that she had assembled were working well. Then something changed. It started when earlier than expected, the base rock changed from a solid and dependable granite, into a loose and difficult metamorphosed mudstone. The fine grain slate was prone to fracture and it would need a great deal of reinforcement to stand up to the pressure of the water pushing on the dam. With a sudden change in the levels of hard work, the crews embraced the difficulties, throwing themselves into the challenge and accepting that the geological survey could only be so accurate. But something else was wrong too and silly little accidents started to happen. A snapped drill bit sent the remaining hard steel bit juddering into the soft leathery foot of one of the trolls, with a resultant loud scream and a sudden stop in work as the crew surged into care giver mode and rescued their work mate. The ambulance arrived quickly and the troll was taken to Winscombe hospital where it was found that the injury was serious enough to require an overnight stay. Luckily although very sore, it was not disabling and after a couple of weeks, the troll was back on site, albeit working light duties until her foot was fully healed. The next accident was more serious and made rather a mess of the work site. The metal storage shed that held the explosives used for blasting the tough granite bedrock, suddenly exploded. Felicity Hopeforthebest had dispatched one of her forensic science graduates to investigate the cause of the explosion and it was found that a single tiny detonator cap, that should never have been anywhere near the explosives store, had been dropped in the shed. The investigation continued and given that each cap was carefully catalogued and signed for by the explosives master when it was needed, there was no explaining how a single cap that had not been signed out of the cap store, on the other side of the site, had found its way into the explosives shed. The next incident was more expensive than dangerous. The storage shed that held the bags of cement powder ready for mixing into concrete, had inexplicably got wet, the whole five tonnes had somehow been soaked with a hose and it had then cured into solid rock. The whole five tone load had to be broken up and replaced at huge cost.

Florence turned and picked up yet another short incident report, that she had been given by one of her forewomen when she had stepped into her office on her arrival. Someone had moved some of the flag markers that outlined the trenches to be dug and it had not been discovered until the trenches had been completed and something felt wrong. Wall markers failed to line up, concrete footings had been poured in the wrong place and then when Florence had climbed up a scaffold to see the damage, it was revealed that the workings, rather than building a safe footing for the dam, instead formed the letters of a very rude word in the Somerset language. It was a word so foul, it even shocked Florence, who was well known among her crew as having the ability to out-swear a sailor who had caught his genitals in a slamming porthole!

With a deep sigh, Florence picked up the telephone and dialled a number as she rested the handset against her head. For a moment, the line was silent and then it started to ring. A few seconds later, the handset at the other end was picked up and then there came some muffled swearing as it was dropped and then retrieved. Finally a voice came through in the slightly strained annoyance of the Magician Brianco Oxx. "Hello, what do you want?" Florence took a breath. "Good morning your grace, this is Florence Grim, site engineer at the dam construction site."

The Magician smiled and with a slightly softer tone, he spoke again. "Ah, hello my dear, what can I do to assist you on this truly beautiful day?"

There was no way to say it delicately, despite the

taboo of even admitting to the problem. "We have a Gremlin at the site and we need you to come and sort it out please, your Grace."

The line went silent for a moment and Florence wondered if she was about to be laughed out of the industry. Finally the Magician spoke again. "By even considering this, you are taking a terrible professional risk, admitting the existence of a Gremlin also gives them even greater power and they do tend to get worse." He stopped to think and the line was heavy with silence from both ends. Finally, the Magician spoke. "You must stop work immediately and get your crews to safety. DO not even pick up your tools, just go and take nothing with you."

"I have already seen to this your grace." She stated firmly, squeezing her fingers to the point of pain to avoid dropping her usual number of F-bombs and other profanities into her speech.

"Jolly good Ma'am," said the Magician respectfully. "These little fuckers can cause havoc if they are not caught!"

"Too fucking right they can, the little cu..." She just managed to stop herself from dropping a C-bomb into the conversation.

The magician thumbed through his mobile phone

contacts list and found the person he wanted to be with him on this mission. He grinned and returned his attention to the phone call he already had. "Now listen, take your girls for a Norfcorean and a couple of beers, just to keep you all out of harms way and then sit tight. I will be there ASAP."

"Thank you, your Grace," Florence stated calmly. "You're a fucking gent."

The Magician laughed. "Yes, quite likely."

Florence slid the handset back onto the cradle and then slid the plans into her desk drawer and locked it closed. She stepped outside her office and slammed the door closed before locking it. In as carefree a way as possible, she wandered across to the waiting transport and climbed up the steps to face the twenty trolls all sat waiting for her. "Right then girls, I've just spoken to some clever-bollocks about our little fucking error this morning and the little bugger is on his way here to sort this shit out." The listening trolls applauded and cheered. When they fell silent, Florence spoke again. "So then you lucky cunts, I am authorised to take the lot of you greedy fuckers out for a Norfcorean and a few jars of the finest angel piss, all compliments of the company shiny arses!" There was more cheering and clapping of huge leathery hands. "So then, before you all get wide ons for beer and scran, you need to make sure that you have nothing from the site on your person or even stuck up your flaps!"

They all knew what she meant and very slowly and rather carefully, the trolls began to examine themselves for anything that could contain the hidden shadowy form of a gremlin. The voices began to sound off as each troll checked themselves and their workmates and found nothing to worry about. Finally there came the soft quiet voice of Muriel Grindingstone. She was fairly new to the industry and was technically still a year one apprentice brick layer, but she was such a darling and so determined to work hard on any task given to her, that Florence had asked the other trades women to train her up with as much as she was prepared to do. "Excuse me, Ms Grim?" Said Muriel, her voice a little worried.

Florence turned to face her and used the young girls nickname. "What's up happy minge?"

Muriel held up a small metal tin, that in the human world would have looked like the sort of old tobacco tin that an ancient Granddad would use to hold rusty drill bits of a size that he never used, but kept for just in case. Her face was stricken, it was obvious that this tin was not hers and she had no idea how it had ended up in her pocket.

Realising what the problem was, one of the trades women threw a roll of strong duct tape to Florence who caught it in the air and then she carefully found the end and then told Muriel to carefully hold the tin up for her to see. Muriel pressed the lid on tightly and Florence began to wrap it in the thick, strong tape. Having wound several times around the tin, she tore it off the roll, before throwing the roll back to the owner. "I'll be right back you lucky fuckers, I've forgotten my fucking keys ain't I." She held the tin gingerly in her finger tips as she carefully climbed down from the bus and then wandered across the gravel yard area to the special post box that the office used for internal mail. She opened the flap and slid the tin into the dark cavity before carefully closing the flap. Gingerly she reached for her nail gun that lived in her utility belt and with several loud retorts of the explosive caps, firmly nailed the post box shut. She took off at a run and leapt the last six feet onto the steps of the bus. "Fucking go, you lazy cunt!" She hissed at the driver, who being a quiet human man from Winscombe and not being used to such strong language from a lady, floored the pedal and caused the bus to lurch forwards and stall the tired diesel engine. Florence glared at the driver meaningfully and silently pleaded with him to get the vehicle going. He twisted the ignition key and pumped the throttle with his foot and finally the engine roared into life, the tyres bit into the gravel and they were off to the safety of a Norfcorean restaurant. Seconds after the bus had vanished into the distance, the long thin nails holding the post box closed began to slowly work their way out of the wood. As each nail popped out and shot across the yard, the next began to squeakily wobble as it too started to work its way out. Finally the flap sprang open for les than a second before it then fluttered shut.

It was the first day of the summer semester at Winscombe University and Felicity Hopeforthebest was teaching the Criminology Module. Felicity stood at the lectern and tidied her sheaf of notes. In front of her sat the entire first year of the university Criminology course and she noted that quite of a lot of them were gazing at mobile phones or whispering to their friends. She cleared her throat and began to speak. "For those of you who have not read beyond the introductory text, I shall remind you of the quote about crime among Werewolf clans." She looked up and found that she held the attention of the majority of the class. Picking her note card up, she read the quote from the rare book, knowing full well that it was a trap. Would the students find it lascivious and silly and thus ignore the more serious issue? Having read it to herself, she turned back to the class and read it aloud. "There is the obvious advantage to being a newly made werewolf, that being the extra flexible spine that one would not find in a standard human body." She paused and looked up again. This time all of her students were suddenly fixated on her as she continued to read. "It is for this very reason that it is very common among young male werewolves to spend a lot of time in their early months after conversion, at home rather than causing problems for the more civil authorities." Polite laughter came sporadically from around the room. Felicity continued to read the quote. "As such, it is extremely unlikely for juvenile male werewolves to be involved in any serious criminal activity for much of their primary learning experiences." She finished her quote and placed the card back down with her notes. When she looked up again, she felt the world weary sigh of every teacher that has ever lived, when the keen but naively innocent student puts up their hand during reproductive education.

Meridian Whiteowl had raised his hand. "I'm sorry to ask this, but what is the reason for them staying at home?"

"You should not be sorry to ask a question Meridian," stated Felicity flatly, masking the fact that she had no desire to explain the intricacies of male werewolves and their masturbatory habits to the class. "However, you will find the answer to your question in chapter one of your copy of Ventress et al." Meridian reddened slightly as he tried to hide the fact that he had not read the first chapter of his course reader. However, some of the students towards the rear of the room had started to snigger. Felicity cast a gaze over the others and found that a good portion of the room where still waiting for her to speak. "Other forms of anti-social behaviour among werewolves that tends to lead into criminality is pack hunting and even tagging." Meridian Whiteowl's hand shot straight up again and this time Felicity stoically ignored him. "As you have no doubt read in the course reader, tagging by werewolves involves them spraying to mark out territory and even to the nose of non-werewolf species, the urine is horribly pungent." Meridian's hand dropped as he worked out what it was that werewolves used for tagging. Another student did raise their hand though and Felicity took a breath before answering. "Oleander Thorntree, you have a question?"

"Thank you Doctor Hopeforthebest," said Oleander politely. "We have read a lot in the course reader about violence and criminality among the werewolf population."

"Yes..." Said Felicity hopefully, waiting for the actual question to come.

Oleander continued, "Yet in their work, Steadman and Darkflower state quite firmly that Werewolves can also be fantastically helpful as criminal investigators and they go on to state that the biggest societal problem with the Werewolf community is actually racial profiling by authority figures."

Felicity beamed with joy, the Steadman and Darkflower book was number sixteen on the reading list and it was an obscure book at best. She spoke to the whole class, although keeping her eyes on her best student. "That is exactly where I was leading." She stated firmly. "Racial profiling causes untold levels of harm to all minority groups within our communities, however the greatest impact is often felt by the werewolf and vampire communities, all of whom suffer with terrible endemic racism for their supposed crimes against ordinary Fae." She turned back to Oleander Thorntree and smiled. "As investigators, it is our duty to rule out any forms of discrimination or bias in our practice. This is imperative to ensure that we are dealing with only the 'facts of the case' in a scientific manner."

Oleander looked very pleased with herself and Felicity turned back to her notes, the year ahead was going to be interesting, one or two of her students were showing real promise and another still was looking very much like she had the drive and understanding to follow through into service after leaving university. At that moment, the special mobile phone in Felicity's pocket began to vibrate and she pulled it out and spoke calmly. "Speak!"

"Felicity, bit of a strange one, gremlin at the dam. I need some support, any suggestions of whom I should take with me?"

Felicity blinked in surprise. Confirmed sightings were unbelievably rare and with no one she could think of, she had no other choice. "Only me I am afraid." She could almost hear the Magician's grin down the phone.

"Righto oh then, young Lady. I shall meet you in twenty minutes, if you can be ready in that timescale?"

"Excellent, I shall be ready in ten."

"Jolly Hockey Sticks, aye what young lady?" Replied the Magician.

"Jolly Hockey Sticks, old boy!" Felicity closed the call and slid the phone back into her pocket before turning back to the class. "Unfortunately for you all, I have an urgent case to attend to, however," she grinned at Oleander. "I suggest that all of you read the section in the class reader that discusses the work of Steadman and Darkflower, unless you have the actual book. In which case, read chapters three and four and make notes for your end of semester assignment." She paused and looked around the lecture theatre as some of the students diligently wrote down the suggested reading. "Don't forget though, you are attending University and you are here to read, to increase your knowledge and underpin your understanding..." She smiled as if she had told a private joke. "So, the wider reading you can do, the broader your understanding will be of this subject, especially when the subject is as complex as criminology and racial bias."

She dismissed the class and then walked as fast as she could while leaning heavily on her cane, towards her office. At the door, she found several notes left for her, none of which required urgent attention. However, her overnight bag was under her desk and on the shelf above her desk was her work case with her crime scene examination kit. She shouldered her overnight bag and hefted her work case, which felt heavier than she remembered. As she turned back to her door, there was a firm polite knock from the other side.

"Enter." She called and the door creaked open and the slightly shy features of Oleander Thorntree peeked around the door. "Excuse me Doctor Hopeforthebest, I understand that you are about to leave on a case." She smiled hopefully at Felicity. "I was wondering, would you permit me to come along and observe some real work out in the field?"

Felicity smiled kindly, but Oleander continued. "I am up to date on my reading, in-fact I am slightly ahead on the course reader and have read the wider texts too. Plus, I have no other classes for the remainder of the week and only one essay due for the end of the month, which is on the third draft, although I am currently eight thousand words into the appendix."

Felicity put down her case and sat on the edge of her desk and looked at the earnest young woman. "Oleander, while I admire your determination and your drive." She smiled kindly, "I cannot take you onto an active crime scene, where I am unable to ensure your safety. Not only that, but you are not yet eligible for the insurance needed to work in the field and as a first year, you are not yet accredited for field work anyway, something which will come for you in your third year." She could see the disappointment on Oleander's face, but the young woman nodded her understanding. "There is one other thing, this case in particular is highly sensitive and has risks associated that are not common to ordinary cases. I hope that you can understand why I am unable to take you with me."

"Doctor Hopeforthebest, I do understand, but you have to admit, I had to try?" She grinned, trying to hide the disappointment of not being able to go with her mentor.

"I would have been disappointed if you had not at least asked." Felicity replied kindly with a warm smile.

Oleander took the compliment and grinned again. "If I may say one last thing though Doctor Hopeforthebest, I have read some of your papers and read about your exploits in the newspaper since I was a little girl." She took a deep breath and gave in to her inner little girl who had hero worshipped Felicity. "You inspired me to read criminology and I would love to follow in your footsteps one day, well, when I leave University that is." She blushed and tried to hide it, her face lowering.

Felicity leant down slightly and in a very quiet voice she spoke again. "Tell me Oleander, how are your foreign languages?" She grinned again. "Do you have a strong keep fit regime and have you looked into military service after you graduate?"

Oleander smiled shyly. "I am at grade two Norfcorean already, I used to run cross country for my school and I still run now, although it's just for fun and yes, I have thought about applying to the General when I graduate."

Felicity nodded and stood up straight. "Jolly good. Keep it up, but not at the expense of your studies and come the time and if you still wish to pursue such a career, I will give you a reference to the General myself."

Oleander beamed and it was only her manners that stopped her leaning over and embracing Felicity in a hug.

Felicity spoke again. "However, at this time, there is one thing that you can do for me, providing that you do not mind, please?"

"Certainly Doctor Hopeforthebest, what is it?" replied Oleander.

"Would you carry my bag for me please?" Felicity held out her work case, which Oleander instantly took.

"No problem at all, Doctor Hopeforthebest." She replied proudly.

Outside of her office, Felicity locked the door and using her cane, began the short walk to the front of the University to meet with the Magician. At her side, Oleander walked quietly, suddenly hyper aware that she was carrying her teacher's bag. But this was not school and University was a much more rewarding place for students of her calibre anyway and so not caring what any of her other peers thought of her, she hurried on to keep up with the famous and heroic, Doctor Hopeforthebest. For the rest of the short walk, she wore a huge beaming smile, because the chance of a personal reference from her mentor to the General, was worth a little teasing from her peers. As it turned out, not a person noticed her or said a single negative thing about it. Oleander quickly discovered that as one of the harder working students in the university, she found herself in good company. She found a common urge to excellence with a group of friends who were similarly driven, including a young woman who was reading for a degree in political science ready for a career in the diplomatic service, Aurora Fireskies. It did not take them long to become close friends, despite their different areas of interest.

King Bobney sat at his desk in his private office and pushed a hand through his hair. The note he held in his other hand was from Deborah, the young woman who acted as his chief environmental advisor, the fact that she was the spirit of Mother Nature in Fae form, also came in rather handy. The note contained some worrying news and it concerned the increasingly warming summer and the effect this was having on the Realm. The crux of the issue was that she was worried about the water table below the city and the ability of the city to provide enough clean drinking water for everyone living within it. The dam would eventually supply plenty of clean water, but not for another few years, because there was still a huge amount of work to do on the project. The more immediate problem needed a quick, temporary fix, but very soon before the city ran out of potable water. The options were not great and he needed to call in both Wuffles and Deborah for a meeting to discuss his ideas, despite knowing that both people would find the ideas almost impossible to put in place. He placed the note back on his desk and instead picked up his mobile phone and started to type a group message to his advisors. '@Advisory Group... Meet Urgent. Water Shortage coming. Planning needed'. He hit send and watched as the message went out and then became seen by his council. It was immediately given a thumbs up from Wuffles and a love heart from Deborah. The General sent a salute and Mr Klemp replied with a formal and polite, "Yes Sire." Felicity and the Magician were away at the dam, but the University Chancellor replied with the emoji of a clock face and a question mark. The last emoji to pop up came from Colonel Thrashgood, who gave the sign of an egg timer to indicate that he was away on mission and would be back when he could.

Having received as many replies as he was going to get, he typed again, an emoji of the palace and then the numerals 1630 and then a smiley face.

The first advisors started to arrive at four fifteen to find King Bobney in his meeting room, pacing up and down. On the table in front of him was a large, scale map of the city and beside that was a cloth covered object. When everyone was seated and ready, King Bobney started to speak. "My friends, we are facing a water crisis. The Dam is going to solve the crisis, but not for a few years yet, which means that we need a temporary solution to getting drinking water for the city."

Wuffles gave a slight whine, waggled his ears and then curled his lip to give a low slow growl.

King Bobney nodded his agreement as he spoke. "Mayor Wuffles has as usual got straight to the heart of the problem. Not only are we wasteful with the water resources we currently have, we have numerous leaks in the supply network that must be fixed."

Mr Klemp raised his hand, "excuse me Sire?" He asked meekly.

Wuffles whined and rested his head on Mr Klemp's shoulder and wagged his tail a few times and Mr Klemp spoke again. "Sorry, I forgot. It still feels strange calling the King of the entire Realm by his first name."

"You have the floor Eli." Said King Bobney sagely.

"Thank you Sire, I was only going to ask where we stand on water storage? Do we use rain collection or let it soak away for ground water?" Asked Mr Klemp.

The Chancellor, Professor Sophie Daphodils spoke

up. "If I may answer your question Eli?" Mr Klemp turned towards the woman of learning and nodded agreeably. She continued. "The problem we have is that the aquifer below the city is already dangerously low, which is causing the ground to sink as it dries out in some specific places below the city and this is causing significant damage to some of our buildings in the city above. Thus, when it rains the water must be allowed to soak into the ground, to try to fill the aquifer. However, the result of climate change is that we are making the atmosphere warmer and this is giving us less seasonal rain than we usually get, which again means less rain fall to top up the aquifer."

Wuffles whined slightly and wriggled his eyebrows and yipped a sharp tone.

"That is possible," stated Sophie in reply. "But sadly grey water still needs to go through treatment because it contains bathing residues, clothing detergents and other pollutants that are damaging to health."

"So, once treated, it could be pumped into the ground which would stop any further drops in ground level which in turn would prevent any further damage to the buildings.." Said Deborah thoughtfully.

"I have an idea on how to get more water," said King Bobney quietly. "But I don't think that you're going to like it."

"What is it?" Asked Deborah and Mr Klemp together.

Bobney carefully picked up the covered container and placed it on the table where everyone could see it. Before he could even uncover it, Deborah reacted as if she had been stabbed with a pin, that no one else could see.

"NO!" She half shouted, pushing back away from the table and knocking her chair to the floor. "You cannot bring that in here. It must be returned to the flow."

Wuffles jumped down from his seat and padded over to Deborah and put his head on her shoulder where she stood against the wall. Her arms embraced him and she buried her face into his fur.

King Bobney was somewhat taken aback and left the cover on the object, but lifted it up and took it back to the original table.

"I am sorry," he said quietly, "I had hoped that it was an answer, I didn't realise that it would upset you so much Deborah." There was no judgement in his voice, only tones of sadness and concern for the young woman and regret for not understanding another important piece of knowledge about the Faerie Realm.

She looked up and gazed at the King, her eyes had lost their usual Fae qualities and had become dark, cold emeralds. "You must return that to the source. You do not understand what it contains."

"I thought it was just dirty water." Said King Bobney very concerned that this was something that he should have known about before. "What else is in there?"

"The souls of the lost." Said Deborah flatly. "It must go back to the source so that they can be free."

"I had no idea." Said King Bobney quietly. He picked up the object and turned back to the group of people. "I'll be ten minutes. Have a cuppa, I won't be long."

"No, wait." Said Deborah quietly. "You will need me too." She stood up and followed the King as he left the room. Professor Sophie Daphodils stood up and wandered over to the kettle and switched it on to boil. "Who else wants a cup of tea?" She said, trying to break the tension of the moment.

The autocart slew into the gravel car park and screeched to a halt outside the Forewoman's office and then continued to screech as the odd creatures that propelled the large drive wheel, fought and wrestled until Felicity dropped in the kilo of carrots that she had bought for the journey. The screeching silenced, to be replaced by the loud crunching of carrots, a few large and airy farts and then indelicate snoring as all three of the creatures curled up together and went to sleep. The site was deserted, all of the contractor trolls were away enjoying a feast in the nearest Norfcorean restaurant. The Magician climbed down from the autocart as soon as he was able to release his grip from the hand rail that passengers were provided with to cling, bite or otherwise hang on to throughout the journey. The colour slowly returned to his face and although he had an urge to bend down and kiss the ground with gratitude for having survived the journey, he was not sure that he had the strength to stand up again having done so, at least not for a little while anyway.

Felicity approached the Forewoman's office with great care, the last thing she wanted to do was trigger another carefully planned accident that had been left waiting to just 'happen'. She was about to touch the door handle when she felt the hairs on the back of her hand tingle. She put down her bag of equipment and pulled out a test meter and touched the probe to the door handle. The needle shot across the scale, indicating an electrical charge of several million volts, the jolt of which would have stopped her heart and then cooked it in her chest. Reaching back into her bag, she found a thick rubber glove and pulled it on, before then pulling on a chainmail over glove. Taking a thick lead and a crocodile clip, she attached the mail glove to the lead and then attached the end to a metal stake that had been hammered deep into the earth. All set, she reached out for the door handle. A bright blue arc sprang from the handle and cracked against the mail glove, before surging into the ground, leaving a blackened burn mark around the stake. On the other side of the door, a whine started for a few seconds, but with a sudden and revolting smell of burning plastic, it slowly faded to silence. Whatever had given the door handle its killing charge, had finally burned out. Felicity pushed open the door and felt the resistance of something heavy behind it. When she was able to look inside, she found the gutted remains of an electrical heater that had been wired to the door handle. "Hey Brianco, you should see this?" She called out to the Magician as he staggered towards her from the autocart. When he reached her, he looked around the door and grinned.

"Nasty, that would have hurt."

"So," said Felicity playfully, "how do we catch the little blighter who built this hellish contraption?"

"Bloody carefully!" Joked the Magician with a forced giggle. "I have a trapping spell, but we need to know where our joker is first."

"Any ideas?" Felicity asked quietly.

"Not yet, but these little trouble makers thrive on chaos and destruction. So let's keep looking and triggering any little jokes left for us."

"Jokes?" Asked Felicity quietly. "These death threats are meant to be jokes?"

The Magician gave a felicity a wide terrifyingly manic grin. "The thing that it is absolutely essential to remember here, is that these are just simple jokes. Nothing more and thus you just need a good sense of humour to 'get them', if you know what I mean?"

Felicity grinned. "Well no one has ever told me that I lack a sense of humour."

The office was empty, with no further traps left to catch them out, but a trail of chaos led across the storage yard and into the construction site. Felicity and the Magician followed carefully, triggering a few small traps along the way. A subtly hidden rake nearly hit the Magician in the face when he stepped on the head and then a small tin of paint fell from a sloped shed roof and nearly soaked the pair of them in a violent bright orange paint that was used for marking out digging sites. The Magician sidled across to a volatile looking Felicity and whispered to her as she furiously dismantled the remains of the paint trap. "Remember my dear, you need to keep a sense of humour."

"I'm trying," hissed Felicity with a forced grin on her face.

"Try?" Asked the Magician quietly. "There is no try!" He started to laugh and as he did so, he slapped the side of his thighs playfully. "Sorry, that is a quote from one of my favourite films in the human world."

Felicity gave the Magician a mystified shake of her head and he laughed again. "It's said by this little green warrior monk guy, to the son of his enemy. It's a great film, I'm telling you."

"I'll take your word for it." She said, quietly chuckling.

A sudden loud crack startled them, Felicity stood up and leant on her cane looking for the source of the noise. In the near distance, a branch fell from a remaining tree and landed on the hard packed ground close to the footings of the dam. "Got him, said Felicity with hiss of anger."

"Remember, keep on smiling or it will evade you." Said the Magician with the hint of laughter in his voice.

Felicity grinned. "Got you." She said laughing and shaking her head. Looking back at him she gave him a wide grin. "I just need to keep thinking of you and your little green warrior monk!"

Chapter 4

King Bobney looked out of the window from his office and gazed at the yellowing lawns and sparse flowerbeds that made up the royal garden. It had not rained for over six weeks and Mayor Wuffles had been forced to introduce a hosepipe ban and strict control of the city's water resources that supplied everyone with drinking water. Bobney's Mother, Queen Linda, had complained that the garden was not looking great and as King, he had a right to a prettier garden, but Bobney had stood his ground and insisted that water rationing applied to the Palace too. Deborah had spent some time at the Palace discussing the disturbing events of the illegal miners who had struck yet again. Not even the SFS was able to discover who the miners were or where they came from, even with tip offs from Deborah. It almost seemed like the illegal miners were able to open a portal and disappear into another world, leaving no trace of where they had gone, but everyone knew that such things were impossible, even with the best, oldest and strongest Faerie magic.

In front of Bobney, was a letter from the King of

Norfcorea, who had requested a summit meeting with the rulers of all of the nations in the Faerie Realm. As over-all ruler of the entire Realm, Bobney was technically the only one who could demand such a meeting, but with the state of the environment, Bobney was in agreement with the Norfcorean King. Kindly, the Norfcorean King had offered to host the event at his own Palace and stated that he would welcome input from Bobney and his team of ambassadors. Just as Bobney was about to pull his quill from the pot and start writing his official reply, the door to his office burst open and Queen Linda pranced into the room and in a shrill voice demanded Bobney's attention. "Bobney, how dare you ignore my calls, my notes and even my conversations?!"

Bobney closed his eyes and let his head rest against his clenched fists. "What is it this time, Mother?" He said, his voice weary, despite the early hour of the day.

"You bloody well know what!" She shrieked back, which caused the Butler to open his small door and enter the office and bow to them both.

"Is there something that you need, your Highnesses?" Queen Linda scowled and turned to face the man.

"Not at this moment thank you, Butler." She tried to give him a smile, but it came out as a grimace.

"Thank you for your inquiry, Butler." Said King Bobney politely. "You may return to your duties."

The Butler bowed again and left the room to return to his office. Bobney turned back to his mother. "What are you twittering about this time, Mother?" He pointed to the pile of documents on his desk and leaned back in his chair. "As you can see, I am rather snowed under with work at the moment, but by all means, feel free to add your own melodrama to my already busy schedule."

Linda frowned. "Don't be so passive aggressive my boy." She said quietly. "You may be the King, but that does not give you the right to speak to me quite so rudely."

For a moment, Bobney day-dreamed about how previous Kings had beheaded the various relatives that had annoyed them or when they had just become an inconvenience.

"Bobney!" Shrieked Queen Linda, as she realised that her son had drifted off into a moment of quiet reflection. "What are you going to do about the coronation?"

Bobney let out a sigh and crossed his arms across his chest. "You know what I am going to do." He gave her a cold smile. "I am going to sit here and ignore the whole sorry mess."

Queen Linda sat down in the left hand of the two chairs facing Bobney and gave him a sour look. "He is family, so you should show your face, especially when the royal family is in such disarray."

Bobney sighed his contempt. "Their royal family, not mine." He hissed back angrily. "We are distant cousins at best and to be honest, fuck him! He does a good job of pretending to care about his people and yet have you seen how he reacts when one of them tries to ask him to justify his actions?"

"BOBNEY!" Shrieked Linda suddenly, "how dare you speak about our family like that?"

Bobney leant forward, his face dangerously calm and his icy voice low, barely hiding his anger. "That bastard is an anti-science, hippy bullshit following toss-pot. He has dubious views on nature that even my friend Deborah finds peculiar. Plus he interferes in their democracy in ways that he should not." He sat back in his chair. "Also, he has shot more than a few Fae folk who found themselves on his land, when he was out murdering birds for fun!"

Linda sat quietly for a moment and then let out a deep sigh. "I can see that there is no changing your mind."

Bobney smiled. "I am glad that you can finally see that." He pressed a button on his desk and a small computer screen slid up from a carefully hidden slot on the back of his desk. "However, I am happy for you to attend the event, if you so wish, you can also take Craig with you, if he can stomach going to the event?"

"Thank you, Bobney." Queen Linda was resigned and could tell that she would get no better offer from her son the King. "Shall I ask the palace tailors to make me a new dress for the event?" She saw that Bobney's face had soured again. "I can hardly fit into any of my old clothes, can I?" She pressed the tiny, barely visible bump of her belly, where Bobney's sister was gestating peacefully unaware of the horrors going on in the world.

Bobney nodded his head, his voice was quiet. "Yes of course, Mother. I trust that Craig can help you with this matter?"

Queen Linda looked at Bobney and studied his face for a moment. "Do you like Craig?" She asked quietly, her voice filled with concern.

Bobney's eyes narrowed and then he smiled, realising that his mother just needed a moment of comfort. "Mother I am aware that when I was growing up, you were a single parent and you did your very best to keep me hidden. However, if I could have had a father, I could not have had a better father than Craig is going to be to your new baby. To be honest. I am amazed at his levels of tolerance and I am actually very fond of the man."

Linda smiled slightly, but her eyes were moist with tears. "Fatherhood changes people, what if he stops loving me and the time we have together?"

Bobney stood up and rounded his desk in a couple of steps and bent down in front of his mother. "I may not know Craig was well as you do, but what I do know of him is that he is loyal, undeniably kind and that he loves you with all of his heart." He gave her a wicked grin, "the poor mad sod!"

Linda sniffed and let out a small chuckle. "Do you think that I am hard work for him?"

Bobney stood up and grinned. "I am sure that he is more than man enough to face the challenge!"

"BOBNEY WOLFGANG JONES!" She shrieked, but quickly started to giggle. "Actually, he really is." She raised her eyebrows suggestively and let out a deep contented sigh.

Bobney shook his head and wandered back to his chair. "If you would excuse me Mother, I really must get on with this work, the Realm is in trouble and unfortunately, the buck stops with me."

Queen Linda gazed at her son, her eyes full of love and admiration. "I am so proud of the man you have become. Wherever I go in this life, I know that the entire Realm will always be safe with you as its guardian."

Bobney closed his eyes for a moment and rubbed them with a thumb and forefinger. "I wish that was the case, but thank you for your words of support Mother."

Queen Linda stood up. "I will organise this coronation thing with Craig and have the details delivered to your desk, so that you will be kept in the loop, so to speak. However, I can see that you have a great deal to do, so you can trust me to be the envoy of the Faerie Realm."

"Thank you Mother, I hope that you have some fun."

Magician Brianco Oxx stood with Felicity Hopeforthebest and he gazed at the distant small post box that rested on top of the wooden pole that was firmly hammered into the stony ground. Felicity was bent down, rooting in the bottom of her work bag and suddenly let out a small yelp of satisfaction. "Got it." She stood up and looked at the Magician. "Are you ready?"

The Magician grinned, "baby, I was born ready!" He saw a sudden shadow flash across Felicity's face. "Sorry, not baby, I meant grown woman." His cheeks reddened and Felicity changed the subject.

"This jar has a tight screw top. Do you think that this will be big enough?"

The Magician nodded his head. This little guy will not be able to resist, they absolutely cannot refuse a practical joke. Felicity carefully placed the small mousetrap in the bottom of the jar, then dropped in the box of matches and finally added a single boot lace. She placed the lid on the jar, but did not tighten it down before handing it to the Magician. The Magician took the jar and whispered words that only he could hear as he carefully spun a small spell over the top of the jar. The lid jiggled slightly and then settled perfectly still as the Magician wandered a few steps towards the post box. Being very careful, the Magician bent down and placed the jar on the ground, before he twisted on the balls of his feet and sprinted away towards the small brick blast wall that Felicity was already walking towards. When they were both hidden behind the wall and squatting down, Felicity let out a long slow breath. "So, we just have to sit here and..."

A loud pop, like the bursting of a large water balloon sounded and was followed by screech that could have been an eagle that had just received a shockingly high gas bill and divorce papers in the same postal delivery. The Magician stood up and grinned at Felicity and offered her his hand. "With no disrespect meant, would Ma'am care for some assistance to stand up?"

Felicity smiled kindly and took his hand. "Thank you gallant sir." He helped her to stand and allowed her to hold on to his arm as she retrieved her walking stick from where it lay next to the wall. "Do you think we got it?"

The Magician grinned. "It was a good joke if we did."

There was a sudden noise in the air and then the shattering of a glass jar as it hit the other side of the wall. Both Felicity and the Magician froze.

"Fuck it." He hissed. "Sounds like our little joke failed."

Felicity nodded her agreement. "I told you that we needed to use the whoopee cushion."

Deborah stood in the vast dusty scoop that resembled a bite taken out of the landscape. Her heart was filled with rage and she stood in silence as around her, the investigative team of the SFS looked for clues as to who the miners were. Half a hillside had been dug out, sifted, treated with chemicals and left as a heap of poisoned spoil. In places, small puddles shimmered with the rainbow shine of chemical pollution. Silently Deborah felt someone approach her from behind.

"Anything?"

"I'm sorry, not a clue." said Gladys Meuchelmorder quietly. She put her hand on Deborah's shoulder and gave her a comforting squeeze. "We will catch these people and we will stop them."

Deborah reached up and put her hand on top of that of Gladys. "It would help if we knew what they were looking for."

"He's no Felicity, but we have an excellent chemist here." Gladys squeezed her shoulder reassuringly. "He says that it looks like precious metals, but can only be ninety percent sure."

"Ninety percent is sure enough, we need to stop them. Before they damage something that cannot recover."

Gladys looked around the area of devastation. "This can recover? It looks barren, dead."

Deborah smiled and slowly knelt down, a painfully sharp sparkle of lightning forming where her fingers touched the ground. Shooting out from her soul, came the stems of plant life that erupted and exploded across the dust. Within seconds, small shrubs were spreading out over the bare earth and between them, flowers and grasses burst from the ground with almost violent popping sounds. Gladys watched in silence as the life proved that it would exist no matter who or what tried to stop it. Finally Deborah stood up, tired and breathing hard. "The damage was deep, but the poisons are locked away and the land is healing." She looked up as a green clad soldier sprinted across the newly grassy meadow towards her. He stopped and saluted Gladys and then spoke, his accent a mix of Winscombe and human. "General," he turned to Deborah, "Ma'am."

Gladys saluted him back "Don't be shy Guillaume, tell us what you have found."

"I think that I have identified what it is they are looking for." He held out a sheath of notes. "I think that they are Lithium miners."

Gladys nodded. "Thank you Guillaume, how certain are you?"

"I would put money on it." He answered.

"Thank you Guillaume." Said Deborah quietly, despite her tiredness.

Guillaume grinned sheepishly. "You are welcome, Ma'am." His face reddened slightly before he spoke again. "Anything I can do to help you, Ma'am, I will gladly do."

Gladys smiled and swallowed down a chuckle that she felt rising in her chest.

Deborah held out her hand to the young man and he shook it gently. "Thank you, we all need to do what we can."

He turned to Gladys and nodded his head respectfully. "General." He turned on the spot and sprinted back across the new fresh meadow.

Deborah watched him go and then turned back to Gladys. "I wonder why they want lithium?"

Gladys nodded. "Indeed." She smiled slightly, her lips barely showing the humour she felt. "So young Guillaume, he seems very taken with you."

Deborah looked up. "What do you mean?"

Gladys leant in close to Deborah. "What do you think I mean?"

Deborah looked into Gladys' eyes, she could see her soul, a gentle softness filled with love, duty and kindness. "You think he likes me?"

Gladys nodded her head from side to side, "who can say with you young people today?" She took Deborah's hand in her own. "Before you ask, I would trust any of my troops here with my life, him included. He's a good lad."

"Sort of like the King?" Deborah said, her voice indicating that she was aware of something that Gladys was not.

Gladys seemed to stiffen, "The King is more than a man, Deborah." She said primly. "He is the embodiment of the Realm, he is the shining light that leads us."

"He also looks pretty fit, it must be all of that training he does with Colonel Thrashgood." Deborah said happily.

"I don't think that I have ever noticed." Said Gladys firmly. She was quiet for a second or two before she continued. "He is likely just as fit as any of the SFS troops, he loves training with them."

Deborah let out a guffaw. "That is not quite what I meant, but you are probably right."

Gladys looked at Deborah puzzled. "You know young lady, sometimes you youngsters say things that mean something entirely different from what you think they mean."

"Youngsters?" Asked Deborah tartly. "I am older than all of you put together." She gave Gladys a warm smile, "well parts of me are anyway."

"Well, back to business," said Gladys firmly, but

kindly. "If we know that they are mining for lithium, can we predict where they will go next?" Deborah fell silent and her face darkened as she gave it some thought. Gladys continued. "If there is anywhere you can give us a clue to, maybe we can catch them before they start?"

"There is one place, but it is a sacred place. They wouldn't dare desecrate it, surely?" Deborah looked stricken.

"Where is it?" Asked Gladys gently, "I can deploy a unit there, to keep watch."

Deborah looked up into Gladys' face with eyes that had turned black with anger, worry and despair. "Home." she said. Her voice haunted.

"Your house, your garden? What do you mean?" Said Gladys, hiding some of the urgency from her voice, while trying to sound reassuring.

Deborah reached out a hand for support and Gladys took it gladly. "The river, by Herbert's house, it goes through an area that has a seam. If they find it, they will destroy my home and all that I love there." Gladys still holding the young woman's hand leant in and in a quiet voice, spoke forcefully. "I will do everything in my power to not let that happen."

"I know." Said Deborah just as quietly.

Letting go of the young woman, Gladys reached

into her pocket and pulled out her mobile phone, she pressed a single number and held it. Three seconds later, it started to ring. It was answered almost immediately. "General, what do you need?"

"Colonel, can you get a troop to Deborah's home ASAP. There is a chance that the miners will arrive there, we know what they are looking for lithium and there is a seam close to the river by her uncle's house."

"They will be there in two hours, I will put Troop Sixty Six on it, The Princess will fly them in." Thrashgood replied.

"Thank you Colonel." Said Gladys calmly, "I will let our young charge know that her home is safe."

"The house and the land for ten square miles will be under our protection, if anyone even so much as throws a pebble in the pond, we will know about it!" Thrashgood grinned, "tell our girl that we will keep a discrete eye on Herbert and Katie too, she doesn't have a thing to worry about."

Felicity pulled out her last specimen jar and checked the lid. "If this one fails, we will need to find another way to catch the little clown."

The Magician shuddered. "Don't say clown, they give me the creeps!"

Felicity smiled and looked up at the Magician. "You don't like clowns?"

The Magician frowned, "why is that so odd? They are terrifying to look at, with their shiny red noses, wild hair and teeth like needles."

Felicity chuckled, "I think that you have been in the human world too much, that is such a human thing to say."

"I was born there and both of my parents are human." Said the Magician conversationally. "I only came here when it became obvious that I had magician skills. It was either come here to attend the University, or stay there and get judged by the nutty God botherers back home."

"I'm sorry, I didn't know." Said Felicity kindly. "It was not my intention to be racist."

The Magician chuckled. "The problem is societal, racism is ingrained into every level of the societal structure. Mind you, if you think that it is bad here, you should see the human world, they are fucking awful there, it's not like they have the different species the way we do here. They are all the same, so they segregate based on skin colour or national differences or the fucking class system."

Felicity nodded, "yeah, I never got that." She said quietly.

The Magician continued. "Racism is so bad there, in most of what they call the 'first world', as if it is somehow better than the other parts! Anyway, people with black, brown or other forms of dark skin, face horrendous discrimination to just find the simple things like housing, education or even the ability to get health care." He sighed sadly, "they call the areas with less of the industry and wealth, the third world." He spat on the floor with disgust. "The implication is that the third world does not have the wealth or power of the rich, white first world. Which is somewhat skewed given that the rich white people made lots of money by stealing land, wealth and even people from the nations of black or brown people."

Felicity nodded. "I have read about their slavery history, it sounded awfully evil."

Again the Magician sighed. "It was and it remains evil. Four hundred years later and the darker skinned people are still suffering from the repercussions of slavery, meanwhile there is a global rise in white supremacy!" He shook his head incredulous. "It is as if they deliberately choose to be wilfully stupid and believe in such nonsense."

"What has this got to do with clowns though?" Asked Felicity gently.

The Magician glared at her for a second or two. "Well, ahh... Um."

Felicity grinned, "don't worry, I won't say another thing about it." She handed the glass jar to the magician. "So, what do we put in this one?"

"I have an idea, but you won't like it." Said the Magician with an evil glint in his eye.

"Try me?" Said Felicity jovially.

The Magician took the jar, raised his robes and placed it firmly against his bottom before he screwed up his face and squeezed hard. After a second or two, a high pitched and very squeaky fart sounded and the Magician quickly grabbed the lid and screwed it on tightly. Felicity gaped for a second or two and then she started to laugh.

"What?" Said the Magician defensively. "They find this kind of thing funny!"

"Oh really?" Asked Felicity. "Are you sure that it's not just you who finds this funny?"

The Magician rolled his eyes somewhat dramatically. "Madam, I will have you know that the fart is the oldest, universal joke in all of creation." He checked that the lid was tight on the jar and turned back to Felicity. "For as long as species have evolved the ability to comprehend humour, they have laughed at farts, poop and other disgusting bodily functions." He gave Felicity an imperious look. "Anyway, young missy, it was you who suggested using the whoopee Cushion!"

Felicity nodded her head as she spoke. "Well, yes, guilty as charged."

"Have you got a sticker and a pen?"

Felicity checked her bag and passed a pen and a sticky label to the Magician. He carefully filled in the label and stuck it on the jar and then showed it to Felicity.

"This will catch the little fucker." He once again performed his spell on the jar and gave it back to Felicity. "If you can my dear, place this over by the post box, then run for cover as fast as you can."

"Well, I shall hobble for cover!" She replied with a smile.

The Magician looked up at her from where he was squatting down behind the wall. "Oh Felicity, I am so sorry. I didn't mean anything by it."

Felicity smiled again, it was a radiant smile and her face was lit with an inner joy and beauty. "I know," she said quietly. "Don't worry." She rounded the wall and paced carefully across to the post box and placed the jar on the ground. Next to it, she placed the freshly inflated whoopee cushion and then she turned on her heels and marched carefully back to the wall, leaning on her cane as she did so. Back at the wall, she carefully sat down next to the Magician and they waited.

King Bobney got dressed in his finest blue silk coat and green pantaloons and then sat on the bed to pull on his brown leather boots. He secured the straps and then stood up again before he wandered out of the room and headed towards his office. As he ambled along, looking out of the window, the Butler managed to walk at a running pace towards the monarch. When he caught the King, he bowed low and then stood up, his spine as straight as a builder's level. "Sire, the General has returned to the palace and is waiting for you in your office, as you instructed."

"Thank you Butler. I was just heading there now." The Butler bowed low and spoke again. "I shall ensure that refreshments are delivered there right away Sire."

"Thank you very much, Butler. You are a true gentleman." The Butler stood up straight as the King wandered away and as he watched the King go, he realised that he was grinning from ear to ear. As much as he had not wanted to, he had come to really like the new King.

Bobney walked into his office and shut the door. At the window, looking out across the parched gardens stood the General, dressed in her finest dress uniform. Her hair was tied up in a tight bun that was held captive below the rear of her cap and her arms were behind her back, her hands on each end of her pace stick. On hearing the door, she turned and lowered her head in a delicate bow. "Your Highness, thank you for asking me to join you on your trip." She smiled her professional polite smile. "You have no concerns about my intrusion into your activities, my team and I will be in the background, we will be as non-intrusive as possible, but will ensure your safety."

"Thank you General Meuchelmorder, but I had actually asked you to attend this conference purely for your company as my friend, although your security knowledge will no doubt be of great use while we are in Norfcorea." Said Bobney quietly.

He could feel his heart beating in his chest and the blood racing throughout his body, which was a remarkably strange sensation and he had no idea why he felt such a way. The General smiled at him and he felt his heart almost flutter and the strangest feeling in his tummy, as if he were suddenly terribly excited, but about which he did not know. "Will you join me for refreshments while we discuss the itinerary?" He almost whispered to her.

"I would be honoured, your Highness." The General replied. Bobney could see that she was wearing a small amount of make up, her eyes were exquisite and her lips were a soft pale red, that matched the red of her jacket, with its gold braid and medals. Her long green skirt was the usual heavy wool of her daily military uniform, but the jacket was new and had been issued by the regimental tailor so that she would look her best as she accompanied the King.

"Please, General Meuchelmorder, call me Bobney, just as my friends do when we are in private." His voice felt like it shook in his throat and for a brief moment he felt both vulnerable and shy.

"Sire, usually I would gladly use your name, but given the journey we are about to undertake, I do not wish to slip up and embarrass you in an

136

important situation." She replied, but as she did so, she ached to call him Bobney and to spend hours just listening to him talk as they sat together, watching the world go on around them.

"I understand General Meuchelmorder and you are right." His voice was almost breathless. "We have a duty to all of the realms and we must ensure that we carry out that duty with the decorum and dignity required by the event. Thank you for the reminder of this duty." With a quiet knock on the door to the King's office, the Butler opened it and pushed in a small trolley that contained a china tea pot, two small cups and saucers, a small fruit cake and a number of biscuits. The King was puzzled, he and the Butler had grown used to the man entering the King's office politely, but without the need to knock.

"Sire, my Lady." He turned to Gladys and gave her a formal bow. "Please enjoy afternoon tea, while we prepare for your flight to Norfcorea." Said the Butler gently. The King noticed that the Butler was smiling, not his usual firm professional smile, but something softer, somehow more gentle and with a subtle hint of quiet amusement. He placed the cups onto the King's desk and carefully poured the tea, before placing a side plate and adding a biscuit to each and small slice of cake. He turned to leave and as he did so, faced the General, whereupon he clicked his heels together and then gave her a stiff military Salute. "General, your tea is ready, Sir." She returned his salute and also clicked her heels as she did so. He then turned to the King and bowed his head. "Sire, I wish you both," He couldn't help but smile. "A very pleasant afternoon."

The King narrowed his eyes and turned his head slightly as he watched the Butler leave. This behaviour was new. He was fairly sure that the Butler was up to something, but for the life of him he could not figure out what.

Outside the office, the Butler raced down the corridor to the kitchen and burst into the warm, well-lit room and took his usual stool at the table. The head chef was off for the day, leaving the assistant chef in charge. She was a tall thin and proud looking Fae, with thin gossamer wings that stood erect on her back. Her face although thin and lined with age, was gentle and her smile was warm, her voice a soft purr. "So..."

The Butler shook his head. "I have given them your lover's cake and served them flower tea with warm heart biscuits."

The assistant chef chuckled and shook her head as

she kneaded the next day's bread. "Every one can see it. Well, everyone except them."

The Butler took a deep breath and puffed up his chest. "She is a magnificent woman, just imagine the children the pair of them would breed. The Realm would be safe for a thousand years."

"You are not wrong, Butler." Said the Chef quietly. "So when do you think they will work it out?"

The Butler let out his breath, somewhat sadly. "I worry that they will concentrate on duty alone and not see each other for what they are."

"Well, we must do our duty and cannot interfere." The chef said, her voice filled with mirth.

"Absolutely Chef, absolutely." The Butler grinned, "although, there is no harm in a gentle push every now and again, is there?"

They both laughed.

The air was still and everything had become so quiet, that the noise of a tiny bell flower swaying in the wind was all that could be heard as the Magician and Felicity sat in silence, waiting for the sounds of a successful trap. Suddenly came the loud, long rasp of a whoopee cushion being activated and then came a loud raucous giggle, followed by a loud, if somewhat obnoxious pop!

The Magician stood and thrust his arm up in the air in exultation. "Oh yes, get in!" He shouted joyfully. "We got the little fucker!" He proceeded to perform a little dance in victory. Felicity shook her head with amusement and waited for the Magician to finish his triumphant dance and offer her his hand. "Who's your Magician? I am, I am !" He began to chant and then he looked sideways and saw Felicity starting to laugh. He stood up straight and turned to face her. "Madam, please forgive me." He offered her his hand and gently helped her to stand up and then passed her her cane.

Her voice was filled with soft laughter as she spoke. "My dear friend, you have nothing to need forgiveness for."

The Magician bowed his head. "Oh my girl, if only that were true."

Felicity smiled kindly, "well, in that case I forgive you and you now have a fresh sheet to start with." She looked around the wall and could see her jar, it contained something, but she could not see what. "We have certainly caught something, but I am not sure what."

The Magician wandered across to the jar and picked it up. Inside was a swirl of dark smoke that thrashed like storm clouds, without the lightning. The

Magician held the jar up and spoke to it firmly. "I say there, to whom do I have the honour of addressing?"

The Smoke suddenly stilled and formed into the shape of a tiny, dark imp. "I am Gregor, to whom do I owe the gratitude of my capture?"

"I am the Magician Brianco Oxx and my accomplice is the Royal Scientist and honourable Doctor, Felicity Hopeforthebest." The Magician replied, his voice filled with noble gravitas. "Sir, it is our honour to meet you." He bowed slightly to the Imp and then turned the jar so that the Imp could clearly see Felicity.

"It is my pleasure and delight to meet you Sir." She said sweetly as she too bowed her head slightly.

The Imp looked at her sternly. "Madam, you are hurt." He stated. "I am most sorry and I hope that my jokes were not the cause of this."

"No Sir, not all." Stated Felicity firmly. "However, someone in our employ has been hurt quite badly and may struggle to walk again in the future."

"This was a result of my actions?" Asked the Imp politely.

"I am afraid that it was, old boy." Said the Magician sombrely. "You caused a malfunction with a power tool, which then slipped and very badly hurt the foot of one of our operatives."

The Imp sat down in the bottom of the jar and allowed their head to sag. "I am truly, truly sorry, I had no intention of causing harm to your friend. I was just trying to have some fun with those who have disturbed my land."

"I understand Sir and can see the truth in your words and manner." Said the Magician solemnly.

"What can I do to make amends?" Asked the Imp.

The Magician turned to Felicity. "Madam, would you care to discuss this with our new friend?"

"I thank you Master Magician, I would be indebted to you." Said Felicity. She bowed once to the Magician and turned to the Imp and bowed again. "Sir, I ask you, with respect that you cease playing your jokes on our friends as they work this land."

"All of my jokes?" Asked the Imp, somewhat quietly.

Felicity smiled. "Well Sir, what is life if all humour is removed? That sounds like no life I would wish to live? However, humour has no place in the world if it causes harm to the innocent, especially when they are performing a duty that will help save the future of the entire Realm."

"Madam," declared the Imp, "I concur with you. We may all enjoy a joke, but I have no desire to harm anyone living or otherwise." He smiled kindly. "May I enquire what task it is that your friends are here to undertake?"

Felicity nodded her head. "You may indeed Sir," she turned the jar to show the footings of the dam and then turned it back again. "My friends are here at the behest of King Bobney, to create a dam in the river valley. This will create a lake which will hold enough drinking water for the whole Realm." She turned again and pointed to one of the footings. "That area there will contain a turbine which will generate electricity that will supply all of the people in the Realm too, so that they can put an end to the dependency on fossil and other polluting fuels brought in from the human world." She turned the jar again and pointed out to the distant hills. "The lake will change the habitat of the area, but this was not a decision that was taken lightly. However, it was made with the guidance and blessing of Mother Nature."

The Imp stood up to attention at once, "you have spoken with Mother Nature?" His voice was urgent.

"I have Sir, may I ask why this is of importance?"

"Madam, I was under the misapprehension that your friends here were the vandals that are damaging the Realm."

The Magician spoke up. "Sir, excuse my interruption as you discuss this important matter with this lady of great learning, but may I ask what you know of these vandals?"

"I have knowledge that must be passed only to Mother Nature herself." Said the Imp flatly.

"I am sorry for asking Sir, I meant no disrespect." Said the Magician.

"You are absolved of any fault Sir," replied the Imp. "However, are you able to take me to the Great Lady herself?" The Imp turned to face Felicity again. "I include you in my request Madam, are the both of you in contact with the Great Lady?"

Felicity nodded once. "Sir, it is our honour and our duty to take you to Mother Nature. However, should you wish to speak to her immediately, I have her telephone number."

The Imp bowed down very low and stood up again. "I am aware of your telephone technology and this is acceptable to me." The Imp raised an arm and pointed to the office building. "Please take me to that building and place your telephone against the glass of my cell."

"I am happy to do so Sir, but do you require to be released from this container?" Said Felicity kindly.

The Imp pressed his face against the glass and his

features slowly melted through the glass and he grinned at her with a toothy smile. "This container is not the prison that you understand the word to mean. However, I choose to stay in captivity because of the guile and the great humour you have shown in my capture."

"Then I am honoured to do as you ask, Gregor." Said felicity gently. She made her way to the office and the Magician followed, shaking his head.

The King of Norfcorea bowed low to King Bobney as he stepped from the carriage of the Royal Dragon, onto the rich red carpet. He stood up and with his best formal Somerset, welcomed King Bobney. "Oh Arrrr, oi would like to welcome yuze, King Bobney, to moy Kingdom of Norfcorea." Behind him stood his two closest friends and advisers. The first, a young woman dressed in Norfcorean traditional dress, stepped forwards and presented King Bobney with a bunch of freshly cut flowers. The Norfcorean King spoke again. "Oi wuld like to prezent moy best frend an advizorr, Sha Wren Ston. The young women curtsied and stepped back behind King Jong. Next an older man stepped forwards and presented King Bobney with a small box of freshly baked cakes. He bowed and stepped back. The Norfcorean King spoke again, "my dear friend and faithful adviser, Fred Bear Rug, presents you with some of the finest baking our nation has to give."

King Bobney bowed to the Norfcorean King and then stood up and spoke, his voice loud, but clear in his polite, but basic Norfcorean. "My gracious friend, King Jong the First, it fills my heart with Joy to be welcomed into your home nation." He held an arm to the General who was stood silently behind him. "May I present my colleague and close personal friend, General Gladys Meuchelmorder." Gladys stepped forwards and bowed to the King before stepping back behind King Bobney. Bobney continued speaking as Gladys stared straight ahead, stood like a soldier made from solid steel. "I am saddened that we have been forced to call for this summit among all the realms because of the danger that global climate change presents to us all."

King Jong nodded and using his more natural speaking voice spoke again. "You are right my dear friend and we your subjects, are honoured that you would come to Norfcorea to hold these talks." He smiled at Bobney and then Gladys. "I hope that during your stay here, you and your companion can enjoy some peaceful times together."

Puzzled Bobney looked around himself and then smiled. "I am sure that the General has endured more than enough of my company, to then be forced to spend her own time with me during any down time we get, is beyond what I can ask of her."

"Forgive me," said King Jong, "I do not speak Somerset very often, I must have misunderstood the General's role and relationship to you."

Bobney nodded. "I can only apologise King Jong, my Norfcorean is very poor."

King Jong smiled gently and spoke kindly. "Well, I can tell that you must be more than able to order your fine Norfcorean food when you visit Winscombe's finest Norfcorean restaurants."

Bobney began to chuckle and bowed his head slightly to the King. "King Jong, you are of course right and while I am in the Kingdom of fine foods, I hope to sample some of the delights you yourself are reported to create."

King Jong stepped forwards and put a friendly arm around King Bobney's shoulders. "My dear friend, I have such culinary delights to show you. He turned his head and smiled at Gladys, "and the General if she too would care to sample our cuisine?"

Sha Wren Ston fell into step behind King Jong and walked next to Gladys, followed by Fred Bare Rug.

The two women nodded to each other and after a few seconds Sha Wren Ston whispered to Gladys. "As soon as these two self important tits have buggered off, do you want to join me for a drink and a gossip?"

Gladys nearly choked and barely managed to keep her passive looking military face. Finally she whispered across to Sha Wren Ston. "Although that does indeed sound fun, I am here as King Bobney's security detail, so will be with him for most of the summit." She smiled slightly. "I am not sure that I will be able to step away."

Sha Wren Ston nodded her head. "I understand, you commendable career military types are duty above all else. Maybe there will be a quiet moment when we can share a bottle of wine?"

The two Kings stepped through a large doorway and Sha Wren Ston and Gladys followed. At the door, Fred Bare Rug stopped and closed the door after the women had passed through into the near gloom of the meeting room. Turning back to the waiting dragon who was having his wing muscles massaged by a flight engineer, Fred set off to deal with the royal baggage. He was most surprised to find that King Bobney had brought only a simple, military style backpack and the General had brought something similar. Dismissing the team of baggage handlers, he picked up both bags and set off for the palace, whistling. This was going to be an interesting summit.

The sudden gentle shade of the meeting room was almost impossible to see through after the bright sunshine of outside and for a moment Gladys stared hard trying to keep her eyes on King Bobney. The two kings showed no such difficulties and King Jong showed Bobney to a small, but comfortable dining table. "As the ruler of all of the realms, I ask you chair our summit and lead our discussion so that we can find the answers that we need?"
Bobney sat down and smiled brightly at Gladys who took a seat nest to him. King Jong sat down opposite Gladys and then Sha Wren Ston sat down next to Gladys. A series of waiting staff entered the room, poured drinks and quickly left the four people alone. As soon as they were alone, Sha Wren Ston let out a deep sigh and rested her elbows on the table. King Jong nodded to her and she started to speak in the not so formal tones of normal Somerset. "Basically, this drought is giving us a damn good kicking in the privates and we know damn well that it is the energy we use that is the

cause." She took a sip of the tea that had been poured for her before continuing. "We have looked at the data sent over to us by your Chief Scientist and our team cannot find even the slightest possible error in her calculations or conclusions. If anything, we would ask that she liaise directly with our offices, if that is acceptable to you, King Bobney?"

Bobney grinned. "She is good isn't she?" He turned to Gladys and nodded at her. Gladys smiled back and took a breath. "Chief Scientist Hopeforthebest is a closer personal friend of mine, I shall have her contact your offices forthwith."

Sha Wren Ston grinned. "Thank you General Meuchelmorder, that is most kind."

King Bobney took a breath and then let it out slowly before speaking. "Listen, we are all friends here right?" He looked to Gladys, King Jong and Sha Wren Ston and they all nodded. "Good, so let's stop all of this annoying diplomacy speak and just speak plainly, as friends?"

"Thank fuck for that." Said Sha Wren Ston. She turned to Gladys, "I'm Sharen," she indicated the King with her thumb. "He's Jong. Shall we get some of those cakes out and sort this shit out?"

Bobney nodded his head. "That sounds good, sadly I shall have to avoid the cakes otherwise I turn into a fat bastard!"

King Jong almost spat out his drink as he laughed. "I remember your coronation Bobney, can I say that you look a whole lot healthier now though?"

"That will be thanks to the efforts of the King and his best friend Colonel Thrashgood." Said Gladys. "You should see them both running around the field in all weathers." Her eyes seem to mist over, as if she were day dreaming. "He works and trains harder than any recruit the regiment ever has." She turned to Bobney, "you should be more proud of yourself than you are."

Bobney smiled at her, it was an innocent smile, almost cherubic. "You know that I love training with you, well with your troops that is, Gladys."

King Jong and Sharen exchanged looks and Sharen rolled her eyes in amusement, which made King Jong chuckle slightly, not that Bobney or Gladys noticed as they gazed into each other eyes for several seconds. Finally Bobney looked back to the innocently smiling faces of Jong and Sharen. "It has to be said, Thrashgood is a damn good man, loyal, brave and he just happens to be in love with our chief scientist."

"They are a lovely couple." Agreed Gladys, "but discrete so that they don't have to tell anyone, even though everyone can see that they are in love." She smiled almost sadly. "It is always nice to see one's friends fall in love, but one does wonder if it will ever happen to us?"

Sharen blinked and then bit her lip to stop from laughing, finally and making sure that she did not look at her close friend Jong, she spoke. "Gladys, I know that we have only just met, but trust me, you are a hottie and I just know that somewhere, there is some who loves you."

Bobney nodded his agreement. "Absolutely and when you find him, he will be the luckiest man in the whole of all the realms."

Jong shook his head and deliberately did not make eye contact with a quietly chuckling Sharen. This was going to be a fun summit.

Chapter 4 and a bit more

It was the morning of the British King's coronation and King Bobney had successfully managed to avoid having anything to do with it, having been immersed in finding solutions to the environmental concerns facing the Faerie Realm or just staring out of the window while burbling his finger over his lips just to fill a few quiet and silly moments. He was, however, grateful for one thing; it had temporarily created a diversion for Queen Linda, away from her obsession with his love life, or lack there of. Her obsession had become problematic for Bobney and it was starting to make him feel distinctly uneasy, to the point that he felt sure people around the palace were likely talking about it behind his back. He'd confided his doubts to Colonel Thrashgood but was gratefully reassured when the Colonel had told him that he was completely unaware of any such discussions taking place. So Bobney chided himself for being paranoid and focussed instead on preparing for the day ahead and the meetings he must attend.

Elsewhere in the palace, the day had begun

peacefully. Dawn had broken and the sun rose majestically, the palace was cloaked in serenity; Craig was sleeping peacefully beside his beloved Linda and all was well with the world. This idyllic picture was, however, not to last.

"CRAIG!" Linda shrieked so hard that Craig fell out of the other side of the royal bed. "What am I going to wear today? I've got nothing to wear! Nothing!"

Craig, who was now knelt on the bedroom carpet, looked at her with incredulity. "My darling, you have twenty new royal frocks hanging right there in your wardrobe, all of which would look equally enchanting with you in them." These were no throwaway words, Craig knew that Linda would look beautiful in any of the gowns. Additionally, they were indeed enchanted, having had a spell woven into the very fabric. The spell, cast on a full moon on midsummer eve, ensured the wearer would sparkle brilliantly like the sun.

"But Craig", Linda cried desperately, "what about the TV cameras? What if the enchantment doesn't work in the human Realm? It'll be broadcast all around the world too and I... I will look like a...a..."

"You will look like a beautiful and radiant Fae woman". Craig finished the sentence in a kind and gentle manner, understanding the crisis of confidence which would occasionally hit Linda, borne of her time in the cruel human Realm. "In any case, Deborah wove a bespoke spell into the gowns, specifically to counter the negativity and judgement in that country. After all, she is partly from that Realm and she understands the complexities of that perplexing and primitive society."

"Excuse me!" countered Linda in mock outrage. "I was NOT a primitive when I lived there and neither was my darling Bobney! We were merely fitting in!"

Craig and Linda glared at each other momentarily before bursting into laughter until tears streamed down their faces. When they had recovered themselves, Craig took on a more serious expression. "My Queen, you need no fancy robes, nor enchantments to enhance your beauty. It is already there, both inside and out. I know though, that your time in the human Realm still haunts you sometimes. But, know that I will support and protect you in every way a husband can whilst we enter back into that world for a short time".

Linda fell silent as she absorbed Craig's words. She felt in awe and wonder of his perception and of his love. In turn, she loved him with all her heart. Without uttering a word, she got up and hugged him before stepping over to her wardrobe. She selected a green silk robe, with living flowers springing from the fabric, and held it up in front of her.

"Absolutely perfect", cried Craig. "You are the very embodiment of Spring!" It was the 6th of May, 2023.

Two hours later, Linda and Craig were finally ready to go. They walked through the palace corridors, arm in arm, until finally they found King Bobney waiting for them in the rose gardens. He was impressed by their elegance when he saw them. Not only because of his mother's dress, but she wore her long red hair entwined with a tiara made from white jasmine and dew drops. The green silk dress adorned with Spring flowers cascaded gracefully to the floor. It smelt heavenly. Craig complemented her perfectly, dressed in a black velvet jacket and black trousers, set off with a green cummerbund. He wore his favourite black DM's which had been polished to within an inch of their life by Colonel Thrashgood's personal boot polisher.

"Perfection!" Bobney grinned broadly. "You both make the perfect envoy to represent our Realm." Wuffles, who had just arrived, let out an excited bark and wagged his tail furiously. Bobney smiled. "Go get 'em, Mum!"

With that, Queen Linda and Craig stepped into the Palace vortex, delineated by a beautiful fairy ring of red and white spotted mushrooms.

Almost instantly they disappeared from sight, being pulled swiftly into the Fairy Arterial Rapid Transport System (or FARTS) with a loud rasping sound, which enabled travel across the Faerie nations and between realms. In the rush and excitement, it was only Wuffles who noticed a shadow being sucked in behind Craig and Linda, but he couldn't discern who or what it could have been. Wuffles looked quizzically at King Bobney, but the King seemed to have seen absolutely nothing out of the ordinary.

One minute Linda and Craig were waving goodbye to Bobney and Wuffles in the glorious sunshine of Winscombe; the very next minute they found themselves standing in a puddle on a muddy thin strip of dog shit covered grass, next to a chewing gum splattered grey pavement in London, in the middle of a huge crowd of people from every nation and to cap it all, it was pissing down with rain. The human Realm, it seemed, apparently had climate problems too. On the opposite side of the road there seemed to be some kind of disturbance. The police were busy rounding up a group of people and bundling them into the back of a police van, along with a collection of variously sized placards. One man got away, wearing what appeared to be a very large and disturbing full head mask of Jimmy Saville. Queen Linda was genuinely alarmed until Craig explained that the man in the mask was a musician and a good friend of King Bobney, by the name of Kunt.

"That's nice", said Queen Linda. Having not fully heard the man's name. "Perhaps he could come and play at Bobney's wedding?"

Craig appeared to choke on his boiled sweet before managing to blurt out, "er, yeah, perhaps!"

Queen Linda looked suspiciously at Craig; he was keeping something from her and she resolved to have it out with Bobney as soon as they got home. "What have those other poor people done, Craig?" She asked, her voice sorrowful.

Craig shook his head and took a deep breath before replying. "I believe they were just trying to raise their concerns about the vast amount of public money used to support the British royal family, at a time when there's a chronic inflation problem. Many people cannot afford food or heating or both and there's also a severe rise in homelessness, while the Government has spunked millions on Charlie's big day. It seems you are not allowed to question the state or protest here any more, no matter how just the cause."

Queen Linda shivered. It had been bad enough when she and Bobney had lived in the human Realm but now it seemed to have got even worse, just like the horrible weather. It was no wonder that King Bobney felt so strongly about making Winscombe a place where everyone was valued and could contribute to the well-being of the entire populace.

At that point, the crowd started to surge forward and point excitedly. An umbrella nearly took out someone's eye which made Craig wince. A group of soldiers passed by, playing some jolly sounding music on some highly polished instruments. To Linda's dismay, none of the soldiers looked even remotely jolly, as they would have done had they been the Faerie Army, marching for King Bobney. Instead, they looked rather cold, very wet, horribly bedraggled and remarkably miserable. Just behind them was a rather old-fashioned coach, being pulled by several horses. The poor animals looked just as miserable as the band, with them flinching each time the big bass drum was thumped hard. Inside the coach was yet another ancient looking human man who was staring miserably out of the window. He half-heartedly lifted a painfully swollen, uncomfortably pink hand and waved disinterestedly at the crowd. Beside him was a cadaverous white-haired old lady who was wearing a plastic smile and she too gave a half hearted wave at all the sodden on-lookers.

"Fuck me!" Exclaimed Craig in shock. "Is that the new King? The one that's related to you and Bobney?"

Queen Linda nodded, unable to think of anything useful or indeed positive to say about the man. At that moment something caught her eye and she looked up. A Goblin was stood on top of a red phone box next to her. As soon as the coach rolled by, he pulled his trousers down, bent over and exposed a rather hairy arse at the new King and his wife.

"Craig!" screamed Linda, but it was too late. The new King had, in one moment, glimpsed both the hairy bottom and then Queen Linda and in an absolute rage, had shaken his fist at the pair, waggling five red and angrily swollen sausage fingers at them.

"How on earth did that Goblin get here?" shrieked Linda, just in time to see a furious Metropolitan policeman trying to climb the phone box and swat the Goblin with a truncheon. He missed, upon which the Goblin blew a large raspberry at him and disappeared into the crowds.

Craig sighed, as a raindrop slid off the end of his nose. He was cold, wet and angry that his beloved Queen Linda had been subjected to such an undignified charade. As another troop of miserable soldiers stomped past them, Linda turned to Craig and spoke in a shaky voice.

"Craig, how did that Goblin get here?"

"I don't know", said Craig, "maybe he slipped into the FART with us and we didn't notice".

Linda nodded, and then giggled. "I can't believe that poxy relative of mine shook his fat old sausage fingers at me", she said, "I'm glad that Goblin flashed at him! Speaking of which, how do we get him back to his own Realm? I have no idea where he went".

Craig paused momentarily and looked sheepish. "Actually, I think I know where he's gone."

Linda looked at him with curiosity. "Craig, did you know something like this was going to happen?"

Craig tried to look innocent but failed miserably. "Might have" he said casually, in a non-committal way. "I believe he's now making his way to the balcony at Buckingham Palace. He's planning another grand flash when the new King and Queen step out to have their photograph taken!"

Linda rolled her eyes before bursting into giggles. "Did Bobney have anything to do with all this?" She enquired, already knowing that the answer was going to be an absolute yes.

"I couldn't possibly comment" smiled Craig, tears of mirth rolling down his face.

It took quite some time before Linda and Craig managed to pull themselves together enough to breathe and have a sensible conversation. Finally Linda spoke, "Craig, when Bobney finally gets around to proposing to Gladys, we're not going to subject the residents of Winscombe to this sort of entitled nonsense, are we?" Her face was serious and full of concern.

Craig shook his head furiously. "Never," he said, his face serious and his eyes glinting. "It will be a joyous occasion in the true spirit of the Fae Realm.

Everyone who wants to be, will be involved and the sun will shine. King Bobney wouldn't have it any other way. And he wouldn't waste any of Winscombe's precious resources on this sort of rubbish."

He looked at his beloved Linda. Although they had laughed until they cried, he could see the pain etched in her face at having to confront traumatic memories of her past, and the rejection she had felt when her relatives in the British royal family had denied her very existence. She had become a recluse along with her son, Bobney, the shame of which still haunted her. Craig suddenly felt very strongly that he needed to protect her and to get her far away from the toxicity of Britain and back to the land where she was not just accepted, but actually loved by the populace. He was about to speak but Linda got there first.

"Craig, do you think we could just go home now? I don't care to watch some old git get his crown, I want to look to the future, not be pulled back to my past."

"Of course," said Craig. "By the way, should Bobney and Gladys ever tie the knot, we'd better start planning which gown you'd like to wear – you'll need plenty of time to prepare!"

Linda aimed a playful punch into Craig's arm. "Ow!" cried Craig, pretending to be hurt. "Come on then, let's go home. I hear there's a rather lovely FART in the middle of Buckingham Palace gardens. Let's go and find it; I'd rather we avoided the two old farts in the palace, though!

"Agreed!" said Linda wholeheartedly. With that, they linked arms and made their way to the magical ring of mushrooms growing in the palace gardens. Even the rain had started to ease off as they prepared to step into the vortex, Craig had one last pressing thought. "We need to protect these mushrooms from the new British King, he likes anything organic, especially if he can flog them to Waitrose! Linda and Craig stepped carefully over the mushrooms and into the vortex, whereupon they were transported back to their own precious, sunny and welcoming Realm.

Chapter 5

The Norfcorean palace was very busy, people rushed about like ants in front of a flood, as the delegates for the summit arrived and were put into their various places of accommodation. Some of the delegates complained that the Norfcorean palace was an austere and overly disciplined place, while others commented that it reeked of opulence and wealth. The Norfcorean palace staff rushed about trying to keep the delegates happy within reason, however there was one voice that remained gracious and grateful and that was the King of the entire Faerie Realm, Bobney. King Bobney along with his chief of security, General Gladys Meuchelmorder, had asked the Norfcorean King if they could join his troops for their daily exercise. King Jong had at first been only too happy to oblige, but after a moment of consideration, had had a quiet word with the guard captain and told him not to go too hard on the King of the entire Realm. So it was that at half past five the very next morning, the Guard Captain stood outside the guard house with six of the fittest royal guards, King Bobney and General Meuchelmorder, all dressed in military sports kit and ready to go for a nice life affirming run. They started with gentle stretching exercises before moving into more traditional aerobic exercises in the form of dancing and stretching to a fast form of Norfcorean pop music, known as N-Pop. Bobney was stood next to the General and every now and again, their eyes would meet and their smiles would beam across at each other as they worked up a sweat. When the music finally stopped after thirty minutes, the guards, the King and his General barely looked like they had worked hard, so the Guard Captain set out for their usual ten kilometre run. Bobney quickly fell in step with the General at the rear of the group and had a gentle and quiet conversation as they ran.

"Do you think that they are going easy on us?" Asked King Bobney quietly.

Gladys grinned, but kept her voice low. "Very likely, they don't want to embarrass us by making us look old and unfit."

Bobney laughed gently. "Can you imagine how it would look if they killed the King of the Realm by making him run too hard until he had a heart attack?"

"I would never allow that to happen." Gladys whispered back, the smile on her face looking strangely serious.

Bobney looked at the General as they ran and felt his heart soar with respect for her. "I have never felt safer than when I am with you, General Meuchelmorder."

Gladys smiled and nodded her head. "Your safety is my pleasure, my King." Her smile was beaming, filled with something that Bobney could not read. "It is also my duty. I would give my life for you." She faced ahead as the running group changed from the smooth well made gravel road onto a grassy and muddy track.

Bobney felt his heart fill with emotion. "I would give my life for you too General." For the first time in his life, Bobney knew that he meant it.

The Norfcorean guards who spoke Somerset grinned, even if the General and the King did not know what they meant, the Guards did and it was beautiful in its purity and its innocence.

The official breakfast on the first day of the summit was a hit with all of the delegates present. The Queen of the Hell Hounds spoke with her companion, her subtle wiffles and growls spoken softly. "I have been informed that the King himself has prepared our first breakfast."

Her companion growled an agreement and then added another point. "My Queen, I understand that your son spent time here, teaching the King some of his best recipes."

The Queen nodded, her eyes filled with pride. "He is now the Mayor of the great city of Winscombe and yet still finds time to occasionally visit and cook with his friends there."

The King of the Imps gently leaned into the conversation, "excuse me Madam, but I have to congratulate you on the skill of your son. Not only is he a magnificent chef, he is also a very talented Statesman and a wonderful political negotiator."

The Hell Hound Queen let out a quiet yelp of thanks and wagged her tail three times.

The Imp King bowed to her. "You are too gracious my dear Queen, but the gratitude should be mine alone, your son has been a wonderful Mayor of Winscombe and has welcomed my people into the city with the open arms of friendship."

Across the table The Queen of the Trolls held a delicate rock cake in her enormous fingers. Her eyes were tightly shut as she allowed the flavours of the cake to roll across the rest of her olfactory senses. Finally she swallowed and then placed the rest of the rock cake into her mouth and continued to slowly and silently chew, her eyes shut with delight. At the other end of the table, the King of Demons sat with an exquisitely iced cake on a bronze plate. He took a tiny crumb and placed it into his mouth. On the table, the plate shuddered slightly and the remains of the cake turned to ash as the Demon King sighed with pleasure. Finally he looked up to see King Jong the First carrying a plate of eggs and bacon into the room to place on the breakfast table. Quickly the Demon King stood up and strode across the busy room and stood in front of King Jong and bowed so low, his horned forehead almost brushed the floor. He stood up straight and addressed the King, his voice a soft and delicate sound. "Your Highness, I am compelled to thank you, the breakfast you have provided is beyond anything I have tasted in any Realm." He smiled, which to those not used to conversing with demonic entities, he looked absolutely terrifying. "I understand that you yourself prepared and cooked these food stuffs, so I would like to offer you my heartiest congratulations as a chef and give you my eternal gratitude and the friendship of my Realm."

King Jong beamed with pleasure before leaning forwards to whisper conspiratorially to the King Demon. "Your Highness, I must admit that although

I cooked the pastries and fancies, for your particular delicacy I used a recipe given to me by the Grandmother of my closest friend."

The Demon King sighed conspiratorially and then whispered to the King. "Well Sire, this woman must be the pride of your nation, please pass her my kindest regards when you speak with her next."

King Jong bowed his head solemnly, his voice filled with gravitas. "It will be my pleasure my dear friend."

King Bobney and General Meuchelmorder had got back from the morning training session and had both returned to their respective rooms where they had showered. Once dry and dressed, they met once again in the corridor outside their rooms. Gladys looked immaculate in her red jacket and green skirt. Her face was radiant and her eyes sparkled when she saw the King. He was dressed somewhat more sombrely, his pressed green lightweight military trousers, carefully folded at the ankle to fit into his military boots. His chest was covered with his usual military green high wicking shirt and on his head he wore the beret of the SFS, with two cap badges. He smiled as he stood opposite the General. "How do I look?" He asked humbly.

The General looked him up and down. Her first thoughts were that he was dashing, handsome, maybe the word she wanted to use was beautiful. His hair was freshly cut in a smart military style, his face freshly shaved and his eyebrows were perfectly styled. His shirt was carefully tucked into the waistband of his trousers and the belt buckle was highly polished and engraved with the entwined birds of the Special Faerie Service regiment. She reached out gently and brushed a tiny mote of dust from the side of the King's beret. "You look perfect, your Highness. You make the regiment very, very proud."

Bobney grinned. "I had better do, otherwise I will have to do twenty laps of the athletics field with Colonel Thrashgood!"

Gladys smiled, her whole face seemed illuminated and King Bobney felt like he was basking in her beauty. She turned her face towards the direction of the breakfast room. "I suggest that we go for breakfast before we miss King Jong's famous cooking."

Bobney nodded sagely. "It would be rather rude and particularly foolish if we were late and missed his food." He turned and offered Gladys his arm. "General, would you please accompany the King to breakfast?"

Gladys bowed her head and then stood up and placed her arm through that of the King. "It is both my honour and my duty, your Highness."

At the door, the footmen opened both doors so that they would not have to part arms and King Bobney stepped into the brightly lit room, with the General still on his arm. As he entered the room, the other delegates turned as one and then bowed to the ruler of all of the Realms. Bobney graciously bowed in return, while Gladys bowed with him. When he stood up and looked around the room, finding King Jong the First and he strode over to him and shook him by the hand. He then turned to the rest of the delegates. "My friends, would you please applaud our host, his Highness King Jong the First, for this most excellent spread, most of which I understand he has cooked for us himself?"

The room seemed to explode with applause and King Jong smiled as he spoke. "My friends, my fellow royals and my guests here in Norfcorea, please enjoy your breakfast. It is my pleasure to serve you all and I hope that when we convene for talks later, you will remember this moment of cooperation and we may strive for a common accord between all the kingdoms of the realms."

Again there was more applause and then came the soft soulful howls of the Hell Hounds.

Felicity sat at the table next to the Magician and watched as the being they had captured finished the small cup of tea that had been made for him by the Magician. He put the cup down and then gazed out at the two people sat with him. "So you want me to, help you, track down these illegal miners and then if I find them first, let you know where they are?" He grinned, "but I can play as many pranks on them as I like?"

Felicity grinned back at him. "My friend, it is your duty to the Realm, to locate these people and then play as many pranks on them as you can. When you think that you have done as many pranks as you can, you have a moral duty to do more, but." Her face turned serious. "No one is to be badly hurt. Are we agreed?"

"So no tying shoe laces together?" He asked quietly.

Felicity laughed, "absolutely you can tie their shoe laces together, but no blowing them up or making traps that will drop acid on them."

"Or electrocute them" added the Magician.

The Gremlin grinned, it was a wicked grin, a wild

grin and Felicity could not help but giggle. "Well, no blowing them up so much that people get hurt." She clarified.

The Gremlin stood up in his jar and patted down the soft canvas trousers that the Magician had made for him, by shrinking down a pair of his own jeans. "Madam, I shall be in touch, he patted the back pocket that contained the shrunken mobile telephone."

The magician grinned too. "Then Sir, I release you from your cell. May you fare well and may all of your jokes be howlers."

The Gremlin stuck out a hand as he stepped from the jar and the Magician took it in his fingers. "It is good to do business with you Sir, most of your kind only want to kill my kind or move us on to the next world. But not you Sir. Instead you are a modern marvel, a peacemaker. We have never been asked to help stop crime before."

There was a sudden flash of light, a reflection from outside that filled the office with a strong glare, but then it was gone, as was the Gremlin, apart from a soft chuckle that sounded from just outside the office door.

Deborah awoke from a bad dream, her heart beating

fast and her mind filled with images of evil. As soon as she sat up, she reached for her phone and scrolled through the contacts until she found the one and hit dial. It rang twice and then was answered. "Thrashgood, speak."

"Colonel, they have struck again, but my mind is fogged, it is somewhere south of you, please, find them?"

"On it." He paused for a moment. "I know that this is hard for you, but we will find them, no matter how long it takes, we will find them."

Deborah knew that the Colonel was trying to to be kind, but the damage being done to the world was awful and it was harming her connection to the planet too. "Thank you Colonel. I know that you are doing all that you can."

"Rest if you can Missy, we are moving out now, heading south and moving fast." Thrashgood said.

"Good luck." Deborah replied.

The SFS unit mounted their truck, a fast moving, six-wheel drive, off-roader that could carry six of them. The Princess however, could carry two more and was already in the air and directing the unit towards the target. In the distance she could see a shimmer in the air of dust and dirt being sent up into the sky. She fled across the sky, wings tucked in close to her body to give her the most aerodynamic shape, the troops on her back tucked in low like motorcycle riders on a race track. At full speed, she could fly at one hundred and eighty knots, in warm air, the truck below her could manage one hundred and sixty kilometres per hour depending on the terrain, so was half of her speed, but as reconnaissance, there was no one better than the Princess. She flew over the miners as their huge machines bit chunks out of the earth and dumped them into refining machines that ground up, crushed and spat out the unwanted rock and soil into heaps of contaminated waste, poisoned by the chemicals used to extract the minerals they wanted. Whipping past the workings, she turned and pushing her wings as hard as she could, she accelerated to her maximum and sped back towards the troops of Colonel Thrashgood. The truck was no more than a couple of kilometres away when she flew down to speak with the Colonel.

"They are there now Sir." She said as she hovered just above the truck, "your ETA is roughly four minutes at this speed, providing the ground does not become difficult." She grinned, which was a fearful sight in a Royal Dragon, with teeth like daggers and her riders stayed low on her back.

"Well done Sergeant," said Thrashgood. "Would you care to start the attack? Fast fly by and roast. Try to keep prisoners from leaving site, for the purposes of interrogation."

"Sir, yes sir!" She shrieked as she flapped her powerful wings and accelerated once again to full speed. At five hundred metres above the ground, she levelled out and made herself as long and slender as possible to ease her passage through the air. The truck driver kept his foot on the 'fast pedal' and drove the vehicle almost brutally across the rough landscape. Mud, ripped up grass and grit plastered the side of the vehicle and the screen wipers were working hard to keep the windscreen clear as they splashed through another small brook. Ahead, the sky suddenly lit up a brilliant blue.

"The Princess has made contact!" laughed the driver. Thrashgood nodded and grinned as he turned to face the troops in the back of the truck. Despite the hard buffeting that the truck was taking, the troops were in good humour, apart from a young female Fae, with the violet wings of a fast attack Faerie, whose head lolled to the side peacefully. Thrashgood shook his head and shouted, "we touch down in three minutes, get ready to take control of this site and someone wake up Corporal Hixx!"

"Sir, Yes Sir!" Shouted the troop, except for Corporal Hixx who grunted when her friend sat next to her thumped her playfully on the shoulder to wake her up!

The miners were half way through their latest crash and dig raid when a sound from the air above them caused the foreman to pause and gaze upwards. The sky was dark and then suddenly it was filled with the bright blue flames of a fast diving Royal Dragon with two Fae riders that swept past. The dragon roared flame and when it looked like she was about to smash into the ground, she extended her wings to act as air brakes, coming close to a complete stop in the air, before she flapped again and began to rise, just as the two riders leapt free and she shot back into the sky, only to swoop down onto the next vehicle and blow flame into the engine of the digging machine. The two Fae, dressed in the black combat armour of the SFS, burst into the worksite and put a suppressing fire down from the flame thrower that one of them carried. The Princess rounded in the air and came down on the other side of them and blew a jet of blue flame into one of the large front loader machines that was shovelling crushed rock into another machine. The engine of the front loader roared and then died as the driver panicked and tried to jump free of the burning cab.

The foreman watched incredulous, this was the first time that they had been caught and he was rather used to having as much time as they needed to strip-mine the chosen area. Suddenly remembering his job, he reached into his pocket and drew out long thin whistle and put it to his lips, blowing a surprisingly loud blast. The machines stopped digging and all vehicles suddenly turned, dumping waste or ore where they found it. The Foreman drew a symbol onto the ground and spoke a silent curse, which caused the symbol to glow painfully bright and then open into a wide tunnel entrance into another world. Those vehicles still able to move, sped into the tunnel, while drivers of the two damaged machines flailed at their controls trying to make them work again. The two Fae stepped in front of of them and again lay down a covering fire as Sergeant Rupertina prepared to land and blow flame at anyone stupid enough to try and push past her. One of the mining trucks engines finally restarted and tried to pass the sergeant, but she lashed out with her strong, muscular tail and smashed the side of the vehicle, forcing it to slide sideways to a halt in the mud, while the driver struggled to restart it once again. Admitting defeat, the driver leapt from the broken vehicle and tried to run around the dragon, only to be tackled to the ground by the two Fae warriors. The last of the machines were abandoned and the Foreman gave the Princess, Sergeant Rupertina of the Special Faerie Service, a nasty grin and then the tunnel was gone, just as the truck carrying the rest of the troop burst through the night into the brightly lit quarry.

King Bobney sat down at the table and smiled gently at the other royals sat around him. For a brief moment he felt strangely alone, as if something or more importantly, someone of great importance was suddenly missing from his side. He looked around puzzled and then stood at the far wall by the main door, his eyes found her and he felt a dizzy peace enter his soul. She smiled at him and bowed her head slightly and with a smile Bobney took charge of the meeting, relieved that his dear friend was close by. "My friends, for that is what we are in this room, be we human, faerie, vampire, demon, hound and troll. We gather as equals because Mother Nature needs our help to heal a wound to the planet that we have all helped create."
From the edge of the table came a low moan of

lament from the Queen of the Hell Hounds and Bobney bowed his head to her before he continued. "Our developing society since I took my familial throne has taken what we have named, the 'Great Leap Forwards' and the introduction of a lot of the technology from the human Realm has been accepted by all gathered here. However, our societies were not engineered for such energy usage and we imported a lot of energy production methods from the human world, increasing generation of our own energy." He opened a folder on the table in front of him and indicated that everyone else was to do likewise. The folders were all designed for the beings individually. The document for the Troll Queen had been carved into thin sheets of slate. For the vampire Queen, the document had been inked onto papyrus. The Queen of the Hell hounds had been given a scroll of leather. The other delegates had been given simple card wallets with the papers carefully presented inside.

"The first page shows the alarming amount of Carbon dioxide that has been released into our atmosphere in the last few years, similar in quantities to what was produced in the human world at the high point of the industrial revolution, a particularly dirty blight in their history."

The Vampire Queen let out a small snort of horror. "This cannot be true?" She turned to face Bobney, her black gemstone eyes pleading for better news. "This is deeply worrying." She lamented, her voice barely a whisper.

King Bobney nodded his head in agreement before he continued. "Indeed, also due to the rather special nature of the Faerie Realm, the effects of the change in atmospheric composition, have had an accelerated effect plus a far greater impact than in the human Realm, where a lot of this tech has come from."

The Hell Hound Queen made a few low growls, howled once or twice and then snarled, with one ear down and one forwards. The rest of the delegates nodded in agreement or gave small words of support.

"That is something that we have started already," said King Bobney. "Especially with guidance from Mother Nature, but the sad truth is that we need to do something other than put scrubbers into the chimney flues or planting more trees." He looked around the room. "As some of you already know, we have started a project that will see the entire Realm under my reign leaving behind fossil fuels altogether and swapping our energy production to renewables within seven years."

The Troll Queen raised her hand to ask a question. "Are we to infer that this is the hydroelectric dam that is currently under construction outside of the Winscombe constituency?"

"Indeed." confirmed King Bobney, "this is the hydroelectric dam that will allow us to shut down all coal, gas and dragon fart powered generating stations."

The Vampire Queen raised her hand. "May I ask why we do not have a representative from the Dragon Realm? I am sure that they will have interest in this project."

Bobney again nodded. "Queen Nightsoul, we do indeed have a representative from the Dragon Realm, Princess Rupertina." He said firmly. "However, she is with a team of the Special Faerie Service and is currently on mission trying to locate the rogue miners who have been destroying areas of our land."

"As I would expect from her," replied the Vampire Queen, a hint of amusement singing through her voice. "I know Rupertina's family well and she was always a little wild at heart."

"If I may?" asked the King of the Goblins, "what

progress has the SFS and the Princess made?"

King Bobney smiled. "If I may redirect your question by turning you towards my colleague, General Gladys Meuchelmorder." He smiled again at Gladys, a smile she returned and he felt it lift his heart. "General, would you please update our delegates on the current situation?"

"Yes your Highness." She purred, her eyes sparkling almost like stars. Gladys stepped forwards and handed out a series of maps, that the rulers took with some gravitas. "If you have a look at these maps, you will see all of the sites that have been hit by these rogue miners, including the site that was hit in the early hours of this morning."

There was some murmuring and gasps of shock among the delegates. The Queen of the Trolls stood up and turned to King Bobney. "How have these miners been able to escape your forces, surely such infrastructure takes weeks to implement?"

Gladys cleared her throat gently and all of the delegates, including the Troll Queen turned towards her. "The miners have been using some kind of portal travel technology that we have never seen before and do not yet understand."

"Is this similar to the mycelium network that we have used for hundreds of years?" Asked the

Vampire Queen.

Gladys shook her head. "As I have stated, we do not yet understand the intricacies of this technology." She paused and waited for the sounds of dissent to stop. "However, on their last raid, despite them evading us yet again, we were able to damage two of their machines and take one of their people prisoner, who is currently in the custody of my colleague, Colonel Thrashgood."

"Will this captive be interrogated?" Asked the Goblin King, his voice dark with concern.

"Questioned? Yes." Said Gladys coolly. "However, we do not use any form of barbaric or torturous techniques."

"What sort of information are you looking to attain from this being?" The Queen of the Vampires asked. "Is the prisoner being cooperative?"

Gladys looked to Bobney, her face dark with concern. Bobney nodded to her and she nodded back once before speaking again. "The prisoner is of human type, but of a race or species we have not encountered before. At the moment, language is our biggest barrier, although some similarities have made basic communication possible."

The delegates suddenly began asking questions, shouting over each other and the noise of the room steadily increased until it seemed that chaos had taken over. Finally, Bobney took action. He placed two fingers in either side of his mouth and blew out a loud, piercing whistle. The room fell silent and all faces, despite the sudden shocking sound, all turned to him. "As soon as my colleague General Meuchelmorder has more information, she will update you. Until then, I am calling a break in this meeting."

Gladys gave Bobney a smile of thanks, her eyes brilliant in the light streaming through the bright windows. For a moment, Bobney felt his heart race, his stomach constrict and the room seemed to fall away from everyone except Gladys. Bobney spoke again. "Delegates, I understand that our host has prepared morning coffee and cakes, please head towards the minor dining room, we will return to this room in ninety minutes." Slowly, the delegates filed out of the room and followed the signs that led to the small dining room where King Jong the First was dressed in fresh Chef's whites and was serving speciality pastries to the guests while his other staff served drinks. Gladys hung back in the room as did Bobney. For a moment they stood in silence and then as one they began to speak. "General, I thought that you..."

"Your Highness, thank you for your..."
Gladys smiled and Bobney gave a small laugh before speaking again. "I am sorry, please go ahead General."
"You have nothing to apologise for, your Highness. I am here to serve you and the Realm."
"Your service is greatly appreciated General, the Realm as a whole has a lot to thank you for." Bobney replied, his eyes never leaving those of the General.
"I give my service willingly, your Highness." Said Gladys, her voice almost a whisper. For a moment their hands hung in the air, almost reaching for each other, when there was a low knock at the door that made both of them jump with surprise.
"Excuse my interruption your Highness, General Meuchelmorder." Said the chief aid to King Jong the First, "I wonder if I may steal the General away for a brief moment to discuss the security arrangements for the closing ball?"
Bobney nodded once, his face carefully hiding the feelings he felt at the loss of his friend, even if only briefly. "Yes of course Minister, I shall not take up any more of her time." He turned to the General. "Maybe I shall see you later today?"
She smiled, it was a beautiful smile on her gentle

face. "Yes of course your Highness, I shall keep you informed of all details of the prisoner as they come in."

Sharen grinned, she looked at the couple as they parted, the King watching the General leave, his face barely hiding the sadness he felt to lose her for even a moment. The General seemed to retreat inside of herself, in a way that she did not do when she was with the King. Did they even know that they were in love? Sharen mused. Because it was so obvious to everyone else around them. Sharen led the General out of the meeting room and towards her office, she opened the sliding paper door and showed Gladys inside to a small but comfortable chair. Sitting down opposite the General, Sharen smiled. "Are you enjoying your stay here in Norfcorea's capital city?"

"Indeed." Replied the General, "everything is very well organised and I am sure that King Bobney is very happy with how the summit is progressing."

"That is very good to hear." Said Sharen, "will yourself and King Bobney be using some of your free time to take in the sights together?" She smiled kindly. "We have some very beautiful places, perfect for couples to spend time together."

"As the King's security officer, I will attend

anywhere that the King chooses to go, as my duty demands."

Sharen gently shook her head. "But what about your quality time together?"

Gladys nodded. "King Bobney does indeed choose to spend time with us, he is often found training with Colonel Thrashgood and myself." For a moment she fell into a silent reflection. "I am so lucky, not many people get to spend quite so much time with our Sovereign."

The smile that spread across Sharen's face was devious and pushing into mischievous as she mulled over the words. How extraordinary! Apparently Gladys either didn't know or had blocked out the fact that she was deeply in love with the King! Sharen's thoughts remained unspoken as she concentrated on carefully controlling her face so as not to put Gladys into a difficult situation. "I am sure that the King enjoys every moment that he gets to spend with you, you must be his closest friend?" She asked instead.

Gladys smiled, her eyes glinting with pleasure at being able to talk about the King. "I would say that Colonel Thrashgood is the King's closest friend, they have a kinship and they are both fanatical athletes."

"I remember well how he was when he first took the throne." Said Sharen warmly. "He has changed so much, I would say that he is one of the most handsome men in all of the worlds now."

"Oh yes indeed." Said Gladys, "I just hope that when he finally finds his queen, she is as beautiful as he is."

Sharen almost choked as she suppressed an exclamation of surprise. When she was able to speak, she did so with all of the diplomacy she had learned to use as King Jong's chief advisor. "She is indeed and I imagine that the children will be just little darlings."

Gladys smiled again, but her eyes betrayed an emotion she did not fully understand. "It will be my honour and my duty to protect the royal family. Whether they have children or not."

"Do you think that the King could marry someone from within his circle?" Sharen asked innocently. "What if his queen was someone he already knew?"

"Unfortunately, royal protocol states that the woman the King of the entire Realm chooses to be his wife, must also be of equal rank and status. There is no one in the court who currently has that status." Replied Gladys, her voice neutral, her face hiding whatever emotion she was half feeling and half not understanding.

"I see." Said Sharen. "Here we have a similar tradition. But King Jong is very happy to break traditions that are no longer relevant if they improve society."

"Without wishing to be indiscrete," asked Gladys, "does King Jong have a fiance?"

Sharen grinned. "If he does, he hasn't told me. Strangely, he spends most of his spare time in the kitchen. I used to think that I was his best friend, but I am starting to think that it is now my Gran, because they are always discussing baking together!"

Gladys grinned. "Can you imagine what society would say if he married her?"

Sharen laughed, it was a hearty laugh and it brought tears to her eyes. "I would not be surprised, but I think that Gran's boyfriend would be!" She turned to Gladys. "What do you think people would say if the King chose you?"

Gladys laughed. "That would never happen. I am a General in the army and he is the ruler of all of the Realms. We are barely in the same league."

"Hmmm," mused Sharen. "Totally different leagues..." Her face was neutral once again and she looked at Gladys. "It would make a great story though."

Again Gladys chuckled. "What kind of a loser would read a story about King Bobney falling in love with a General of the army?" She shook her head. "No one would believe it anyway, because Bobney is far too noble and true to do anything that would risk the throne."

"Oh I don't know." Said Sharen, "you would be surprised at how many people would be turning the pages hoping that the King and his most senior General would get it on!"

Gladys laughed again. "Well people do seem to love such nonsense." She gave Sharen a sideways grin, "well, people in the human Realm do."

Sharen nodded and offered her arm to her new found friend. "Shall we head to the ball room for you to check the security details, before we head back to the summit? Hopefully, they have not agreed to anything too silly while us great minds have been gone!"

Deborah sat at the kitchen table in the Mayoral residence as Wuffles finished up a quiche to put into the oven to bake. She had been feeling at a loss as how to stop the miners who were destroying the environments that they had burst into from their portal. As such she was feeling in need of some gentle company while she was in the city, away from her chosen family home. It would not take her long to get back home and into the gentle company of Uncle Herbert and his close friend Katie. But she had work to do in the city and so, as she often did, she found herself sitting with Wuffles. He gently closed the oven door and dropped his specially made oven glove onto the counter before he wandered across the kitchen and put his head on Deborah's lap. Deborah felt his love for her and almost without a thought, her hand dropped to the soft fur behind his ears. Wuffles whined and wagged his tail a couple of times, which made Deborah smile.

"Thank you, but I am OK." She replied. Wuffles let out a sharp yip and a small whine, then tapped his paw on the floor.

Deborah sat up. "I know you are right, but I just feel so useless."

Wuffles growled and then whined, exposing his teeth, which made Deborah laugh. "I know, you would never let anyone else say that I was useless." She stroked his head again and then he sat up and looked her in the eyes, giving a small, stern whine and then a slow wag of the tail.

Deborah let out a soft sigh. "Yes, OK. I will, I promise." She stood up and pulled her cardigan around her shoulders. "I am sorry that I always come to you when I feel sad, but you are so wise and your company is so gentle and lovely." She gave him a small smile. "You feel like family." She laughed again, "not weird family, but good family obviously."

Wuffles shook his head and wiffled his version of laughter. With a deep breath, Deborah made her decision. "Right, I shall leave you in peace, thank you for giving me space to think." She opened the kitchen door and stepped outside, but half a second later popped her head back around the door. "Save me some of that quiche, it smells lovely." Wuffles growled playfully, his tail wagging, his eyes bright, which made Deborah laugh again. "Oh you and whose army?" She replied playfully.

Chapter 6

King Jong the first's summit was considered to be a universal success by all of the rulers, elected representatives and court advisors, all of whom had come to the same conclusions. The state of the Realms was indeed of great worry and with their decree, King Bobney had ruled that new directives needed to be put in place to combat the extreme environmental damage caused by mining, building, agriculture and industry. Water quality and provision was discussed and the concerns over the increasing drought had led to the private water companies in the Realms all being told in no uncertain terms to clean up what they are were doing or else they would become owned by the state. Bobney had tried to have the water taken into ownership by the Realm, but this was a sticking point that some of the human representatives would not agree to. Nevertheless, everyone could see that it would not be long before Bobney took a greater stand against them. Although the summit attendees walked away from the meeting pretty much happy with the outcomes, the businesses who had an interest in the areas facing new and stricter regulations were less than happy. King Bobney had an autocart to take him to the dragon port where he would catch a flight home and as he said good bye to all of the summit guests, the Queen of the Hellhounds approached him and bowed low. He bowed in return and then spoke quietly. "Queen Lupa, thank you for your wisdom, we needed to hear what you had to say."

The Hellhound Queen waggled her ears, yipped a couple of times and let out a soft whiffling sound in reply. Bobney nodded, "Well your Highness, I appreciate your support in these matters." He took a deep breath, realising that she had approached him for a reason. "How may I be of service to you, my royal friend?"

The Queen sat down and let out small halting whimpers of distress. Concerned, Bobney sat down on the ground opposite her and opened his arms to her. She rested her head on his shoulder and he embraced her as she expressed her sadness. When she finished, Bobney released her from the hug and leant back again to speak to her. "I can only imagine how it feels to have gone so long since you have seen your son, I will gladly offer you space as we journey back to Winscombe and as a Royal Guest, I offer you a place to stay at the Royal residence."

Queen Lupa yipped her gratitude and wagged her tail before she stood up, bowed and turned to her team to explain the change in her plans.

King Bobney stood up and turned to his aid who was packing the cart ready for the journey to the dragon port. "I am sorry to be an annoyance, could we make room for Queen Lupa? She will be accompanying us back to Winscombe."

The aid nodded his head low. "Of course your Highness, you always pack lightly, so there is only one small bag each for yourself and the General. The rest of this is baggage for the other Royals who are coming to the same port."

With space cleared for the Hell Hound, she trotted across to the autocart, her own small bag clutched in her teeth. Bobney showed her to her seat and she jumped up and settled onto the bench quite comfortably. As soon as she was settled, Bobney climbed up next to her and a few seconds later, General Meuchelmorder climbed up and took the front passenger seat. She had been having a quiet talk with Sharen, who stood with King Jong at the entrance to the palace, watching the guests leave. The General gave her a last wave and then nodded to the aid who had taken the driver's seat. Bobney looked to see who she had waved to and smiled. "I see that you have made another friend here General Meuchelmorder." His voice was gentle and filled with soft humour.

The General turned on her seat and faced the King. She looked into his face and saw the rugged handsomeness that he had grown into, the strong jaw, the kind eyes filled with sparkles. Her heart felt like it was going to burst out of her chest. "She is a wise woman, Your Highness. I shall seek her council again in the future, no doubt."

Bobney grinned. "Well, if you trust her, then so do I." He shifted in his seat slightly, "were you able to enjoy some time off with her?"

"Indeed Highness," she replied happily. "I was introduced to her husband, who was a charming man. I also met her Grandmother, who is also an advisor to the King on all things culinary."

Bobney nodded, impressed. "Given the quality of the food served in Norfcorea, I can only assume that she is a fantastic cook."

The General also smiled and turned to face Queen Lupa, "Your Highness, I understand that your own son has spent some time here in Norfcorea teaching the King some of his secrets."

Queen Lupa whined and wagged her tail several

times, which made Bobney laugh with surprise.

"I cannot believe that Wuffles would not even wash his own plates when he was a youngster," said the general, smiling. "He is so fastidious in the kitchen these days."

Queen Lupa yowled and yipped a few barks, her ears forwards and her tail wagging.

"Oh he sounded so adorable when he was a child." Said the General laughing at the stories. "I can just imagine him covered in mud, using your best china to make mud pies."

"Well," said King Bobney with gravitas, "the city would be lost without him now. Wuffles is the finest Mayor the city has had for generations.".

Queen Lupa whined, yipped and let out a few barks, her ears flat and her tail still.

"Indeed your Highness," said King Bobney. "He brings an integrity and a humanity to the role that it has been sadly missing for decades. I also know that he is greatly loved by the city populace."

The General smiled too, "he is a credit to you Ma'am, you must be so proud of him and what he has achieved."

Queen Lupa nodded her head and settled down on the bench once again as the autocart turned erratically onto the straight track that led into the

Dragon port. At the gates, the guard waved the vehicle to stop, until he saw King Bobney. He instantly went rigid with a salute and hit the button that raised the barrier. Bobney asked the driver to slow down and as the autocart drew level with the guard, Bobney stood up and returned the guard's salute. Inside the compound that served as the waiting and resting area for the great Dragons, several of the great beasts were being loaded with passengers or baggage and Bobney's autocart was directed to the far end of the field and a waiting Greater Red Dragon. The animal was curled up on a bed of straw, while a groomer was checking the animal's claws and scales, a huge metal file in his hands. As the King approached, the Dragon rolled over and stood up before bowing his head low. "Highness, I await your instruction to return you back to the great city of Winscombe."

Bobney climbed down from the autocart and approached the great lizard and then bowed before the creature. " Highness, I am honoured that the King of the Royal Red Dragons would fly me himself." He stood up and turned back to the autocart and grabbed his small green backpack, a piece of kit he had purchased on advice given by Colonel Thrashgood. He opened the lid pocket and pulled out his royal purse and removed three large golden coins before turning back to the Dragon. "I present you, Highness, with these tokens of my esteem."

The dragon took the coins in delicate, giant claws and closed his eyes as he sniffed the gold. Next to King Bobney, Queen Lupa sat down and she too presented the Dragon King with a golden coin.

The Dragon settled low and spoke with a soft voice. "Thank you, my dear friends, it is my honour and pleasure to fly you home." He took the gold coins and placed them into the hands of his groom who placed them into a small bag that was then secured around the neck of the great beast. "If you would care to board your carriage, I will take off as soon as you are comfortable."

"Thank you Highness." Said King Bobney. He turned to Queen Lupa, "your Highness, if you would care to enter the carriage, I will join you shortly." Queen Lupa nodded once and climbed up into the small, comfortable carriage on the back of the Dragon's back. Bobney then turned to General Meuchelmorder. "General, would you care to board with me?"

"Yes, Highness. As your security lead, it is my duty to fly with you and to keep you safe in the event of an incident." She replied, her voice firm and proud.

Bobney smiled, "bugger duty or incidents, once we are in that carriage, you are back to being my friend, no arguments!"

Gladys bowed her head. "Yes, Highness," she purred, a soft feminine smile on her face. For a moment Bobney gazed at her, his eyes seeing nothing else but her. Realising that she was still waiting, her offered her his arm. "Shall we board then, Ma'am?"

Gladys lifted her small bag and then placed her hand through the crook of the King's elbow. "It is my pleasure Sire." Together they climbed the small set of steps and entered into the plush and comfortable carriage. Already fast asleep in a large soft basket, Queen Lupa was almost coiled, her nose resting on the tip of her jet black brush of a tail, her deep red eyes closed fast asleep as she dreamt and occasionally let out a soft whiffle. Bobney showed Gladys to a seat beside the window and once she was sat down, he joined her and got comfortable. The carriage was just large enough to seat six comfortably, or twenty if they were crammed into economy seating and didn't mind not having enough legroom to even satisfy a legless lizard. The walls were decorated in a soft pink so pale it was almost white, with a deep red tartan on the well-padded seats that somehow matched the very dark grey carpet. The seats themselves were firmly bolted into the floor of the carriage and included a reclining back and built in foot rest. As the King got comfortable, Gladys adjusted her own chair and took a deep breath, after almost a full week of the summit, she was fairly tired and was looking forwards to the flight home and some much needed sleep. The Dragon's groom stepped up the door of the carriage and with a final nod, sealed the door and carefully locked it from the outside. A few moments later, the great Dragon's voice could be heard in the carriage. "My dear passengers, please secure any luggage and sit down with the seats in the upright position. I am about to begin take off and there may be some minor buffeting until I am fully airborne. The weather outside is a warm twenty four degrees and our flight today will last approximately twelve hours." For a moment he paused before continuing. "Once we are in level flight, a steward will enter the cabin from the rear, with drinks, snacks and blankets if required. Should you require toilet facilities, these are located through the door at the rear of the cabin. Thank you for choosing to fly with a Greater Red Dragon, we aim to be the fastest, smoothest fliers in any Realm."

Bobney turned to Gladys, "I love this bit. When I was living in the human Realm, I never flew anywhere. I barely left the house to be fair." For a moment a dark shadow seemed to cross his face, but he quickly hid it. "Now here I am and I get to fly on the back of a dragon." He grinned at her. "How great is this?"

Gladys smiled, despite her tiredness, she found King Bobney's enthusiasm for something as ordinary as an international flight to be quite endearing. "I cannot believe that you did not have dragons in the human Realm, it must have been quite unpleasant if you had needed to use one of their huge flying machines." She shuddered slightly, "how horrible, being stuck in one of those dirty metal tubes."

Bobney chuckled, "they are not that bad you know." He said, "some things in the human Realm are quite good fun."

"Like what?" She asked innocently.

"Well, have you ever seen a racing car?" He asked. "What about a roller coaster?" His voice was bemused as he said the strange words to a baffled Gladys. "Oh my dear Gladys, you have not lived.

There are so many little adventures I would love to share with you in the human Realm."

"Well, maybe one day you will." She said quietly. "After all, I am sure that you will have to visit there in an official duty at some point and as your Chief of Security, it would be my duty to go with you."

For a brief moment, Bobney looked crestfallen, as if a hard truth had just shattered a brief moment of dreaming. "What if I just wanted you to come along as my friend?" He asked, his voice soft. "I do really enjoy the time I spend with you, you just seem to make the adventures more fun."

For a moment, Gladys thought back to her conversation with Sha Wren Ston, the chief advisor to King Jong the First.

"I've been married for about five years now." Said Sharen jovially, "not that you would know. He's hardly ever here since the Norfcorean University program employed him as liaison officer with the human world." She smiled, as much as she loved her husband, there were still some things that she missed about being single. "The hardest things in any relationship are the moments when you have to compromise, it can't all be one sided. So when he landed a dream job, combining his love of science with sharing knowledge across the Realms, I had to let him take it."

"Do you miss him when he's away, even if it's just for a day or two?" Asked Gladys shyly. Some new thoughts were starting to drop into her awareness and she was not overly happy about them or what they could mean. "What about if he is at home, but you have to go away on some business for the King?"

Sharen nodded. "Of course I miss him." She stated kindly, "I miss him when he goes out with his friends to play Fairy Football at the weekend, but it's something that he loves, so if it makes him happy, I'm happy. Also, if I want to go out with Jong and Fred, to do something not connected to work, my husband fully supports me to do so." She grinned, "we support each other and we love each other. We do not limit each other or control each other."

"How do you know that you love him?" Asked Gladys, her thoughts dwelling on something that she was starting to really not want to know.

Sharen narrowed her eyes and smiled slyly at Gladys. "When I am with our King, who I love, it's because it's fun. We laugh, we solve problems and we do stuff for the good of the Kingdom." She smiled as Gladys nodded, somewhat more happily. "But," said Sharen, "when I am with my husband, I don't have to do anything. I can just be quiet if I want to, snuggle up on the sofa with a book and just be in the same room as him. We don't don't even have to say anything, we can just be ourselves, in peace and in love. As much as I love Jong, the love I have for my husband is entirely different." Gladys was looking more and more unhappy. "I can feel the love for my husband in my gut, he feels like a part of my soul, like two halves of the same person," said Sharen helpfully.

Gladys looked grey and uncomfortable, as if she had been given a new wallet and had opened it to find a huge gas bill. "So when you say that you love the King, you don't want to spend every day with him, to be there when he wakes up, to run the assault course with him first thing in the morning, for him to be the last thing you see before you go to sleep?"

Sharen shook her head slowly. "Errrr, nooo..." She said as gently as she could. "Those are the sort of things I want to do with my husband, well apart from running around the assault course, that just sounds utterly hellish!" She grinned. "There are other strenuous activities that I prefer to do instead..." She had a mischievous grin on her face and Gladys was mystified.

"What, like combat practice or overnight manoeuvrers?" Gladys asked, albeit rather innocently.

Sharen tried to hold it in, but she failed and burst out laughing. "No you silly, like kissing, or sex."

Gladys looked appalled. "Oh the Gods, I want to have sex with King Bobney!"

Sharen blinked in surprise and continued to laugh. A harsh look from Gladys just made her laugh harder until Gladys started to cry, forcing Sharen to comfort her new friend. "Oh my dear, don't cry, there is nothing wrong with wanting to have sex with the person you love."

Gladys sobbed harder, "but I love the King. I thought that everyone loved the King. It is your duty, you have to love the King when you join the army." She sniffed and Sharen passed her a tissue. "It's part of the pledge of allegiance, we have to love our democracy and the King."

Sharen wrinkled her nose slightly. "Democracy and Kings, they tend not to mix well."

Gladys sobbed again, "but not with King Bobney, he's so good. He loves the people and he wants to help them. He does his absolute best for them. He loves all of the people in the Faerie Realm, he says that he is their servant."

Sharen nodded. "Well, technically, he's not wrong. That is what a King was always supposed to be." She grinned, "just look at our King Jong." She smiled again. "He also says that he loves our society and that he serves the people and in his way he does. He makes decisions for them, he created a system that cares for them if they get sick. He makes sure that everyone gets a good holiday every year and he has also introduced a lot of care for the elderly who have given so many years to the Kingdom and need some of it returned in the form of a pension."

Gladys looked at her mystified again. "But does your King tell you how he will give anything to make the people happy and how he doesn't deserve to be treated better than them, just because of his birthright?"

Sharen pursed her lips and nodded a little. "Yeah, he has said things like that, but luckily I just shove Grandma at him and she drags him off to the kitchen to bake another cake."

Gladys started to cry again, large silver tears rolling down her cheeks and dripping from her chin onto her bright red military jacket. "King Bobney must never know that I love him."

Sharen giggled. "Well, if he doesn't by now, he is either blind or stupid!"

"Oh the Gods, this is just awful!" Sobbed Gladys again. "I will have to resign, I can't risk any harm to the King or his office."

Sharen frowned. "Why can't you just tell him?" She smiled, "he's nice, not like that last arsehole who ruled over all of the Realms."

"It is my duty to look after the Royal household. What if he marries and I have to spend time with his Queen and I say something that compromises us or I do something that puts them both in danger?" Gladys squeezed the unused tissue in her fingers until it was all but a string of paper. "I will have to resign and leave the army and Winscombe altogether." She finally sniffed and used the tissue rope to dab at her eyes. "When I was undercover at the paper, I used some family friends to act as my parents because my own parents are long passed. I could go and stay with them both, they are nice and they will not mind that I may have fucked up my entire life by falling in love with the King of all the Realms!" She sobbed again and buried her face in her hands. "Oh my fucking Gods!" She looked up, her face stern. "How do I stop it? How do I stop being in love with the King?"

"Ummm, well..." Stammered Sharen. "I suppose that you just have to try and shut it down. You have to make some rational decisions, maybe spend some time away from the palace for a little while so that you do not have to see him every day." She put her hand on Gladys' arm. "It will hurt though, you are creating a rejection and in a way you are not giving it a chance." She grinned, her face filled with the hidden knowledge of having seen Bobney and Gladys together. "Why don't you talk to the King, maybe he is in love with you too?"

Gladys looked up at Sharen, a haunted look in her eyes. "I'm not noble born, when my family were alive, they were farmers. The King needs a proper Queen, so that he can sire an heir to the throne. I'm a nobody."

Sharen shook her head sadly. "So this great democracy that you were talking about earlier, where does that get you with these royal issues?"

Chapter 6 ½

Quotidian Hail

Really sorry Reg, I was listening to the classic Jeff Wayne album while recording the events listed in this report, but you know what it works mate, you just whistle that opening riff as you read what they did to Wuffles. The utter bastards...

Is this bad news for Wuffles?
By Abingdon Gentree

Two weeks after the summit, all was not well across the Faerie Realm. Despite the populace of the city being quite happy, somewhere across the gulf of wealth, minds immeasurably more evil than Wuffles' own, regarded the city with envious eyes and slowly and surely they plotted their plans against him...

That is how it was for the next few days, a flare sent up by the various polluting business, onto their Faerieface pages and with it came falsehoods, disinformation and down right lies. The chances of any of it being true, were a million to one, but still they posted.

♫ ♫ ♫ ♫ ♫ ♫

It was the start of the very public character assassination of Wuffles. He always loved this time of year, those fallen leaves lie undisturbed now, coz he's not here. It was with a deafening roar that you drove at those evil CEOs, moving swiftly through the opinion polls, sensing victory was nearing, people started cheering, "come on Wuffles." But the CEOs just raised their vile disinformation and melted Wuffles' valiant heart...

When the dust of the story cleared, Wuffles had reached the end of his patience, but Mother Nature was safe. Wuffles was soon to vanish into the history books and Winscombe belonged to the greedy CEOs...

Quotidian Hail

For fucks sake Abingdon, cut it out man, you are supposed to be a fucking journalist, not a pot smoking dickhead with a penchant for 1970s cheesy disco! Just write the facts.

Cheers, Reg XX

Oh Wuffles, where for art thou?
By Abingdon Gentree

Wuffles the Mayor of Winscombe has finally snapped and has issued court proceedings against a select group of CEOs, namely those who have been releasing hidden footage of the Mayor in a meeting with someone who attempted to bribe him, to allow one of the major mining companies to open a new mine on the outskirts of Winscombe. Meanwhile, public support of Wuffles remains high with many people saying that they would vote for Wuffles again, if he chose to stand for Mayor at the next Mayoral election. In a statement from his office, a spokesperson stated that "Mayor Wuffles identified the person who attempted to bribe him and then reported that person to the authorities. Wuffles continues to be dedicated to the environmental protection laws brought in across all of the realms recently, following the inter-Realm summit chaired by King Jong the First.

===

Wuffles wins court case against senior Company Executives
By Abingdon Gentree

In a shock move, the courthouse of Winscombe has turned into something of a place of celebration. Wuffles has won his case against the CEOs who accused him of fraud, of taking bribes and of not upholding the values of the office of Mayor.
The Jury look less than fifteen minutes to find in favour of Wuffles, but despite this popular win for the city Mayor, a dark cloud hangs over the city of Winscombe today.

Some voices continue to shout about corruption and even nepotism within the office of the Mayor. Given that Wuffles has just won his case, we cannot help but wonder if another court case is about to begin, to silence those voices once and for all?

==

Outrage as Wuffles continues to be slandered by several senior Company Executives
By Abingdon Gentree

This Wednesday morning, an official press statement came from the office of the Mayor of Winscombe, in the name of Wuffles. Unfortunately, Wuffles has decided that after a period of one year of him taking the office for his three year term, he will step down as Mayor of Winscombe. He has stated that the reason for him making this decision is because he wishes to spend more time with his family. However, some critics of the office of Mayor have stated that his protracted social media war with several high profile companies over pollution, corruption and bad faith adherence to new climate laws brought into the Realm by King Bobney, have finally worn him down. After several years of dubious, if not down right evil mayors of Winscombe, many voices are calling on King Bobney to step in and appoint a new representative for the public. At this time, no statement has come from the palace of King Bobney.

==

An Editorial opinion.
Wuffles, is he all that good?
By Reg Singingtrees

In the last few months, since our beloved King Bobney introduced the new laws to protect the environment from unscrupulous development and pollution, we have seen one person in particular catching the flack. That person is our dear Mayor, Wuffles who has done more for the public good in the few months that he has been Mayor than any of the other Mayors we have had in the last few years.

It is a popular opinion that Wuffles is working hard for the good of Winscombe, but are we just jaded because the last six Mayors that we have had have been swindlers, liars, war criminals, demonic entities and half human chimeras? Objectively, compared with all of those people, of course Wuffles is going to appear to be doing good, but just because he is not planning on taking over the Realm or starting a war with Norfcorea to get back at an estranged ex-husband, is he truly trustworthy?

I went out into the streets of Winscombe and I asked several people what they thought of our

Mayor.

Mr Flatfoot, part of the city guard said that "He (Wuffles) is doing a bloody good job and you lot should bloody well leave him alone!" Yet as a member of the authoritarian forces that we have roaming the streets in the city, is Mr Flatfoot truly indicative of public opinion?

With that question in mind, I spoke with Mrs Dotty Drybottom, Madame of Winscombe's infamous underground house of exotic pleasures. She was of a similar opinion stating the following. "As far as I'm concerned, Wuffles has stood up to them bastard oil, mining and power companies who want to F*** us all up up the wrong un, and who are damaging our environment." The strong language and profanity is a prime example of why we need to clean the streets of these particular workers though, so with Wuffles aiming to provide them with legal protection and health screening, there is yet again, a vested interest in this statement, so we must ignore it, in the name of impartiality.

Not content with just two voices, both from the older generation in Winscombe, I popped over to the University to ask some of the students what their thoughts on Wuffles were. Stanley Higgingbottom, an Engineering student from the Human Realm was nonplussed. "I don't really follow politics and I don't listen to politicians," he stated boldly. He then followed it up with, a clearly decisive and damning view of the current Mayor. "They are all as bad as each other."

However, a differing viewpoint came from Margery Squiggletree, the daughter of a leading philanthropist and CEO of the Winscombe water company, Jerome Squiggletree. She voiced a strong objection to Wuffles. "What I object to most is the near deification of Wuffles, as if he were some kind of second coming of the great leader of Norfcorea. What no one sees though, is what goes on in the background, especially when people like my Father are working so hard to make our drinking water safe, clean and profitable."

Now clearly, this is a small sample, but I am sure that you can agree, although Wuffles record has thus far been moderately successful, can we really judge him on that? What happens if he decides to start a war with the Goblins he invited into our city? What if he was to start discriminating against nonflying Fae folk, shaking up a long forgotten race-war? Until Wuffles is done and dusted, I think that we all need to withhold judgement on his actions until we know exactly what he is up to.

In the meantime, the Quotidian Hail is happy to be supported by our partners in the Energy, mining and water industries, all of whom have made several large donations to the widows and orphans fund of the Army and have even sponsored a new printing press for this very paper.

Chapter 7

King Bobney stared out of the window of his office at the dry and dusty patch of parched grass that used to be the royal lawns. It had not rained in Winscombe for over six weeks, which was unusual. It had also been remarkably hot and the trees had withered, the flowers had bloomed and then quickly died back and even the wine growers and farmers had complained that things were not right. The footings of the dam were well underway and even the best estimates said that it would be three years until the dam could be closed and start to flood the valley. The King had stepped in and warned the energy and water companies to clean up their act or face dissolution and a return to public ownership. As for the mining companies, they had been given such strict codes of conduct and had become so heavily regulated that a single complaint about Wuffles would see them back in court and the damages demanded would be huge.

Bobney sighed, there was still so much to do and then there was the rogue mining group from another unknown Realm. The prisoner being held up in the tower had proven to be remarkably unhelpful, although he was thankful to not be working for the miners again. His lack of help was not however wilful, but had more to do with the sad and awful fact that he had been a slave, who had been physically assaulted and forced to work. When he had been questioned, he had tried to be as helpful as possible, but with little actual knowledge of how the sites were chosen or how the technology worked, he had quickly dried up, but had then begged not to be sent back to his own world, stating that he would rather be a prisoner in the Faerie Realm, than a slave in his own. King Bobney had given permission to house the prisoner who wanted to be as far away as possible from the ground and so had been re-homed in the tower, with access to the Faerie-Net, TV and more books than most people would want to read in one lifetime. The Prisoner became an avid student, learning to speak Somerset and was a dedicated reader, and regularly wrote short, occasionally odd letters to the Quotidian Hail in support of the City Mayor and the King, both of whom had offered him a peaceful life of safety away from the evil rogue miners.

Bobney stood up and looked at his watch. It was half past eleven and if he left his office now, he could catch Colonel Thrashgood for his lunchtime run. Ever since he had got back from Norfcorea and even with Queen Lupa staying as a royal guest, King Bobney felt rather lonely. The General had dived back into her work with the army and when he had sent her messages, asking if she would care to join him for lunch during the week, she had been polite, even friendly, but sadly unavailable, which had left Bobney feeling strangely rejected. Normally, he would accept that someone was busy, given how hard everyone seemed to be working, but the sting of the General's rejection felt somehow harder to bear. It was a sting that he felt in his chest, as if his innards had turned to stone. So it was that he was spending more time filling his time with things that wore him out, so that he could spend as much time as possible asleep when not at his desk. He closed his office door and trotted along the corridor to the main door. Just as he was about to step outside, he was caught up by Queen Lupa who jogged up to him and sat down. She whined a couple of times, whimpered once and then let out a sad bark. Bobney shook his head sadly. "I am sorry to hear that, but do remember that despite what the press says, they are trying to make money and these vile lies sell more papers than the more mundane truth, especially when talking about politicians like your Son."

Queen Lupa whined again and wagged her tail twice, then waggled her ears. Bobney nodded his understanding. "Yes of course, I shall gladly ask the palace team to organise a nice dinner and we shall invite your Son the Mayor as guest of honour. However, I am sure that he is fully aware that he has the support of the people though."

Placated, Queen Lupa barked twice and then bowed to the King.

"You are very welcome," replied Bobney.

Again Queen Lupa whined, barked and stamped a foot twice. Bobney pursed his lips and gave her a sad smile. "Sadly, the General is very busy at the moment, she has some new recruits that are struggling to settle in and the Master has the flu and she has personally promised to look after him."

Queen Lupa put a front paw over her eyes and whined sorrowfully.

"Well, I wouldn't put it quite like that, she and I are just very good friends."

Queen Lupa barked in genuine surprise. Her ears were fully forwards and then she wiffled slightly and leaned her head against Bobney's leg for a brief moment.

"No really," said Bobney quietly, "we don't see each other like that." He frowned, part of him greatly wished that the General could be with him to help reassure Queen Lupa that they were not a couple, despite her insistence. Finally he spoke again. "I know that you mean well, but I very much doubt that she has feelings like that at all, after all if she did, would she be avoiding me or working so hard that she never has time to see me?"

Queen Lupa whined a non-committal answer and wagged her tail. She then stood up and with a low whine wished King Bobney a good day, before wandering away to her quarters and a rest in the cool of her room.

King Bobney stepped outside and pulled the door shut, the words of Queen Lupa were somehow haunting his mind, replaying over and over again. Finally he chuckled, he really must see the General soon so that he could tell her what the Hell Hound Queen has said, he was sure that they would both find it funny. Moving quickly, he jogged down the pathway to the gates of the palace and saluted the Guard who stood in his smart uniform. "Just off for a run with Colonel Thrashgood." He reassured the concerned looking guard. "Will be back by dinner time." He paused for a moment, half way through the gateway. "By the way, what do you think of the General, Trooper?"

Unsure of what he should say, he stood to attention. "The General is a great woman Sir, one of the finest warriors the Realm has ever seen."

"I see," said King Bobney nodding. "Would you say that you loved the General?"

"Excuse me Sir?" Asked the Guard. "I'm not sure what you mean Sir."

"It's a simple enough question. Do the troops love the General?"

The Guard grinned. "Sorry Sir, I understand now, Sir."

"Well?" Asked King Bobney.

"Sir, yes sir." Said the Guard. "We all love the General Sir, she is one of us, a damn good egg, Sir."

Bobney grinned. "That is what I thought. Thank you." He looked up to the palace and then back to the guard. "If I were you, I would take a break, tell your sergeant that King Bobney sent you for a fifteen minute tea break. You deserve it."

The Guard smiled. "Sir, thank you Sir. However, the Sergeant is in the Guardhouse Sir."

A Fae suddenly appeared in the Guardhouse doorway. "Sorry Highness, I was just enjoying a cup of tea and a biscuit."

Bobney grinned. "No worries Sergeant, I suggested to this young man that you should both take a tea break anyway, I'm going for a run with Colonel Thrashgood."

"Sir, yes Sir." said the Sergeant, who stood rigid and saluted the King. He then turned to the young Guard. "Private Smokestone, return to the Guardhouse and make a pot of tea."

The Guard saluted the Sergeant, "Yes Sergeant. Would you like another biscuit Sir."

The Sergeant grinned. "That's the spirit young man, we'll make a fine officer out of you one day."

Bobney was already half way to Thrashgood when the guardroom kettle started to boil.

Felicity Hopeforthebest sat in a low, but comfortable chair in the home of the Magician. The man himself had gone to the kitchen to fetch a plate of home-made buns and was just returning when the mobile phone on his desk and the phone in Felicity's pocket both chirped. Felicity pulled out her phone and then her eyebrows shot up. "Our friendly Gremlin has engaged the enemy. I need to call the Colonel and Deborah." Before she could even dial, the phone rang and she answered. "Hey

Deborah, I take it you have news?"

Deborah was unhappy, her voice sounded hurt. "They're back. South of the city, no more than thirty miles."

Felicity's heart broke for the young woman, she could feel the pain in her voice. "Listen, we have an operative on site and he is staying with the crew, following them and slowing them as much as possible. We will catch these swine. Have you informed the Colonel?"

"That's great news." Said Deborah, a new note of hope sounding in her quiet voice. "Is it anyone I know?" She paused. "Oh yeah, I have told Thrashgood."

Felicity grinned. "You know about the Gremlin we spoke to at the dam site?"

Deborah suddenly grinned. "You sent them a Gremlin?" She started to laugh, "that is genius!"

"Not my idea." Stated Felicity, with a laugh in her voice. "You can blame our esteemed Wizard for that one!"

The Magician grinned and winked. "Send Deborah my love. Also, tell her that we are going to catch these buggers and put a stop to their games."

Deborah laughed down the phone, "please tell him that I heard." She said to Felicity.

"I will." Felicity said kindly. "Listen Deborah, I need to get off the line, Thrashgood will be wanting to get in touch directly, then we can get these people. Do you want us to pick you up when we catch them?"

"Oh yes please Felicity, now go. Send Thrashgood my love." She paused for a second. "Thank you Felicity, I love you, you know."

Felicity smiled, "I love you too little one." She put the phone down and turned to the Magician. "Our young friend is feeling a little more positive now."

The Magician smiled kindly. "That is good, I have been terribly worried about her." Suddenly Felicity's phone began to make an alarming chirping noise. "Thrashgood?" He asked.

"Yes," she said as she put the handset to her ear." Colonel, news?"

"We are on site and have the King with us. Would suggest that you, your colleague and the young one make your way here."

"On our way Colonel, see you in thirty."

"Love you Girl."

Felicity smiled and closed the call. Turning to the Magician, she spoke. "Gather up your skirts, we have some naughty miners to catch."

"Wonderful." Said the Magician. "I shall put my

combat robe on!"

The autocart pulled up outside Herbert's house to find Deborah, Herbert and Katie waiting in in the dark. Deborah hugged them both and climbed up onto the autocart and sat behind Felicity, who was driving. Herbert stepped up close to the vehicle and spoke. "Felicity, please take care of our Deborah. I know that she is an all-powerful Mother Goddess, but she is also our little girl."

"Don't worry Herbert, by the time we get there, all of the fun stuff will be over." Felicity said while grinning. Katie just shook her head and Herbert laughed. Felicity waved and then they set off at speed towards the latest mining incursion.

Colonel Thrashgood was finishing his paperwork when he looked up from his desk and saw the King stood on the dry, course lawn, chatting with a couple of the troops. He could see that although the King was being jovial, chatty and appeared happy, something was not quite right. He signed the last page, put it carefully into the right folder, sealed the cover with the wire and placed it on the tray for collection when his secretary came through later in the day. Finally finished and aching for some exercise, the Colonel stood up and paced through the office door and outside to meet the King. The King looked up and seemed to somehow brighten. "Ahh Colonel Thrashgood, jolly good to see you old bean." Said the King brightly. "I just wondered if you had some training on this afternoon, I seem to be at a loose end and want to take my mind off things, so thought that a damn good run would sort me out."

Thrashgood smiled and nodded at the two young men who stood patiently waiting and with that the two of them took off back to the work that they had left waiting for them. "I was thinking of maybe a brisk ten Kay, then back here for coffee?"

The King grinned. "Just what the Doctor ordered!" He said, "ready when you are."

Thrashgood gave the King an appraising look and then with a soft sigh, nodded. "No time like the present."

The King looked around. "No other troops coming along?"

Thrashgood shook his head. "Not today. I have the team on lockdown, mid mission. Rupertina and section one of the SFS are all holed up, monitoring radio transmissions and intel from Mother."

"So just us then." Said the King expectantly. "Lucky me."

Thrashgood grinned, "yeah, I need a beasting and also it gives us time to talk, have a catch up." He started to stretch and looked over to Bobney who was also stretching out, ready to run. "Come on then, Your Highness, let's put some burn into those lazy royal thighs!"

The King laughed and then had to run hard to catch up with Colonel Thrashgood, who was running harder than he usually did when he was training troops or running in recruits. Soon enough Bobney caught his friend up and was breathing hard for a while, until when Thrashgood thought the time to chat had come, he eased off slightly. "My King, I need to talk to you not as your friend, but as a military advisor."

Bobney frowned, breathing hard, but keeping pace. "This sounds serious, am I in trouble?" He joked. When Thrashgood did not reply. Bobney started to slow. "Of fuck, this is serious isn't it?"

Thrashgood pointed to a small wooden bench overlooking a hill, roughly eight hundred metres from where they were. "See you there!" He set off at a sprint and for the first time in a long time, Bobney found himself struggling to keep up. By the time he got to the bench, Thrashgood was already seated and breathing normally. Bobney sat down, blowing hard and barely able to speak. "Give it to me?"

The Colonel grinned. "I love that you give the troops your love and your support. You gave them a new barracks and have supplied them with new facilities that they otherwise wouldn't have had access to." He shook his head sadly, "but there is something wrong and it is with you."

King Bobney finally managed to sit up straight. "I'm fine, OK I am not as fit as you or the troops, but I'm not bad."

Thrashgood shook his head. "It's not that."

For a moment Bobney looked bleak. "You think that I'm a bad King?"

Thrashgood laughed before turning to face the King. "No, I do not think that you are a bad King, but I do think that you're a bloody idiot."

Thrashgood was not sure how the King was going to take the critique, but Bobney seemed to be waiting for more information, although he looked just as puzzled as he was hurt. Thrashgood took a deep breath. "Felicity and I want to get married."

Bobney let out a deep breath. "Oh Thrashy, I am so sorry. I had not realised." He put a hand on his friend's shoulder, "the regiment can survive without you for a couple of weeks. Take your leave and

Felicity and do what you want to do, if anyone deserves it, it is the both of you."

Thrashgood shook his head. "That is not the problem."

"Oh!" Said Bobney perplexed. "So what do you need from me?"

Thrashgood sighed, "listen there is no easy way to say this, but I can't have you distracting the troops while they are on missions or preparing for combat." He took a deep breath as Bobney seemed to grow somehow smaller. "Those two lads today that you were chatting to, they were running intelligence, under order to run information as fast as possible between offices."

King Bobney sat up straight and sucked in his breath. "Colonel Thrashgood, you are absolutely right. I apologise wholeheartedly."

The Colonel shook his head. "You come into the barracks because you are lonely, even though you are surrounded by friends. However, there is one person who always brightens your day."

Bobney smiled, albeit somewhat sadly. "I am sorry, I was not aware that I was taking up so much of your time."

"My time is not the issue." Said Thrashgood firmly. "What do you think the General wants here?"

"Ahhh," said the King. "I had not given her a moment of thought. Given that she is no longer in charge of the regiment..." He paused for a moment. "I owe her an apology too, don't I?" He shook his head, "I have not been thinking, dragging her away to Norfcorea, not giving her a moment of time off while we were there and now I call her up and ask her questions, all while she is working so hard." He slapped Thrashgood on the thigh gratefully. "Thank you for bringing this to my attention. That woman deserves a damn sight better treatment than I have been giving her."

Thrashgood laughed out loud, "Oh shit, you really are an idiot!"

For a brief moment King Bobney almost looked angry. Instead he sighed and leaned forwards on his knees, resting his chin in his hands.

Thrashgood leaned over to the King. "What do you think of the General as a woman?"

The King blew out a breath. "I do not think of her as a woman at all, I think of her as a damn fine soldier, a bloody good leader of the troops. She is an inspiration to young women everywhere and she puts her life on the line without asking what is in it for her."

Thrashgood grinned again. "Do you like the

General, Highness?"

The King laughed, "like her? What has that got to do with anything? That woman is..." His face suddenly faltered. Thrashgood stayed silent, but raised his eyebrows. Finally the King spoke again. "Ahh, I see what you mean."

"Do you?" Asked Thrashgood meaningfully. "What do you think of the General?"

Bobney settled slightly on the bench. "If I am completely honest with you, I think that I am more than a little fond of the General."

"Really?" Teased Thrashgood, "more than a little fond of her?" Bobney nodded his head. "So." Said Thrashgood, "what are we going to do with the pair of you? You are both so tied up in duty and work and doing the right thing, you can barely see what is right in front of your eyes."

Bobney shook his head. "Thrashy, I've not met a woman before, who well, you know..."

Thrashgood put his arm around the shoulders of his friend. "Fuck man, you're the King. How would you ever? Anyway, I know for a fact that she is just as pure as you."

"So she won't think that I'm defective for not having had a girlfriend before?" Suddenly the King's face flushed red. "I am so sorry, I cannot believe I just asked you such a personal question about another person."

"It's OK, it is just between us and I swear that I will not tell a soul. Also, I am not going to gossip about someone who I respect and love as much as that woman. If you want to discuss things like that, do it politely and respectfully and talk about it with her." Thrashgood stood up, "come on, it is time we got back to barracks and I think that you have something to consider."

Bobney stood up and looked at his friend. "Thank you, I still have so much to learn about life and I seem to learn an awful lot of it from you."

The mobile phone in Thrashgood's pocket started to buzz loudly, he pulled it out and spoke. "Thrashgood, speak!" Suddenly his eyes widened and he grinned. "We are three miles from barracks, pick us up on the way, we have got these buggers. Oh don't worry about telling the King, he's right here."

Bobney looked up. "Tell me what?"

"Rogue miners," said Thrashgood. "We've got their new location. Apparently, there is already an operative on site, giving us intel."

"Fan-fucking-tastic." Said King Bobney brightly. "Some good news and about time too." He looked to Thrashgood who had put his phone away. "Thank you, for being a true friend and also for not being a dick about it."

Thrashgood grinned. "Day's not over yet, friend!" They both burst out laughing.

The Gremlin had been through every function on his phone, he had investigated apps, discovered ancillaries and then discovered some neat little hacks that gave him access to things that the developers would really rather he not have. The result was that he was able to hack anything that had blue tooth, Wi-Fi or a plain old USB socket. So when the miners suddenly burst back into the Faerie Realm, he tracked them almost instantly and was able to get to them using his Gremlin abilities. The first thing he found as they wheeled out their large machines was that none of the computers used USB leads. They did however have a strange phallic nodule that he was able to hack and then connect to and thus he had full access to all of their systems. The ability of a Gremlin to learn a mechanical system was unequalled, which meant that within five minutes, the manager of the main computer system that ran the entire mining operation was finding that his computers were starting to glitch rather badly. These were not the only faults the team were encountering, not by a long shot. The mining machines themselves started to develop strange and unusual problems, so much so that the crews were finding it all but impossible to carry out normal work. It did not stop there however, as soon as the Gremlin was done with the computers, it was time for him to get to the real work. Tools went missing and turned up in the wrong places. Keys to tool lockers mounted on the machines were swapped and then hidden. Maps within the machines were redrawn and then redrawn again, just to add extra confusion. The Gremlin only stopped when he came to the mobile explosives carrier and he remembered Felicity's words. No blowing anyone up. So he filled the locks with chewing gum and super glue. The mining crew were growing more and more annoyed as mechanical problems, software problems and missing tools became overwhelming until eventually everything simply ground to a stop. Not even the computer that activated the portal was working, so until they could fix all of the glitches, there was no way home. The workers unfortunately caught the ire of the foreman, a vaguely human looking male in his later middle years, with a balding head and a greying moustache. His only real methods of making his workers perform was through brutality and as luck would have it, he quite enjoyed the process, so he took the senior crew member from each failing machine and had them line up in front of him and made a show of taking out his most vicious whip. He uncurled the foul thing, flicked a few scraps of dried flesh from the barbs at the end of the leather thongs and was crushed to the ground by a member of Colonel Thrashgood's team who seemed to leap out of the shadows the workers were casting on the ground behind them.

With the site under the control of the SFS, the workers were released from their slavery, but were put into questioning, as soon as they were medically checked. King Bobney strode around the site silently raging at the colossal machines that had already done so much damage to the Realm. Eventually he decided that it was time to discuss the damage done with the foreman, but thus far all attempts at communication had failed. He spoke no languages that any of the Fae spoke. King Bobney shrugged his shoulders and then asked to meet with the hidden operative alone in one of the sheds. He entered the shed and sat down on a small wooden stool, which collapsed because one the legs had been almost fully sawed through. Standing up and dusting himself down, King Bobney came face to face with the Gremlin, who was sat on a dusty shelf, grinning almost from ear to ear.

"I hear that you wished to speak with me, your Kingliness?"

"That's right," said King Bobney, "I do indeed."

"What do you want, I've done what I was asked and no more. Just as directed."

The King was quiet, thoughtful for a moment. "Are you aware that without your help, this mission would not have been successful?"

The Gremlin grinned. "Yeah, it was a shit tonne of fun." He scratched a nail across a paint tin, the lid popped open and he gently pushed the tin towards the edge of the shelf. "So?"

"I know very little about your people." Said King Bobney quietly and the Gremlin nodded his head sagely. "And for now I want it to stay that way."

The Gremlin snorted back a discontented laugh. "So now that you're done with me, you want me gone?"

"Actually," said the King, his voice barely hiding the smirk from his voice. "I wonder if you would care to sign on full time with my military force?"

The Gremlin sat down in surprise. "Excuse me?"

"Well quite frankly... I'm sorry, I do not know your name."

The Gremlin smiled, his mouth filled with glistening white teeth and one gold cap. "If I give you my name, you have power over me. So that is a no can do."

The King nodded. "I understand, however if you would like to take up the position, you would be working with the Colonel of the Special Faerie Service directly."

For a moment the Gremlin was quiet, his face serious. "Why?" He asked.

"You know why." Said the King flatly. "Your intelligence got us here faster than Mother Nature could do alone. Once you were here you created a diversion so great, you wiped out the enemies ability to engage us before we had even arrived." He paused for a moment. "What do you know of human history?"

The Gremlin shook his head from side to side. "Not much, maybe a little."

"Well," said King Bobney quietly, "When I was in school, I learned about a group that fought against tyranny during their second world war. They were called The Special Operations Executive or S O E."

"What does that mean?" Asked the Gremlin.

"They were spies, saboteurs, special operatives." The King smiled. "Those people were bloody good. However what you have just done here bested them all and in under thirty minutes."

The Gremlin grinned. "Why thank you, it is nice to meet someone who has a sense of humour."

King Bobney nodded, his eyes shining, but his face did not smile. "S O E saved many hundreds of lives, probably many thousands more, sadly I do not remember my lesson that well. What I can tell you is that they often worked alone and in places that would execute them if they were caught. The operations I would ask you to go on have the potential to be just as dangerous to you." He let out a sigh before speaking again. "Tonight we stopped them, but this is just one group and I am sure that there are many more out there, primed and ready to come here to rape the landscape of its mineral wealth."

The Gremlin nodded his head in understanding, his face suddenly glum. "That is really not very funny is it?" He sat down on the edge of the shelf and pushed the paint pot back towards the centre of the shelf. "You paint a bleak picture of the future."

"Oh it gets better," said the King. "In this Realm we

are fighting a campaign of dirty tricks, a group of private companies have held us in a strangle hold, supplying us with energy, water and infrastructure. In exchange they are sucking the planet dry and when we tried to make them see sense, they all but destroyed the reputation of the good being I have trying to fix their damage."

The Gremlin stood up, he was not more than the height of a pencil and his small stature did not hide his immense power as an operative. "My name is Gregor. My people have only one name and we choose it ourselves when we reach adulthood. We have only one sex, made up of three separate genders and when we swear our allegiance to someone, it is for life." The Gremlin stood up and took off his small cap and held it over his heart. "I Gregor, swear my allegiance to the Realm of the Faerie, under the leadership of King Bobney." He put his cap back on and held out a small hand to the King. King Bobney took the small hand in his own. "I, King Bobney Wolfgang Jones, do gladly accept the allegiance of the operative known as Gregor, I pledge to keep the secret of his name forever or until he gives me permission to share it with another. I welcome you Gregor to the royal court as a trusted guest and I would be insulted if you did not play the occasional practical joke on my guests. As your Commanding Officer, I grant you the rank of Commander and you will be awarded the pay and pension as appropriate, back dated to when you joined our campaign."

The Gremlin burst out laughing and then quietly released his hand from that of the King. "I will see you back at your palace my King. You will know that I am there, you can trust me on that."

"Until then, Commander Gregor, I would ask that at a time to suit yourself, you report to the office of Colonel Thrashgood." Said King Bobney, "just one thing, Thrashgood is a damn good man, with a great sense of humour. However, even though he is probably the best friend I have and I trust him absolutely with my life. I will only tell him to expect Commander X. It is up to you to decide for yourself if you wish to give him your name." The King paused. "When you have weighed up the man, I want you to think about recruiting a small unit of your people, working as operatives under his direct command. This is why I do not want to know them, so that they can have full confidence that I will never betray them. If you decide that your people would like to join our fight against this destruction, I want it to happen by your choice alone."

Deborah sat at the kitchen table of her Uncle Herbert's house and sipped from a dark and dangerous looking brew. Her Uncle had often gently teased her about drinking witches tea, but he always made sure that there was plenty of it in stock for when she was at home. It had not taken long for her to think of Herbert's home as her home too and she loved her Uncle who had cared for her many times in her young life. Herbert himself was growing old and with age came a degree of fragility, meaning that there were the occasional times when Deborah returned the favour. Also living with them, pretty much permanently, since moving from the human Realm was their friend Katie. Katie had first met Deborah in the distant past, when Deborah had travelled through time to visit the human town where her Uncles lived. Despite a rough start to their friendship, Katie had become a part of Herbert's family and the three of them lived peacefully in the large, beautiful farmhouse that had been designed by Herbert's human husband, Oliver. Oliver had passed away a few years before and all of them deeply missed him, including Deborah who had been a tiny baby when she met Oliver for the second time. There were times when her adventures almost melted her mind when she thought about them and the time paradoxes she had encountered, but the result was that she was happy with her little family and had even introduced a few of her friends to them too. She sipped her tea and found that it had cooled and then as she drained her mug, the doorbell rang, but was quickly followed by urgent knocking. Deborah grabbed her overnight bag from the kitchen floor and was half way to the kitchen door when Katie answered the door. She chatted briefly and then called to Deborah, just as she rounded the corner and into the small passageway that led to the front door and where Felicity stood waiting, leaning gently on her walking stick. "Come on Missy." Said Felicity with a smile. "It looks like we have caught them."

Deborah grinned, but her eyes were the colour of ice from the bottom of a glacier. "I will be right there Felicity," she turned to Katie. "I will see you when I get back." She put her arms around the neck of the older woman. "I love you so much Katie Flowers, I am so glad that you are my friend."

Katie hugged the young woman back, "I'm glad too." She kissed the young woman on the forehead. "promise me that you will be careful?" She started to laugh. "Look at me, worrying about the Mother Goddess of the Earth." She released the young woman. "Go and be brave, save the world for us all." As Deborah turned to the door to follow Felicity, Katie spoke again. "I love you too Deborah and thank you for changing my life." For a second Deborah looked back at the older woman, she could see that the sand in her timer was starting to run low and for a brief moment her heart ached knowing that one day she would lose Katie forever. She smiled and winked and then turned back to the door and followed Felicity to the waiting autocart and the Magician who sat at in the front passenger seat. She climbed up, sat on the bench at the back and strapped herself in, just as Felicity flicked the cane that held the purple plush vegetable that hung on a string from the tip. The strange creatures that propelled the autocart squealed gleefully and the vehicle leapt forwards. The roads leading away from Winscombe were fairly smooth, but at the speed of the autocart, even a small bump felt close to catastrophic. The Magician seemed lost in thought and Felicity was concentrating hard on the parts of the road she could see in the dim lights of the lanterns that hung from the front of the autocart. After twenty minutes, they finally arrived at the site of the latest incursion and Deborah almost sprung from the autocart and sprinted into the site to find Colonel Thrashgood. Finding him and still slightly breathless, she almost shouted when she spoke. "Thank you, you stopped them before they did any damage."

Thrashgood grinned and bent down as the young woman hugged him in gratitude. "We had special help, but yes we stopped them this time."

Deborah looked around the site. "Where are they from?" Are they human?"

Thrashgood shook his head. "We don't know and we don't know. They look human, but then so do we. So who knows? Perhaps?"

"At least you stopped them." Said Deborah firmly.

"We stopped these ones." Said Thrashgood gravely, "but who knows if there are more of them?"

"Let's hope not," said Deborah.

Chapter 8

General Gladys Meuchelmorder sat quietly at her desk, reading the report from Colonel Thrashgood about the mission to shut down the rogue miners. There was one section when he mentioned working alongside Commander X, a special operations spy that intrigued her, but otherwise she was happy with the report. The workers from the mining machines had been debriefed as much as possible, with the help of Piotre, the first miner to be arrested. During the debriefing, it became clear that the society that sent them, used an awful lot of slave labour and so plans were made to re-home the miners in Winscombe where they could be helped to overcome the horrific and appalling treatment they had suffered. The only person not to be treated with quite so much compassion was the Foreman of the operation, who had reacted rather badly to be being arrested and questioned.

A sudden knock at her door almost startled her and looking up, she called out. "Enter." The door opened and with slow careful steps, came a man in a pressed military uniform, a cap on his head and a large uncertain smile on his face. Gladys stood up and bowed her head. "Your Highness, it is a pleasure to see you, how may I help you today?"

Bobney pointed to the seat in front of the General's desk. "May I please sit down? General Meuchelmorder? I feel that you and I need to have a very difficult conversation."

"Yes of course." Said Gladys quietly. "I shall have some tea brought in and then we can talk. I assume that you are concerned about the rogue miners. I am just reading Thrashgood's report right now. It sounds rather harrowing, those poor people have really suffered."

The King nodded. "Indeed they have suffered, but this is not why I came to see you today."

"I see." Said Gladys, her voice suddenly guarded. She pushed a button on the intercom and a voice replied almost instantly.

"Yes General?"

"Can you bring tea for the King and I please Sergeant?"

"Certainly General. I will be there in a few moments."

"Thank you Sergeant." Replied Gladys. She sat back down on her comfortable chair and waited for the tea to be delivered. Less than two minutes later, the office door opened and the Sergeant came in carrying a tray with a large pot of tea, a small milk jug, a bowl of sugar cubes and two large mugs with the SFS insignia printed on them. "Your Tea General." The Sergeant turned to the King and saluted before marching back out of the room and firmly closing the door. Gladys took the two mugs and poured out the tea and added a splash of milk into each one. She placed a mug in front of the King and then held her own in both hands and took a small sip. The King had watched her throughout and then he just stared at the mug. Finally Gladys broke the silence. "What do you need to discuss, Highness?"

Bobney swallowed, but his throat felt dry. He lifted his mug and took sip. "This is probably the hardest conversation I have ever had to have." His eyes dropped to the mug once again and then he looked up at the General. He cleared his throat. "I am going to tell you something General and I hope that you will not be insulted by what I am about to tell you. However, no matter what the outcome, I want you to know that I respect you fully."

Gladys frowned. "Has there been a complaint about my behaviour at the summit? To my knowledge, I performed my duties exactly as required."

The King shook his head. "My dear General, you

performed your duties to the letter and without even the slightest hint of a faux pas." He cleared his throat again. "However, this is a personal matter that I hope you can understand my reticence in discussing this with you."

Growing more concerned, Gladys spoke firmly. "Well Highness, just spit it out. Rip the plaster off so to speak. We are adults and can deal with any problem in an adult manner."

Bobney's head lowered briefly. Finally he looked up and into the gaze of the General. She was a magnificent woman, her eyes glittering with compassion and strength. Her smile radiant. "General Meuchelmorder, I am in love with you."

Wuffles sat in the garden and watched the birds as they hopped from branch to branch. Sat next to him was his Mother and she was starting to look her age. Some of her joints were stiff and despite her grace, she had the occasional wobble in her hip as she walked. She turned to Wuffles. "My Son, I have missed you so very much, even more so since losing your Father and your Brother."

Wuffles lowered his head and spoke, his voice full of sadness. "I know dear Mother, I am sorry, I should have been there with you."

The old Queen shook her head. "No my son, you were always where you needed to be and I can see that now. I can also see how much good it has done you and you were right, you have learned a vast amount, none of which you could have learned had you stayed at home." She leaned across to him and gently licked his ear. "I can see the friendships that you have forged here, the respect you have gained through being compassionate and kind." She licked him again. "I am so proud of you, my son."

"Thank you Mother." He said quietly.

His Mother continued to speak. "I am growing too old to rule our homeland, I am exhausted every day because I have ruled for almost six hundred years." She paused for a moment and gazed at her son as he watched the birds. "I think that you are almost ready to take the throne in our homeland."

Wuffles nodded his head. "I am, but I have some commitments that I must see through to the end here."

"I know," whispered the Queen. "And I know that you will carry out your duties to the best of your ability until you have completed them."

"I have spoken with King Bobney and have told him that I intend to stay for one year and then I shall return home." Said Wuffles gently. "I hope that this is acceptable to you, Mother?"

The Old Queen nodded again. "Of course it is my son and again, I could not be more proud of you." She licked his ear again before continuing to speak. "What you have done here, for all of these people, it has shown me that you are going to make a great King. You have made so many difficult decisions and you have done so without arrogance or indecision. There are many princes who could learn a lot from you, my son."

Wuffles wagged his tail as he spoke. "I am happy that I have made you proud my Mother, I hope that my father and brother can look upon me with such pride."

From behind them came a female human voice, slight accented from Wuffles' home world. "Hello, is there anyone here?" Both Hell Hounds turned as one to face their visitor. The young woman almost froze as she saw them both. Suddenly she bowed low and maintained the bow as she spoke. "Queen Lupa, I was not aware that you had travelled out of our Realm. Please forgive my intrusion."

The Queen turned and yipped a reply. "Rise child, how can you be of our Realm, let me see your face."

Seeing a fellow traveller, Wuffles yowled a friendly

greeting and trotted across to the young woman as she stood up. He gently licked her hand, ignoring the chipped black nail polish and cheap silver rings on her fingers. He turned back to his Mother. "My Mother, this is my friend, she was formerly of our Realm, but she is now of the human Realm. We met as we both travelled."

The Queen gazed at the girl, her face somewhat puzzled. "I am aware that such a change was possible, but I have never met one." She stepped forwards a little. "Please child, tell me your name?"

"My name is Bronwyn." She looked to Wuffles who nodded encouragement to her. "I am a trans person."

The Queen yipped and whined, her ears fully forward. "Well my child, I would not have guessed, had you not told me." She stepped forwards. "I am pleased that you have found your peace within yourself."

"Thank you Queen Lupa." Said Bronwyn shyly. "Meeting your son was a lucky occasion for me, he helped me settle into myself. By giving me his acceptance, I was able to find my own and I am now settled."

Wuffles yipped and barked his pleasure at seeing his friend again.

"Thank you Prince Hatti," said Bronwyn happily.

"If I may ask?" Yipped Queen Lupa gently, "why are you dressed like a Vampire woman?" She nodded to the young woman's t-shirt. "That image is quite shocking!" She gave a small wiffle of laughter.

Bronwyn looked down at her t-shirt, it showed an album cover for her favourite heavy metal band. "I'm a heavy metal fan, we all dress like this, lots of black, lots of band patches on my leather jacket."

"Well my dear," yipped Queen Lupa, "from what I know of the Vampire peoples, you would be welcomed into their society."

Bronwyn gave a large happy grin. "Thank you, your Highness."

"If I may also ask," yapped Queen Lupa, "why are you here?"

"Oh yeah," gushed Bronwyn, "when I was travelling, I met Prince Hatti and he was very kind to me. So when I was passing through Winscombe, I hoped that I would be able to come and say hello to a fellow traveller and thank him for his guidance."

Wuffles wagged his tail and leant his head against Bronwyn as he yipped his happiness to see her again. "I am so happy that you came to see me." He paused for a moment. "Are you staying around for long, I have a friend here about your age who I think would really like to meet you."

"I don't have anywhere to stay yet." Bronwyn replied, "but I was going to look for a room for a few days, before I head back to the human world for a festival."

Wuffles yowled and yipped, wagging his tail as he did so."

Bronwyn could not help but smile. "Ahh, thank you Prince Hatti, I would love to crash at yours for a couple of days." She grinned. "I promise that I won't make any mess, like leaving beer cans around the floor or leave dirty pants behind the sofa. I know what people think of metal-heads!"

Wuffles laughed, while Queen Lupa looked on mystified, shaking her head in mirth.

General Meuchelmorder looked at King Bobney in stunned silence. For a moment he seemed to hesitate before speaking again. "General Meuchelmorder, there is no obligation for you to say anything or for you to return my feelings." He swallowed on his dry throat. "It is not my desire to put you in a difficult position." He shifted in his seat and then stood up. "I am so sorry, I shall leave you now. Please put this conversation behind us. I hope that you can forgive me if I take a few days to sort myself out?"

The General stood up and adjusted her regimental tie and then stepped around the desk and stood in front of the King. "My King," she bowed her head and stayed looking at her feet. "I am not high born, I am honoured that you would tell me this, but I am just a farmer's daughter, who became general in the army, I am not a princess who would be worthy of your love."

"I don't care about your birth status." Bobney winced suddenly at his own words. "Sorry, that is not what I mean." He paused and then stammered. "I love you because of who you are, not because of your assumed lack of social status." She looked up at him and he smiled. "Anyway, let's be honest, almost every member currently serving in the armed forces has way more respect for you than they do for me. Yeah. Fine, I'm the figurehead they salute to or have to pretend to be as fit as, but you are a decorated war hero. I know who I would rather have leading me into battle."

Gladys smiled. "I have a secret, that I have to tell you."

Bobney looked suddenly worried. "I am so sorry,

you already have a romantic partner." He snorted, "I am an idiot, how could I not realise this?"

"No," said Gladys softly. "That is not it." For a moment Bobney just looked at her, waiting for her to speak. "I spent some time with King Jong's chief advisor and I can see why he chose her, she is very wise."

"I am aware that you spent time with Sha Wren Ston, I know that King Jong speaks very favourably of her." Said Bobney.

"She helped me." Said Gladys, her voice a whisper.

"How did she help you?" Asked Bobney, his own voice barely an audible sound.

"She helped me understand that I am in love with you." She leant in closer to the King. "King Bobney, with all of my heart and soul, I love you."

The King smiled as if he were a hungry child who had been given a ham sandwich with the crusts cut off. Then he leant his head down very slightly, with a delicacy that seemed almost impossible between them both, he kissed Gladys and she kissed him back. It was a simple, chaste kiss between innocents and yet it changed everything between them. Their heart rates soared, their pupils enlarged and their skin became more sensitive to each other's touch. The kiss ended and for a moment they gazed at each other, smiling like innocents. "I have never kissed anyone before." Said Bobney quietly, almost shy.

"I have never been kissed like that before." Purred Gladys, her eyes drinking in every detail of Bobney that they could.

"Was it OK?" He asked, suddenly feeling vulnerable, but safely so.

"No," said Gladys gently, "it was perfect." She kissed him again, her hand brushed the side of his face, she could feel the firmness of his jaw, the soft scratch of his recently shaved face. "I think that I am in heaven," She whispered.

"All of my life, I never knew that I could feel like this." Said Bobney, his voice delicate, husky with emotion. "Now, I don't know how I survived without this." He looked at her again, the brightness of her crystal-clear eyes, the slight arch of her brow, the softness of her nose, small scars from combat. Every detail was perfection, his eyes drank her like rain in the desert. "My heart feels freer than I have ever felt before and I know that I love you with all of my being."

Gladys started to laugh and her arms circled his neck. "I have loved you for so long and I was unaware that what I felt was so special. I thought that everyone felt like this about you. I thought that everyone missed you when you left the room."

Bobney laughed too. "I thought that when you were not there, the light in the sky was somehow less bright." He kissed her again. "I never want to let you go."

There was a small cough behind them. As one they turned their heads to the face of Colonel Thrashgood. "Excuse me intruding Your Highness, General. Our interpreter has made something of a breakthrough with the captive miners. I thought that you would want to know right away." He saluted and then turned back towards the door. At the door he stopped and turned back to them. "I am really pleased to see you both finding what all of us could see." He smiled again, on his tough and military face, it was a softer, more gentle smile. "I cannot think of two people who match so well. Felicity and Deborah will be overjoyed when you are ready to share your news with them."

Bobney's face suddenly fell. "Oh shit, I have to tell my Mother."

The small interview room was surprisingly cool, despite the number of people crammed into it, nearly all of them were facing the back wall against which was a chair, upon which sat the foreman of the rogue miners. For most of the interview he had worn a smug, maybe even spiteful smile and had repeated the same harshly barked words in his own language. When the interview had first started, his interviewer had been Felicity Hopeforthebest aided by Piotre the first miner that had been arrested, who had then agreed to act as an interpreter for the Faerie Realm. To give them protection, should the man turn out to be dangerous, three strong guards from the SFS stood against the wall, each dressed in dark green, with the black beret of the military police. Translating the words of the captive foreman was quite a feat for Piotre, given that he himself was still learning how to speak Somerset and then there was the trauma caused to him by the awful suffering he had undergone as a slave. Despite the foreman's indifference to his crimes, Felicity had tried her best to explain to him what his future held, namely a court case and then very probably a long time in prison. The Foreman had laughed in her face and then muttered something that she only half heard. Piotre translated as best as he could. "He say it better here than home, where he get punish dead." Felicity was saddened by what she heard, she turned to Piotre. "What kind of a hell hole do you come from?"

Piotre nodded. "Not nice there, we slave for very bad emperor, we not do as told, we get deaded."

Piotre smiled. "Nice here, Felicity friend, Deborah friend, King very good man to whole peoples."

Felicity gave him a sad smile. "I am so sorry to hear this, you are safe here Piotre."

Piotre smiled. "I happy here, Faerie people no whip me,"

The Foreman leant forwards. "I want to stay here too. I will tell you everything if you let me stay here?"

Both Piotre and Felicity goggled at the man. "You can understand everything I have said?" Asked Felicity, "then you know that we would not treat you in such inhumane ways."

The Foreman laughed. "Do you think that our world was always so awful?" He snorted his contempt. "We started out peacefully enough, but then some politicians decided that they wanted to make some extra money and grab some extra power. After that came a pointless war that bankrupted the world and then just when you thought that it could not get any worse, the old Prime Minister had all of the peace keepers murdered, before he declared himself the eternal

Emperor."

"So how are you coming into our world?" Asked Felicity. "And why are you destroying our environment?"

"I told you, if I tell you, I want immunity and I want to stay in the city too."

Felicity nodded her head. "I cannot offer you these things, but I will ask the Mayor for you." She gave the man a friendly smile. "Can you tell me if there are other groups who will come through to our world?"

The Foreman shook head. "Immunity and then answers." He turned to Piotre and spoke in his own language.

Piotre nodded his head and turned to Felicity. "He say others already here. No tell unless you make safety."

Felicity stood up. "I will go and see the Mayor now." She looked at her watch. "It is nearly lunch time anyway, eat your food and we will come back after that."

The Foreman nodded his head. "Your food here is good, back home, not so much."

Piotre agreed with a smile. "Food there shit, not like much. Food here fuck good."

Felicity smiled and shook her head. "It is good to

hear you picking up the language Piotre." She stood at the door and it was unlocked and opened by one of the guards. "Give him his lunch, as much as he wants. When I'm back it is likely that he will flip and tell us what we need to know."

The soldier nodded. "Yes Ma'am." Then she stood back to give Felicity room to pass through the door. "Good to see you again Ma'am."

Felicity smiled. "You too, Corporal Strongfire."

Piotre stepped out after felicity, followed by the two other guards and then Corporal Strongfire locked it again with a loud click. She turned back as Felicity began to walk away leaning on her cane. "Excuse me, Ma'am?"

Felicity stopped and turned back to face the muscular young woman. "Yes Corporal Strongfire?"

Strongfire clicked her heels together and gave Felicity a stiff military salute. "It was an honour to serve under you Ma'am. Thank you for all you taught me."

For a moment Felicity stood completely still, her face flashed several emotions. Finally she smiled. "I cannot claim that I have not missed serving alongside you all, but I know that the Regiment will continue to have the finest soldiers in all of the realms." She nodded her head once. "Jolly hockey sticks Corporal."

Corporal Strongfire grinned. "Jolly hockey sticks, Ma'am." She saluted again and watched as Felicity walked away.

Wuffles was in the kitchen of the Mayoral residence when Felicity knocked at the door. Wuffles barked once and Felicity pushed the door open. She walked into the warm kitchen and took a deep breath. "Oh it smells wonderful in here, I wasn't hungry until I came in."

Wuffles wagged his tail, whined and then yipped a couple of times.

"Oh yes please," said Felicity enthusiastically. "A slice of one of your quiches would be lovely, thank you." She stepped over to Wuffles and scratched him between the ears, "however, I also need to speak with you about a serious matter."

Wuffles whined, yipped twice and then raised his front left paw to check his watch. He crossed the kitchen and picked up his oven glove and went back to the second oven he was using and took out a perfectly cooked quiche. He slid it onto the worktop and then carefully tipped it from the baking tray and onto a cooling tray. He collected four plates from a low cupboard and then cut the quiche into four slices and pushed one across to Felicity. He then put two plates on a tray and disappeared out through the kitchen door for a couple of minutes before returning to collect his own plate and wandered through to his office, with Felicity following. He slid his plate onto his desk and jumped up into his seat and turned to face Felicity and barked, yipped and whined, his ears forwards, his tail still.

She sat down and took a forkful of her quiche, but didn't put it in her mouth. "I am afraid so, however we have just discovered that the senior operative speaks Somerset. And he wants a deal. Basically, immunity and asylum. Says that he has information about some of his people already hidden here, spying for them."

Wuffles snarled and yipped a couple of times.

"Yes, it does make sense, I suppose. How else would they know where the minerals were?" She finally ate the piece of quiche that was on her fork. For a moment her eyes seemed to close and she took a breath, allowing her to absorb the flavours. Finally she spoke. "Wow, how do you do it? This is the nicest quiche I have ever tried."

Wuffles yipped his thanks, his tail wagging. Then he took a more serious tone and barked, yipped and yelped a couple of times, his lip curled in a small snarl and then he dropped his ears and gave a low growl.

"That is the difficulty isn't it." Replied Felicity. "We know that the general workers were slaves, but he was the slave master and we know that he physically abused them. Immunity means that we have pardoned what he has done to those poor people."

Wuffles whined and then tapped a foot on his desk.

Felicity nodded her agreement. "Do you want me to call him?"

Wuffles yipped and started to eat his quiche. Felicity put her plate down with her half finished meal and took out her phone, pressing down a button as she did so. The phone rang on the other end and then it was answered by the Butler. "Miss Hopeforthebest, you are through to the King's office, but I am afraid that he is out at the moment, due to a meeting with General Meuchelmorder." There was a short pause. "I am sure that he would answer his mobile phone if you consider it important."

"Thank you Mr Butler, unfortunately it is highly important." She ended the call and dialled again, finally getting through to the King.

"Felicity, you rang?"

"Your Highness, nasty situation here, need your input."

"I see." The King replied. "Where are you?"

"I am with Mayor Wuffles at his residence."

"Excellent." Said the King. "We will see you there shortly."

"Thank you, Highness."

"No," said the King jovially. "Thank you. See you in ten."

Felicity closed down her phone and picked up her plate. "The King is on his way here, said that he'll be ten minutes."

Wuffles wagged his tail and finished his quiche.

The Foreman had finished his lunch and was sat comfortably with a large mug of tea when the door opened and the King walked in and sat down at the table. The Foreman looked up and his face drained of colour as he recognised the King.

"I'm guessing that you know why I am here?" Said Bobney quietly, his voice compassionate, but firm.

"I'm guessing no immunity or asylum?" The Forman replied. "So, no information. Get lost."

"You abused the people who worked under you, you whipped them, beat them and forced them to work against their will." Said the King, his voice cold. "Giving you immunity means that we of the Faerie Realm will ignore your crimes." He paused and nodded to Felicity who had entered the room. She sat down next to him and lay a brown paper file on the table before looking up to the Foreman. "We have now debriefed the people you forced to work and they have some particularly brutal stories," she paused as her words sank in. "However, there was an accord among them that said that you were less brutal than some of the other slave masters." She opened the file. "Less brutal is still brutal though. We have thirty-six workers, including Piotre in custody and over fifty percent of them require medical help for serious injury directly caused by your violence." She took a deep breath. "However, there are no signs of sexual violence and they report that you have not directly killed any of their colleagues, unlike others from your world."

The King shook his head. "I can only offer you immunity from the crimes that you have committed against this Realm, but that does not include immunity from charges of slavery against your own people. You will however be offered asylum."

Felicity picked up from where the King stopped. "You will not be transferred back to your Realm, where you would most likely be going to suffer appalling punishment. Our courts are fair here and should you be found guilty of the crimes you stand accused of, you will be housed here in our criminal reformation centres." She took a leaflet from the folder and slid it across the table to the Foreman. "This is an information leaflet that we give to all Winscombe people who find themselves going through our legal system. We do not believe that physical punishment or just locking you away in cramped dirty cells with other prisoners works to rehabilitate you in any positive way at all. Instead we ask that you participate in therapy sessions and that you undertake some form of reparations, be that by performing voluntary work in the community or by helping your fellow prisoners." She flipped the leaflet over to show more information.

The Foreman briefly looked down at the leaflet and snorted his condescension. "I broke no laws in my world and I was just following orders anyway. If I had not done what I did, I would have been on the other side and they would have done it to me."

The King stood up. "Take it or leave it. However, your compliance now will show favourably during your case." He turned to the door and then turned back. "By the way, the people you brutalised, they are going to be re-homed here in Winscombe and they are going to be cared for. Those fit enough to help will be caring for and helping those who are not yet fit to care for themselves." For a moment he let his words sink in. "I am sure that once we have earned the trust of your people, they will have plenty more to tell us. Basically, we don't need you." He turned to Felicity. "Don't waste any more time on him, we can always pass him on to the Dragon Kingdom for incarceration." He knocked on the door and the door was quickly opened from the outside by Corporal Strongfire. Felicity stood up and followed him out of the room. Before the door could shut, the Foreman stood up. "No, wait." He shook his head. "You have four high ranking people from my world in yours. They are the people who are in charge of your water, mining and energy. That is how we knew where to mine." He sat down again, his face dark. "You can do what you want to me, but those people working under me, they are innocent. Please look after them?"

Felicity smiled sadly. "We are, you don't need to worry about that." She turned to Corporal Strongfire. "Please accompany our guest to the Winscombe Police building, to be charged?"

Strongfire nodded once and stepped inside the interview room and waited for the Foreman to walk around the table before taking his arm and leading out of the door. In the corridor the man turned and spoke again. "We were just one unit, there are others hitting other worlds out there. It won't be long before they replace us." He turned and walked away under the guidance of Corporal Strongfire

King Bobney's face was severe, his eyes filled with anger. He strode out of the door and as soon as he was in the sunshine, he pulled out his phone and dialled a number. It rang once and was answered by Gladys. "I'm sorry, I just wanted to hear your voice."

"That's OK my love." Said Gladys softly. "What has happened?"

"It's not great news, looks like we might have been infiltrated by them, some time ago." He swallowed and took a deep breath. "I am calling in the SFS, meeting in Thrashy's office now, can you be there please?"

"Yes of course, Highness." Said Gladys gently. "As General of the armed forces, it is my duty to be there."

"Thank you." Said Bobney. "I am going to need your wisdom, this sounds nasty." For a moment he was quiet. When he spoke again, his voice was softer. "I love you."

"I love you too." She replied. "I'm on my way now, see you there."

Bobney slid his phone back into his jacket pocket and turned back to see Felicity smiling. "Do you want me in your meeting too?" Her smile faded slightly. "I know that I am not SFS any more, but I'm here to help."

The King offered her his arm. "Miss Hopeforthebest, your input is what has given us all the information we have thus far, of course I want you there." He gave her a slight smile. "There is also something I would like to tell you, if you don't mind talking personal stuff for a minute?"

Colonel Thrashgood was stood by the window, looking out at the regiment he was so proud to be a part of, as they prepared for another mission. There was a knock on his door and then the King marched in, accompanied by Felicity. Thrashgood crossed the floor to greet them both. The King stopped in front of him and waited for Felicity to take Thrashgood's arm before he moved over to the office chairs and sat down. Felicity looked into Thrashgood's face and then she kissed him. He grinned and showed her to his own seat at the large wooden desk that had served every leader of the SFS since the regiments creation. Moments later another knock at the door sounded and General Meuchelmorder walked into the room. Instantly the King stood up. Thrashgood turned around and saluted her. "General Meuchelmorder, thank you for coming." Another knock sounded and the door opened again, as a young Fae walked in, her uniform was black, with no insignia, her face was almost fully covered by her combat helmet and mask, from within the dark facial covering her eyes glittered brightly. Thrashgood nodded once and then turned to the people stood or sat around my desk. "I would like you all to meet my two I C, this is Major Chinara Adesina. She has just been promoted, so this is her first mission as lead."

Major Adesina removed her helmet revealing dark skin and a closely shaved haircut. Her eyes were a deep gloss purple and her lips were deep dark red, behind which she had two rows of sharp spiked teeth that made her smile appear terrifying. She turned to King Bobney and saluted him. "Your Highness, it is an honour to serve you."

Bobney offered his hand and she shook it firmly. "Major, the honour is to serve the people and we both do that."

"Indeed, Sir. As we all do." She said brightly, accepting the King's slight admonishment. From her pocket she took a small computer tablet and switched it on before placing it on the Colonel's desk, revealing a picture of four people, three male and one female appearing by Fae standards. "Thanks to the information given to us by Doctor Hopeforthebest, we have targeted these individuals as possible enemy agents." She touched the screen and four small images of buildings appeared. "These buildings are where they are currently located and I have four teams ready to take them into custody. I have eyes on each building and our intelligence shows that each person is currently at home."

Gladys spoke up. "Do we have evidence of espionage by any of them?"

Major Adesina nodded. "Again, Doctor Hopeforthebest has supplied us with detailed information that is currently being explored. Early indications are already looking positive."

"So," asked the King, "what is the mission plan?"

"This is a counter-espionage mission and we have four targets. So, our mission objective is to take each target at the same time to prevent them warning each other. Telephone monitoring indicates that they are as yet unaware of us making the connection to them, so it will be a surprise to them. The second objective is to secure data from any and all sources at the sites."

Colonel Thrashgood rounded his desk and turned to the Major. "Thank you for the briefing, Major. Do please carry on and keep us informed of the mission outcomes."

She picked up her helmet and saluted the Colonel. "Thank you Sir, my teams are ready to go. Mission countdown is at T-minus twenty minutes." She pulled her helmet on and clipped the chin piece into place as she marched from the room.

Gladys' eyes followed her out and Thrashgood smiled. "Still stings, doesn't it?" He said. "Not being on the ground with the troops."

"It does," she said quietly. "But my new duties have responsibilities that are more important, with bigger consequences if I get it wrong."

"Very true." Said Thrashgood.

"I miss it, probably more than all of you." Felicity said quietly. "If it were not for a certain young woman in our team, I'm not sure that I would even be here right now."

"Where is Deborah?" Asked Gladys, "I thought that

given her position within the team, she would be here."

Felicity laughed. "I think that perhaps you should ask our dear Mayor."

"Really?" Said Thrashgood, frowning.

Wuffles finished his day's work, closed the folder of documents and slid it into his out tray ready for his secretary to scan and distribute the following morning. He jumped down from his desk and trotted out into hallway before climbing the stairs up to his private rooms. He pushed the sitting room door open with his nose and wandered inside to find two young women giggling on the sofa, each with game controllers in their hands and some frightful horror of a game being played out on the large television screen. Deborah looked up and watched as he entered and then jumped into his favourite armchair. "Hey Wuffles," She said happily. "Do you object if we call out for pizza tonight?" Wuffles growled, his lips curled, his ears flat and his eyes flashing, but his tail slowly wagging behind him showing his true feelings. Deborah laughed. "I'm sorry, I didn't want to impose when you have been working so hard today." She grinned at her new friend. "I cannot believe that she has not had Winscombe pizza before!"

Wuffles whiffled a laugh and then jumped down from his chair. He yipped a few sharp tones, whined and then tapped his paws on the floor.

"Thank you, your Grace." Said Bronwyn. "I am afraid that I will have to trust your opinion." She smiled shyly. "I'm still getting used to being human and Deborah's right, I've not actually had pizza before."

Wuffles stepped over to the young women and sat down in front of them both. He whined, yipped and let out a happy bark and both women laughed.

"I don't know what you are implying," said Deborah indignantly laughing, "But I will have you know that we have been hugely busy. For example, we spent the day stealing cars, buying drugs, selling said drugs and even shooting people in the face." She bent down and rested her head against his. "Thank you, this was just what I needed and you are right, she is loads of fun."

Bronwyn grinned. "You think this is fun? Just you wait until I get us tickets to see one of my favourite metal bands, we are going to go wild!"

Chapter 9

The raid was flawless, each assault team attacked at exactly the same moment, securing each of the four individuals plus any data they had in their possession. There was no noise, just the soft sounds of rustling and then the bang as the front door of each residence burst open and the SFS troops entered to find the residents either watching television, reading a book, listening to music and one slightly more red faced individual who was caught in an act of self love and was thus allowed to wash his hands before he was cuffed. The first one to arrive at the SFS headquarters to be debriefed was Amanda Blutvine.

To a casual observer, Amanda Blutvine looked ordinarily like a half Fae, half human, apart from the shocking mane of bright blue hair and slightly darker blue eyebrows, hiding pale yellow eyes. She was unusually tall for a Fae, being over two metres in height, but her flesh had the feel and wrinkles of a well used shammy leather. As they led her into the cell, they removed her shoelaces and the thin belt that secured her long tailored trousers before removing her handcuffs. She sat down on the soft foam mattress that was secured to the bed base that in turn was fixed to the floor and put her head in her hands, covering her face and letting out a long sad sigh.

The next to arrive was the smallest of them, a portly, completely bald man with puffy face and small eyes that were rimmed in red. Grendal Halftoof had his fingerprints taken, his mouth swabbed and was then shown to another cell, where he was stripped of his shoe laces, belt and tie. As they closed the door, he ranted and hammered his fists against the thick heavy wood. After five minutes, he finally fell silent and the camera in the room revealed that he had sat down on the bed and was silently crying.

With the cell block quiet once more, SFS team four brought in the third alien to the Faerie Realm. Simeon Whetwissle was smiling with his mouth as he walked into the building, his eyes though were dark blank pools of unreadable malevolence. His dark hair was cut in a dashing and modern style, his clothes would have been equally exquisite, but he had been found naked except for a thick, red, rubber head mask and a strange contraption that resembled a security guard's torch, attached to his genitals. Despite the interruption of his private moment, he had refused to get dressed and had in fact peeled off the red rubber mask, with some effort and had then chosen to cover his nakedness with an ankle length gold satin bath robe. As he was taken into his cell, the belt of the robe was removed and the man allowed it to fall open, revealing his rather small and abraded genitals to the SFS once again. No one commented and Simeon moved into his cell with a curious ambivalence.

The final prisoner to arrive was the leader of the small group, Jeremiah Coldhart, a man who looked like he had suffered with terrible facial acne while a teenager and was heavily scarred by it. His hair was nothing but a thin covering of greying hair that exposed the sun burnt flesh of his scalp and the flakes of dandruff that fell like a constant snowfall to his shoulders. He wore a light blue towelling polo shirt and pale brown trousers, but his shoes were a pair of hand carved wooden clogs that clopped alarmingly loudly as he walked into the cell. At the door he turned around and gave the SFS troops an unnerving smile. "You think that you have done something good here today, but what you have actually achieved is to make me take notice of you all," he sneered. "As soon as my lawyer arrives, I think that you will find that my friends and I will enjoy stripping the assets of your pathetic little garrison town."

Major Adesina pushed him backwards slightly and gave him a grin, exposing her carefully filed and sharpened teeth. "Then I hope that you will enjoy your time with us, I hope that your stay will be as comfortable as possible and maybe you can give us a nice on-line review." She stated coldly, before closing the door. Away from the door, she took off her helmet and run her hand across her closely shaved head, "fuck me, these bloody people think that they own the world!" She whispered under her breath to no one as she walked through the door leading from the cells and waited for it to be electronically locked before moving on. Her report to the Colonel and the King was going to be interesting.

The pizza was richly topped, with a thick crust and the edges filled with garlic and cheese. Little disks of pepperoni had crisped around their edges, without burning, pieces of sweetcorn glistened in the cheese, along with the orange, red and green of sliced peppers. A little addition by Wuffles was flakes of the crushed and dried chillis that he grew himself, to add extra burn to the palate. By his own admission, it did detract slightly from the taste of the pizza, but it increased other sensations and sometimes even the great Wuffles would admit that flavour was not everything. The two women had put aside their game controllers and each had a dining plate with a large triangle of pizza. Deborah looked to her new friend as she picked up the slice in her delicate fingers. "Go on, trust me." She said grinning, "more than that, trust Wuffles, if you don't want to trust me."

Bronwyn gave the young woman a grin and put the sharp tip of the pizza into her mouth and took a bite. For a second her face was thoughtful and then her eyebrows shot up, her eyes sparkled with tears induced by chilli. When she swallowed, she put the plate down and for a moment stared at it hard, before looking up to the expectant faces of Wuffles and Deborah. "I do not know how you have done it, but that is the greatest thing that I have ever tasted." She grinned and tried to blow some of the chilli heat from her mouth before she picked up her plate again.

"Try a bite of the stuffed crust, Wuffles uses a light garlic and cheese filling that eases the heat of the peppers and chilli oil." Enthused Deborah helpfully. She turned to Wuffles who was gently lapping from a glass of wine from a bottle that Deborah had brought for him from Herbert's vineyard. "Thank you Wuffles, you are a true friend."

Wuffles looked up and flicked an ear at the young woman. It was a subtle expression of his love for the young woman and for a moment she seemed to shine as her soul absorbed the love from her friend.

Bronwyn had bitten into the filled crust of the pizza and had closed her eyes as the soft warm cheese had eased the bite of the chilli oils. Finally she opened her eyes to find Wuffles and Deborah looking at her, their faces filled with gentle humour. When she was able to speak she did so with a huge grin on her pretty human features. "I have not been a girl for very long, but I can assure you that this day has been one of the best in my life so far and as of now, pizza is officially my favourite food."

Wuffles thumped his tail on his chair with pleasure and Deborah raised her hand, palm towards her friend who slapped it with her own.

"Well my dear Bronwyn, welcome to the wonderful world of femininity." She grinned, "we have many delights still to show you."

Both women burst out laughing and Wuffles shook his head as he enjoyed his glass of wine.

Queen Linda sat at the lunch table, sat next to her was her husband, the Royal Companion Craig. On the other side of the table sat King Bobney and sat next to him was General Meuchelmorder. The meal had been rather sombre, the chat was unusually stilted and finally Linda put down her cutlery and took a deep breath. "Right then, Bobney, are you going to explain to us why you have dragged this poor woman to our lunch table?"

Craig coughed meaningfully and arched his eyebrows, which Linda ignored equally meaningfully.

Bobney looked up and put down his own cutlery. "Mother, Step Father, I, or rather we have something to tell you."

"I see." Said Linda archly. "Well, don't keep us waiting, what is it."

Craig patted her hand. "Linda my darling, you should be more patient with the young people in our presence."

"Oh stuff and nonsense Craig." She hissed impatiently, "I never brought Bobney up to piss around the puddle."

Gladys almost choked on her ham salad and Craig visibly cringed while Bobney just shook his head and let out a long slow breath.

"Mother, please do not embarrass my guest."

Linda narrowed her eyes and pursed her lips before speaking. "Are you implying that my language can embarrass a woman who has seen combat the heavens know how many times?" She patted Gladys' hand kindly. "I hardly think that this magnificent warrior maiden is that delicate." She grinned at Gladys, "are you dear?"

Craig couldn't help but chuckle.

"I wish to marry General Meuchelmorder." Stated Bobney firmly.

"Good." Said Linda. "She is a magnificent woman and will provide me with many healthy and strong grandchildren."

"If I may," said Gladys quietly. "There is a small issue. I am not high born. My parents are from farming families."

Linda stared at Gladys, her face stony. "I see." She turned to Bobney. "So what are you going to do about this impossible situation?"

Bobney looked to Gladys and then back to his mother. "I am prepared to abdicate, if the people will not accept this woman to be my wife and we will move to the human world."

Linda slapped her hand on the table. "Over my dead body you will. I want my grandchildren to grow up in their home land." She turned to Craig. "What do we do about this?"

"Do you want my honest answer?" Craig answered calmly. Bobney and Linda both nodded their heads and waited for him to speak. "Fuck all." Linda burst out laughing and Bobney looked confused. "It's an archaic law," Craig continued. "So remove it from the charter." He offered his hand to Gladys. "Ma'am, you are a decorated war hero, respected leader of the military and former leader of the most elite force in all of the realms, are you not?"

"I am, your Grace." Said Gladys gently.

Craig tutted. "Right, that is enough of that. As my daughter in law, you will refer to me as Step Father, Craig or..."

"Oi you Wanka!" Giggled Linda wickedly. She turned to Gladys and took her other hand in her own. "Darling girl, my son has made an outstanding decision, there is no one in this Realm more beloved by the people than you." Turning to Bobney she spoke again. "As for you, it is about time you sorted this out. We need to rethink this whole high-born nonsense system anyway, before we end up with completely useless royals, turned into overly entitled dickheads through directed inbreeding." She released Gladys' hand and sat back in her chair. "Craig and I have had enough of those sort of people recently, trust me." She grinned to her husband and turned back to Bobney. "When my baby is born, I want it to grow up in a world where love and kindness and cooperation are more important that social status. It is the duty of you both to make our society better for everyone. This wedding will show that we are changing, that our society is evolving, that we are embracing the goodness within us all."

"Your Mother is quite right." Said Craig kindly as he patted her hand lovingly with his own. "As a Royal companion, your mother cannot recognise my position as husband for social occasions, which is why I was knighted prior to all of this current excitement, but it still does not give me equal status as spouse. You do not want Gladys to suffer that fate." He took Linda's hand in his own and she leaned her head against his shoulder lovingly. "Our society needs to change, you are the King that has already made so much change, what will this one more, tiny little thing matter?"

Bobney nodded his head. "Thank you Step Father, as always your advice is greatly appreciated." He turned to Gladys. "My Darling, having heard all of this, are you prepared to be my wife and Queen of the Faerie Realm?"

Gladys smiled beatifically. "Highness, it will be my honour to serve our people and my joy to be your wife."

Linda smiled, it was a gentle, happy smile and she felt Craig put his arm around her shoulders. "I am so proud of you both." She said quietly, her voice softened by emotion. She stood up and rounded the table. "Gentlemen, if you could excuse us, I wish to have some time getting to know my daughter in law." She grinned at Gladys, "if you would care to spend some time with your future mother in law, my dear?"

Gladys smiled. "I would love to do so, but unfortunately, I have a great deal of work to do after raids last night, as has King Bobney."

Linda looked deflated, but quickly hid it with a warm smile. "Well, I cannot say that I am not disappointed to miss out on some girls' time, but I do understand, you are a modern working woman." She sat down again, "we can at least finish lunch." She grinned again, "I am after all eating for two at the moment!"

"And you look beautiful doing it." Said Craig lovingly as he picked up his knife and fork.

Bobney sighed, his heart at peace but knowing that his workload was still full and that it would be a struggle to drag his future wife away from her desk for the next few days.

Felicity read the transcript of the interviews and snarled with anger. Amanda Blutvine had spoken clearly, almost without emotion as she laid out the plan that her species had for the Faerie Realm. It was almost clinical in her description of the destruction planned, as if she had no fear of the consequences of her actions against the Realm. For a lot of the worst parts of her statement, she had been smirking, as if she had been contemptuously explaining something simple, to a person she despised and thought too stupid to understand.

The next transcript was even worse, Simeon Whetwissle was without remorse. If anything he seemed to think that he would be out of prison within a day or two and had been treating the guard staff like hotel waiters, demanding food and wine, while complaining that he was missing his television shows and asking when his lawyer would be brought in to see him.

The other two prisoners had kept quiet, saying nothing and barely answering questions, other than to confirm their names. Felicity was not happy and her staff were of a similar point of view. She put down her notes and turned to her computer and began to type up her report for King Bobney, when there was a knock at the door. She looked up as the door opened and Deborah entered, her face dark with fury. She approached Felicity's desk and sat down. "You read the transcript?" Asked Felicity quietly.

"I did."

"Two of them admitted everything, we have enough to send them to prison, but I don't think it matters, they don't care and seem to think that we can't hold them."

For a moment Deborah was silent. Finally, her eyes swirling storms of fury, she spoke again. "They are unrepentant, they believe that it is their right to decimate other worlds to amass wealth for their own."

At that moment, the phone on Felicity's desk started to ring, she picked it up and spoke. "Felicity here, speak?" She listened for a few seconds and then replied. "She is with me, we will be right over,

Highness." The call ended and she placed the phone back on her desk. "The King has asked for our presence, shall we?"

"If the King wishes it, it would be rude to keep him waiting." Replied Deborah quietly.

Felicity smiled, "I'm never sure if you are being serious when you say such things young lady!"

Deborah stood up and her features flickered and reformed into that of the ancient Earth Mother. "Who are you calling young lady?" She said through the ancient wrinkled smile of the Earthly Crone.

Bobney stood up from his desk and paced the room as his guests patiently waited for him to speak. When he stopped, his face was determined and his jaw strong. "There are two things that we need to discuss." He looked up to the General and she smiled and gave him a slight nod of her head. The King nodded back and spoke again. "I have informed my mother that I intend to marry. As some of you will no doubt be aware, I have developed a powerful relationship with General Meuchelmorder and her feelings are reciprocated towards me. To do this, I am going to change our ancient laws and I want to change things in really big ways. I am not happy that our society is pretty much ruled by a hereditary heir, so I want to pull back royal power and create a senate for the people. I am a figurehead only and that is how it should be."

Thrashgood stood up, "excuse me Highness, but how can you do this and who will lead us if you step down?"

Bobney smiled. "For a start, it has always bothered me that you all refer to me as Highness. I am a man, I try to be a good man, but I do not always get it right and when I get it wrong, the people suffer. So, I want them to have a say in how we are run. I want a senate that will have elected individuals representing the needs of the people. I have already drafted the laws and they are being checked by palace staff. Once this goes through, it will not be only our esteemed Mayor who will be voted into position. My role will be entirely ceremonial and then in five years, the public can take a vote about whether they still want a King at all." Thrashgood sat down and the room fell silent with expectation. Bobney smiled, his features showing an inner happiness that he had not shown for a long time. "I can still be of use, but I and those who come after me will no longer have absolute power. Absolutism leads to corruption, which in turn leads to the suffering of the people."

Felicity stood up, "Bobney, we have been friends since just after you took the throne and I know that this is not a decision that you will have taken lightly." She smiled and nodded to the General. "I will add though, I truly, with all of my heart wish you and General Meuchelmorder every happiness together."

Bobney bowed his head slightly to Felicity and looked towards the General who also bowed her head. "This leads me to my next point." He pointed to the map laid out on his desk. "The raids we have suffered have ended for now, but a greater evil is building and they will come again and probably in greater numbers. This puts us on a war footing." He turned to the General. "Your input would be appreciated please General Meuchelmorder." He returned to his seat and Gladys stood up. "The King has asked me to organise a force that can detect and defend against an incursion by the other worlders." She turned to Colonel Thrashgood. "Colonel, I want you to put together a fast response unit with air support."

"You want the Princess?" Colonel Thrashgood asked.

"If she is willing, this unit must be volunteers, they

must be aware that as yet we do not know the levels of technological development available to the interlopers. Given the complexity of their mining equipment and the nature of their society, I suspect that their ability to wage war will be advanced and barbaric." The General turned to Felicity. "Scientist Hopeforthebest, I am asking you for your help, but as a civilian you have the right to refuse."

"Never, I am SFS through to my bones, General Meuchelmorder." Felicity stated firmly. "I am in, tell me what you want?"

"Thank you Scientist Hopeforthebest, it is noted that you are so determined. I need a way to detect these people, your budget comes directly from my office, there has to be a way to detect them, I am asking you to find it."

"I have a small team, we will contact your staff and arrange the particulars." Felicity stated again.

The General turned to the King and looked at him, a slight smile on her face. He smiled back and nodded his head. She turned back to the rest of her group, friends and key officers. "There is one more thing I wish to bring to the table, which when compared to these attacks, feels somewhat less significant." She clasped her hands behind her back and stood up straight. "The King and I have wondered if this is the right time to announce our engagement to the people or do we wait until after this crisis is over?" She sat back down and gently took the hand of the King.

Deborah stood up, her eyes smoking pools of darkness. "Herbert and I will supply a special wine for your wedding, I know that he will be delighted to do so. Alas, he is getting old as is his companion, the human woman who became a part of my family, Katie Flowers. I can see in her that she doesn't have long left on this plane of existence." She reached out a hand into the air and seemed to catch an invisible dust mote, which only she could see as it danced through her fingers. "Life among the living is short and that time is taken for granted too often. I have lived many lives, all of them short and all of them hard, so I know from experience that you must marry each other now. Do not wait, otherwise your day may never come." She sat down and Felicity reached over and Deborah took her hand in her own and squeezed it tightly. "One other thing," said Deborah firmly, "I can be of help to Felicity's team and I offer my services."

The King frowned. "No offence Deborah, but you are barely an adult in this lifetime, I cannot with good conscience allow you to participate in warfare, you have done enough for our people already."

The air around Deborah darkened as snaps of tiny lightning discharged against her body. Felicity raised her free hand. "Err, excuse me Highness, I have tried that argument with Deborah, it will not end well for any of us. Remember, her memories go back to before the creation of the realms from out of the great dream of the universe."

A small arc of lightning discharged again with a slightly louder snap against the edge of the King's desk and Bobney grinned. "OK Deborah, I give in, you can be a part of Felicity's team, but as a strictly non-combatant only. Is that clear?" Deborah nodded her consent and the King continued. "Also, I want your working time on this limited, I know what the two of you are like, so this is set in stone from the beginning, no thirty-six hour days for any of you, is that clear? Felicity, as lead I expect you to take care of yourself and of Deborah too, the pair of you are far too valuable to us and Deborah..." He paused until she looked him in the eye. "You are to take care of her too, she still needs you."

"You got it." Said Deborah as the air above her cleared of the tiny, angry storm clouds.

The King turned to the General. "It looks like

Mother Nature wants the wedding go ahead, as the senior being the room, can we argue with her?" He turned to the others in the room. "Do you agree with her?"

As one the King's guests stood and gave applause, General Meuchelmorder also stood as did King Bobney; gently, they leant towards each other and shared a single delicate kiss.

The day of the wedding came quickly and Gladys was nervous. She and Bobney had both decided that they did not want a conventional extravagant and expensive royal wedding, but some conditions had to be given to this and she had agreed to allowing the wedding to be televised to the Realm. Gladys had stated that she would be wearing her finest military uniform and King Bobney had joked that he was going to wear his gym shorts and an old t-shirt with the sleeves cut off. Stood alone in her office, Gladys gazed out of the window. A troop of soldiers were doing laps of the training field under Major Chinara Adesina who was running them hard. There was a small knock on her office door and the sergeant entered with a cup of tea. "Excuse me General, you asked me to remind you when you had twenty minutes until your wedding."

Gladys turned away from the window. "May I ask you a question please Sergeant?"

The Sergeant placed the cup of tea on her desk and stood up straight, her arms by her side. "Yes of course General, I am here to aid you as you carry out your duties."

"How come that when I have been into dangerous combat situations I was able to control my fear? Yet when it comes to marrying the man I love, I feel like my insides are turning to jelly and I want to cry?"

The young sergeant smiled and took a small packet of tissues from her pocket and offered them to Gladys. "If I may speak freely General Meuchelmorder?" She waited politely while Gladys dabbed at her eyes before nodding her head. The young Sergeant continued. "Going into war is a terrible thing, but we know that we are giving our lives to protect our homes and the people we love. But, getting married is not a war, it is a beautiful thing, a moment when we are dedicating ourselves to usually one person for the rest of our lives and we Fae live very long lives." She smiled kindly at the General. "How can such a powerful decision, based entirely on the emotion of love not be scary?" Gladys looked up and wiped a tear from her beautiful eyes. "I think that I understand, thank you Sergeant." The sergeant hesitated for a moment. "Is there anything else you wish to add Sergeant?"

"It is just one question General and I believe that I already know the answer."

"Please, go ahead Sergeant."

"I know that he is the King, but when you remove that aspect from his life, do you still love him as just a man? There is a difference between those of us who love him as our King and the woman who loves him as a man."

"Marrying the King does feel like a huge responsibility and that is what worries me. What if I am not up to the job?" Said Gladys quietly.

The Sergeant nodded her understanding and she leaned forwards against the General's desk in a way that in any other situation, she would never do and in a quiet voice spoke again. "Strictly between us as women General, there is nothing out there in any world that you cannot handle. I would follow you to the end of the realms if you said it was going to be an adventure and that is only a portion of what the King feels about you." Gladys put the tissue into the waste bin and smiled. The Sergeant spoke again. "Would a friendly hug from someone who both respects and admires you help?"

"Yes, it really would. Thank you Sergeant." Gladys stood up and walked towards the open arms of her Sergeant.

King Bobney stood in front of the mirror and looked at himself framed in gold. His skin showed the stretch marks and elasticity of his previous life as a morbidly obese lost royal, there was a large dark tattoo on his shoulder, that no one but his friend Colonel Thrashgood knew about, because they had matching ones. In his early days of his reign, the mirror had not been his friend, it showed him as a mound of grot and fat, but he had dieted, he had exercised and he had worked so very hard to achieve what he had become. He remained humble, knowing that it would not take much to fall back into his unhealthy old patterns and unhealthy weight gain. Turning away from the mirror he stepped into his dressing room, which also had a small amount of gym and training equipment. After twenty minutes of gentle stretching, his first workout of the day was to do twenty pull ups on the bar and then thrash out twenty kilometres on the exercise bike. The bike was a modern marvel of electronics and computing power and it had suffered in the early days of his ownership. These days, the gears had been replaced and having completed the first ten Kilometres, the King worked on intervals of sprinting and recovery. When that was complete, he would swap to the treadmill next to the bike and start running. Running was his joy, he could feel every change that his body had made, the physical and emotional strength he had gained, the power in his leg muscles that he had developed. Having worked up a sweat, he started his cool down and finished his morning regime with a swim in the palace pool, the same pool where the SFS practised their water survival skills, before going out into the wilds of the Realm to practice them for real. Ten lengths of the pool left him feeling physically tired but relaxed, at peace with himself and ready for his shower. As he stepped through to the regimental shower room, a dark thought crossed his mind, was he still too fat, did he need to work harder, eat less food to be handsome? He shook his head, that was a thought to deal with on another day, no doubt it was something he could discuss with his therapist, his fear of returning to what he had been in the human world.

Back in the King's dressing room, the Butler was sat on one of the King's dressing chairs waiting patiently while listening to a podcast on his wireless earphones. This was a gift that the King had given him, a gift that at first had deeply confused the elderly warrior, but he quickly discovered that every subject of interest to him, had a pod cast and some of them were excellent. As his favourite pod cast came to an end, the King wandered into the dressing room, still clad in his bath robe.

The Butler beamed a smile at the King and bowed slightly. The King returned the Butler's smile and greeted him warmly. "Ahh, Butler, my jolly good man, I am so pleased that you are able to be here."

The Butler nodded his approval. "It is your big day today, Highness. It is my honour to assist you as you get ready."

Bobney took the older man's hands in his own. "Thank you." He said, his voice trembling with emotion. "I really mean it." His eyes started to tear up slightly and the Butler reached into his pocket and took out a tissue.

"Sire, this is going to be an emotional day, there will be moments of fear, moments of joy and moments of duty." He gripped the Kings hands firmly. "There is no man in this Realm who can do this day with as much dignity and respect as you will."

The King looked up, his eyes wet with tears. "I

learned from the best." He wiped his eyes. "You have been a teacher to me beyond your duties and I will always be grateful."

"Stuff and nonsense, Sire." Said the Butler jovially, although he understood the King's meaning. "Besides, my family has served the Royal family for generations, it is our duty."

"Well," said the King quietly. "This generation of the royal family is deeply thankful." A dark cloud seemed to pass across the King's heart and he sat down on his dressing stool. "What if I am not good enough for her Butler?"

The Butler put his hand on the King's shoulder, a simple act of love and support. "I never had a son, instead I had three daughters who made me deeply proud. However, if I had been blessed with a son, I would have been proud if he had been even half the man that you are." He sat down on a small stool opposite the King. "Wedding nerves get us all. It is a big day and not just because of your station. You have the people of the Realm cheering and waving flags in celebration as they welcome your wife as their Queen. With all of that on top of a normal wedding, how could you not have wedding nerves?"

"Gladys won't have wedding nerves." Said the King

brightly. "She knows what she wants and she works towards it, no matter how fearful she could be."

The Butler smiled. "I wouldn't stake my life on that Sire, that woman is far braver, cleverer and stronger than any woman I have met before. The consequence of which is that she will understand the enormity of her position. As such, she too will have nerves, but she won't deny or belittle herself for having them and neither must you." He smiled kindly at the man he suddenly saw as so young and brave. "To deny our feelings or to hide them away is deeply unhealthy." He sighed a knowing breath. "I know, because I have been there and I have suffered because of it."

There was a knock at the King's bedroom door and then the door swung open and Colonel Thrashgood stepped into the room and turned towards the dressing room, popping his head around the doorway. "Jolly hockey sticks Butler!" He said brightly before turning to the King. "Highness. Are we ready for this day to come?"

The Butler stood up and saluted the Colonel, "jolly hockey sticks Colonel, just about to help his Highness get dressed."

The King grinned at his friend. "Sorry old chap, the old body is struggling today. I won't be long."

Thrashgood nodded his head. "I understand, I have something that might help." He stepped into the small dressing room and reached into his pocket and pulled out three small boxes. "These two are your rings, but this one is special." He gently tossed the box to the King who caught it easily and opened it. His eyes went wide and he snapped the box closed and stood up.

"I can't wear this, this is special."

"Nonsense," Thrashgood chuckled. "Anyway, Dad would approve." He took the box back from the King and held it tightly. "So get your dancing clothes on and then I will pin it on."

The Butler nodded his approval and helped the King to get dressed, finally pulling the light, smart jacket of the SFS across the King's shoulders. He buckled the belt and closed the shoulder strap and then held out his hand to the Colonel. "If you please, Colonel Thrashgood."

Thrashgood nodded and handed the small box over to the Butler who opened it and nodded his approval. "It is rare that we see one of these, they are given out once every generation, to an outstanding Fae, who has shown exceptional bravery."

"It belonged to my father, Butler." Said the Colonel

quietly, his voice stiff with pride. "Not only was he a formidable warrior, but he taught me how to be a good man, to be kind, to be compassionate and to stand up for what is right. I know that he would admire our current King, a man who has all of these qualities too."

The Butler pinned the medal into place. "This alone is all that you need. No sash, no long service medals and no cub scout badges. I know that the General will approve too."

All three men chuckled. "The General is one hell of a woman Bobney, she deserves one hell of a husband." Said the Colonel as the King pulled on his military cap.

The Butler stepped back and looked at the King, happy with his work. "Magnificent, if I say so myself. The General will love how you look." Bobney smiled, his heart tender and hopeful for the future."

The State wedding was to take place in the largest hall of the palace. An honour guard of SFS lined the corridor that led to the entrance door which stood open and inside, a large crowd had gathered. Honoured guests and foreign ambassadors all stood together and among them was Aurora Fireskies and her Mother, Muriel. Stood next to them was Queen Nightsoul of the Vampires and her Daughter Ivanka. The two families had been friends since the two young women had met in school and formed a friendship that would last for all of their lives. Aurora was dressed beautifully in a dark trouser suit, her hair was carefully styled to compliment her face and she seemed to be glowing with a healthy vitality. In comparison, Ivanka was deathly pale, her face and blood red lips were without make up although her naturally dark hair was dyed a glowing red, like coals on a fire. The Vampire Queen occasionally gave Ivanka a loving look, but spent most of the time happily talking with Muriel Fireskies, who held the hand of her dear friend as they chatted, laughed and shared news. A shape seemed to move through the crowd and then as if condensing from the air, a shadow stepped into a small gap next to Aurora. Ivanka looked up and smiled as Aurora suddenly gripped the hand of the person who had seemed to melt out of shadow. "You made it, I'm so pleased." Aurora kissed the young woman and then turned back to her dear friend. "Ivanka, I want you to meet my girlfriend, Oleander."

Ivanka smiled, the light glinting on her milk white

fangs. "I have heard so much about you from Aurora. I'm really pleased to meet you at last."

Oleander grinned, she was slightly shorter than Aurora, had light brown wavy hair and wore a smart blue tunic over black trousers. Her most striking feature was her eyes, which were a deep gemstone blue, with a tiny ring of golden stars around the edge of the iris. "Aurora has told me a lot about you too." she said happily. "You are who she calls her best friend ever since school."

Ivanka laughed. "Yeah, that long. Even though we live in different realms now, we see each other as often as we can."

Aurora laughed. "Yeah, but your university department is in the human world and that can be a weird place because it smells of rocket fuel and science nerds!"

Ivanka laughed again. "Oh yeah? Meanwhile you are reading languages and diplomacy in as many universities as can get you. They are probably fighting over which one is allowed to give you your degree!" Ivanka turned back to Oleander. "What is your field, she did tell me, but it sounded strange?"

Oleander smiled gently, but her eyes showed a devilish glee. "I am on a special course that will lead me into the military. I want to get into the SFS one day."

Ivanka nodded. "That is a tough career path. I have met a couple of them through Mum, from what Aurora said, I am sure that you will do it though."

Aurora squeezed the young woman's hand. "She took me camping, and introduced me to all sorts of adventures. Come the summer holidays, you really must come with us Ivanka. Olea is so much fun." She turned and grinned at the young woman. "You can play rockets with Ivanka, she's a bit of a weirdo, but I wouldn't change a thing about her."

"Actually," said Ivanka quietly. "There is a small thing I should tell you."

Aurora looked to Ivanka, her eyes suddenly suspicious and Ivanka continued. "I have met someone, it's very early days, but we have even had a kiss."

Aurora seemed to burst with happiness. "That is wonderful Ivanka, I am so pleased for you." She reached out and took her friend's hands in her own. "I know that in your society, such matters of the heart are taken very seriously, so I am really, really happy that you told me." She squeezed Ivanka's hand gently. "Am I allowed to know their name?"

"I even have a picture to show you. They would have come with me today, but they are unfortunately stuck at the European Space Centre, back in the human world." Said Ivanka quietly as she reached into her jacket pocket to pull out a mobile phone, which she opened and started to flick through the apps until she found the gallery. A second or two later, she passed the phone to Aurora and there on the screen was a picture of a gentle looking young scientist, his face was covered in a scraggly ginger beard and he had large, fluffy ginger eyebrows, but his pale blue eyes glinted like gem stones. The white lab coat had a small name badge and she could just read the name, Dr Lukas Hunziker.

Aurora smiled and passed the phone back to her friend. "Have you told your Mum?" She whispered conspiratorially.

Ivanka nodded slightly. "Mum has even met his Mum too and although it was a bit strange for them at first, they have become good friends now." She paused for a moment and looked to her Mother, who smiled and nodded her head a tiny amount. "They have even been out for lunch together, in the Fae Realm obviously, the human world is still a bit weird towards our kind."

Aurora's mouth hung open in surprise. "Ivanka!" She exclaimed in surprise. "This is properly serious, he is not just a boy friend, he is your one!"

Ivanka nodded her head and smiled at her friend. "I did say that I had something to tell you."

Aurora couldn't help herself and even in the busy crowd, she threw her arms around Ivanka's neck. "I am so happy for you, can we both come to the wedding?"

Ivanka hugged her friend back. "I really, really hope so. You are like family to us all, so you are the first name on the guest list."

Aurora stepped back a little and pulled Oleander into the small circular hug. "Olea, you have no idea how special this is and you are coming to the wedding with me."

Chapter 10

Bobney stood at the front of the hall and could feel his heart pounding in his chest and hear his blood roaring in his ears. Next to him stood his closest friend, the Leader of the Special Faerie Service, Colonel Thrashgood. The hall was filled with the quiet noise of a lot of people gathered together and having whispered chats. In the right hand front row of seats, sat Queen Linda and her husband Craig. With no other family in their lives, they sat alone and Linda held Craig's hand tightly, her belly finally showing signs of the new family member growing within.

With Gladys having no living family left, the front row of the left-hand side seating held Gladys's friends. Deborah was sat with her family and was quietly whispering to her new friend Bronwyn, while Uncle Herbert and Katie Flouers were having a whispered conversation too. Next to them sat Wuffles, quieting chatting with Colonel Olajlámpás and, in her smallest form Princess Rupertina, the only royal dragon serving with the SFS.

Behind Linda and Craig were sat the many various royal visitors from other nations in the Faerie

Realm. King Jong the First sat with his Royal Advisers Sha Wren Ston and Fred Bare Rug. Queen Lupa of the Hell Hounds arrived and spotted her old friend Queen Nightsoul of the Vampires, so wandered to her and yelped a happy greeting to the Queen and her family. Ivanka gently knelt down and opened her arms and the Hell Hound gently placed her forelegs onto the young woman's shoulders for a hug. Suddenly the small quartet of musicians at the back of the hall started to play.

The music was martial, somehow sounding like the sort of tune that a maniac fell runner would have in their headphones as they ran up a mountain, in the darkest winter rain. With quiet squeaks, groans and the rustle of clothing, the audience stood up and turned to face Gladys as she appeared in the doorway, dressed in her finest military uniform. Her dark green skirt came to just above her ankles, her white blouse was buttoned to the throat around which was a tie with the SFS insignia. Her jacket was a gloriously deep red, with a row of medals on her left breast. Her belt was striped with the three colours of the Faerie Army and her cap had a highly polished peak and badges of both the SFS and of the Fairy Army. Her only concession of femininity was that her usual functional military shoes had been replaced with black low-healed court shoes over her usual jet-black tights. Hanging from the belt on her waist was a ceremonial scimitar, the handle encrusted with gem stones and the scabbard was a deep gloss black. Stood next to her, gently leaning on both Gladys and her cane was Felicity Hopeforthebest. She was dressed in a beautiful deep blue dress with delicate lace edges and on her breast was a line of military medals. Her hair was carefully styled and when Colonel Thrashgood saw her, his heart began to pound in his chest too. Behind the two women stood a man in an old brown military uniform that was impeccably brushed, pressed and the buttons polished like stars. The Master had been like a father to many in the Faerie Army, and when Gladys had taken over the office of General, she had gone to him many times for his advice. The main reason for his presence though was that along with Felicity, he was the chosen family for Gladys, for this most special of occasions. Slowly, Gladys began to march towards the front of the hall, taking care of her dear friend Felicity. Behind her marching with his baton under his arm and his highly polished peaked cap, the Master could not help but smile, his eyes damp with tears of pride in the young women marching with him. Finally at the front of the hall, Felicity gave Gladys a small kiss on her perfect cheek and sat down next to Deborah. Gladys nodded her thanks and stood up, next to King Bobney who had joyful tears glistening their way down his cheeks. Thrashgood gently nodded a bow to Gladys and then to the Master. Gladys bowed her head back and Colonel Thrashgood stepped forwards and asked the gathered audience to take their seats. There was some hushed mumbling and the squeaking of seating as the various beings sat down again. When the room was quiet Colonel, Thrashgood addressed the audience. "King Bobney and General Meuchelmorder have asked me to lead this ceremony without reference to any form of religion and they have written their own vows." He paused for a moment as his words were absorbed by the crowd. He took a deep breath and spoke again, his powerful voice loud and full of love for his friends. "I would ask you to respectfully give them this moment to express their feelings." He stepped backwards and Bobney and Gladys faced each other. Gladys reached up to touch the face of the man she loved and allowed a tiny tear to fall onto the tip of her finger, which she put to her lips. She smiled, her heart a gentle drum in her chest. "Your Highness, I, General Gladys Meuchelmorder, pledge myself to stand at your side as your wife, as you lead this Realm. To be your council and to be your friend, to hold your hand through good times and hard times. I will help you in your duty to the people and I promise to always love you, with all of my heart for the rest of my days."

Bobney took her hands in his own and kissed her fingers. "General Meuchelmorder, I, King Bobney Wolfgang Jones, promise to be your husband, to stand at your side through all of life's adventures, to support you through tough times and good, to be your friend and to love you without reservation of condition until the end of my time."

Gladys smiled and gazed into the eyes of her beloved husband, for a brief moment, nothing but the pair of them existed for her, despite the mass of people watching them in person and on the many TV screens that were broadcasting live from the venue. "My King, my love, you fill my heart with joy, I will always be with you, even when we are apart. My love for you knows no end."

Bobney spoke again, his voice soft, with a slight tremor of emotion. "My Queen. Your presence brings comfort and love to me, I know that there is no darkness that could come between us, I will love you with all of my soul for as long as I live."

A sudden loud sniff of emotion came from Queen Linda as she wiped tears from her eyes and buried her head into Craig's shoulder to stifle her sobs of joy as her son became a married man.

Thrashgood stepped forwards again. "Your Highnesses, I now must ask you to turn and take the chalices of the people and sip the wine before you confirm the marriage."

Deborah stood up and presented two small ancient silver goblets. The silver metal was old and tarnished, the surface decorated with tiny filigree showing the images of the ancient first King and Queen of the Faerie Realm, hundreds of centuries before. The wine in each cup was a very special vintage made by Herbert and Oliver many years before and there was only one bottle of it in existence. Gladys took a goblet first and then Bobney took the second. Again they turned to face each other and as one, holding the goblets in both hands, put the tiny cup to their lips and drank the delicate wine within. Bobney smiled as the flavours swirled in his mouth, he could taste the summer sunshine that had gone into the grapes, the tenderness of their care as they grew and love of the two men who had grown them. Gladys closed her eyes as smokey scents washed through her, reminding her of the moments in her life when she had been happiest and she realised that quite a lot of them had been with the King. With the wine drunk, the bride and groom returned the goblets to Deborah who beamed a smile at them and then sat down again.

Wuffles stood up and lifted a small tray from a member of palace staff who approached him. On the tray was an old silver plate, parts of it blackened with tarnish, but engraved into the rim of the plate was a story of the original King and Queen of the Realm as they lived their lives together. On the plate sat two small, perfectly formed cakes. They looked simple, but again having been made by Wuffles himself, they were very special. He presented the tray to the King who bent down and took the tray from his friend with a broad smile and a tickle behind his ears. Wuffles turned to the crowd and with a few small yips, barks and ear waggles he explained the next stage of the wedding. With a smile, King Bobney lifted the tiny cake and turned to Gladys and waited for her to take her own. When she was ready, she lifted the tiny cake to his lips and he allowed her to place the morsel on his tongue. He closed his eyes in pleasure as he tasted the flavours and then opened them again to place his cake into Gladys' mouth. She smiled and could taste the spices that Wuffles had used to make a cake that was just for her. With the cakes done, Wuffles returned to his seat and Colonel Thrashgood stepped forwards once again and waited for the King and his Bride to be ready. They stepped forwards and took each others hands in their own. The room fell silent and Thrashgood grinned. "King Bobney, ruler of the Faerie Realm, patriarch of all of the Fae peoples and friend to all who live." He grinned and the King grinned back. "Are you ready to take the sacred rope and tie the knot? Do you take this woman to be your wife?"

The King turned back to Gladys and looked into her gemstone eyes. She was radiant, with the ferocious beauty of a warrior. In that instant, he knew with absolute certainty that he wanted to spend the rest of his life with her. "I do." He said quietly, his voice breaking with emotion and tears flowing down his cheeks.

Thrashgood bowed his head and then turned to Gladys. "General Gladys Meuchelmorder, Are you ready to take the sacred rope and tie the knot? Do you take this man to be your husband?"

Gladys smiled, she looked to Bobney and she could see him as he truly was, brave, compassionate, thoughtful and filled with love for her. Her heart was singing his name and she turned to Colonel Thrashgood. "I..."

The explosion outside the building shook the windows in their frames shattering the glass across the people inside. The emergency exit doors blew inwards and the thick broken frame fragments scattered into the air. The audience began to yell as the broken glass fragments fell on them causing cuts and lacerations. Gladys had instantly leapt into action and had shoved the King backwards and into safe cover under her delicate frame. She checked him quickly for injury and found a superficial cut on his face. Thrashgood charged down the centre aisle to the broken side doors of the hall and leapt through the smoke to the outside, with his weapon drawn only to come face to metal grill, with a mining machine. The machine had been either remotely driven or abandoned, with a shaped charge fitted to the blade of the scraper on the front, leaving a black into brown burn mark on the scratched and rusted steel. Whomever had delivered it had gone back into the vortex that led to their

Realm. Thrashgood called out and from the dust and smoke, seven of the SFS seemed to coagulate out of the air. They were bruised, a couple of them had bloodied faces and the final one had a broken arm. "Report." Said Thrashgood firmly.

"They opened a portal and shoved the machine through with another machine." They pointed to a slab of burned melted metal that resembled the front half other machine. "It closed before their man had even got back through. I think that he was killed when the machine was cut in half."

A second SFS operative stepped forwards, "The weapon was triggered by the closing of the portal. We had no chance of stopping this."

"The bastards." Hissed Thrashgood angrily.

"Colonel, what about the King and the General?"

Thrashgood turned to face his questioner, "Both safe. The General took the King down to cover before he could be hurt. I'm more worried about her."

He turned back to the exploded entrance. The charge had not been accurate and a large portion of burned wall showed where a lot of the weapon had been pointed. "We were fucking lucky."

Medical crews appeared, along with a troop of soldiers and they rushed up to the Colonel, "here to help Sir, priorities please?"

Thrashgood nodded. "Guests and dignitaries need medical attention. Secure the wreckage and be prepared for a secondary attack." He turned to the SFS troopers. "Bins, get that arm fixed. The rest of you with me." He turned and sprinted into the building and ran to where he knew that the King would be and found the King holding Gladys where she lay on the ground. A spear of wood had hit her in the back and pierced her flesh, her lips were blood stained and she was struggling to breathe. As soon as he saw Thrashgood the King spoke. "She needs urgent help." One of the people helping her was Deborah, who was deep in trance while uttering arcane incantations, a powerful green glow of magic pouring from her hands into the body of Gladys. The SFS crew bent down and the medic began to wrap the General with bandages, securing the jagged wooden spear to prevent it doing more damage until it could be safely removed. Deborah sat back, her face grey with fury and desperation. "I have nothing left that I can do, it is up to her now." She whispered as she turned to the King, "stay with her, help her fight."

"I will." He whispered back.

The medic from the SFS issued an order and as one

the team lifted Gladys to lay sideways on a stretcher and then stood up. She still held the King's hand, but her eyes seemed less bright, her face pained and covered with flecks of bloody spray. Then the medic turned to the King. "Can you run Sir?" The King nodded his head. "Good, now we run." Thrashgood watched as the King and his bride left the left the building at a full run. Other medical staff were treating the guests and somehow, none of them were badly hurt, apart from a few cuts and scrapes and a lot of smoke inhalation. Aurora Fireskies found her way to Colonel Thrashgood. "You don't know me, but I can help. I am here with The Nightsouls, they know medicine and healing magic." Thrashgood looked at the young woman. "Aurora, I know your Mother and your girlfriend, come with me, bring all of them with you." Aurora found Ivanka and her Mother, Queen Nightsoul. Mrs Nightsoul was using her healing magic to help Mrs Fireskies who had a nasty cut on her face. Aurora turned to Ivanka, "where is Oleander?"

Ivanka pointed, it was faster than speaking. Oleander was knelt down helping an older guest with a cut hand, she looked up and her eyes met those of Aurora and she smiled. "Nearly there."

Aurora gave a worried smile back, "that Colonel

needs our help with the General."

Oleander put a knot in the bandage and stood up. "On my way."

Collecting Mrs Nightsoul and Ivanka on the way, Aurora and Oleander left the building and met the Colonel outside. He had ordered a soldier to drive them all to the palace on an autocart as fast as possible. Even with the horrible situation that awaited them, the young women found it hard not to be excited by the journey, while Mrs Fireskies and Mrs Nightsoul huddled together in terror, around every corner.

The palace felt cold and unwelcoming when Bobney arrived with Gladys. The grip she had on his hand had weakened to the point that it was hard for him to know if he were holding hers or she holding his. They rushed her through to the medical unit that served the soldiers of the palace and found the Doctor sat at his desk, his face ashen. "I saw it live, I have been waiting for her." He pushed open a cabinet of instruments and began to work on Gladys, he found her pulse, but it was weak and she was going blue with blood loss. Her chest was rising and falling, but little oxygen was getting through to her. A sudden crash at the end of the room was a small team of nurses rushing through the door.

"Sorry that we are late Doctor, we were watching on the TV and came as soon as we saw what happened." The Doctor waved to them and they immediately formed a team and set working on Gladys, rolling her gently almost onto her front as they cut away ragged blood soaked clothing. A few moments later, the door swung open again and Mrs Nightsoul entered. She could smell the blood and she could sense the closeness of death. She barely seemed to move as she crossed the floor like a wraith and stood opposite the King. Her eyes were smouldering black holes of darkness and her fangs seemed to grow from her jaw as she awakened her full vampire powers. Her voice was a harsh lisped whisper, "I am here to offer what magic I have to keep her with you."

At the back of the room, Aurora stood with her Mother, Oleander and Ivanka and then Mrs Nightsoul looked to her daughter, her voice a cold hiss. "Ivanka, I need your help."

Ivanka shook her head, her voice came as a soft, sad lament. "I can't Mum, I gave up that part of me to study science. I don't have it in me anymore."

For a moment, the room darkened as Mrs

Nightsoul's eyes seemed to suck all of the light from the room. "Nonsense child, the magic is tied to your soul, to your heritage. You just need a reminder."

With a reassuring smile from Aurora, Ivanka stepped towards her mother and as she did so, her pretty blonde hair turned raven black and seemed to crawl down her back. Her already smokey dark eyes grew blacker and her fingernails extended into ebony claws.

Oleander watched slightly askew. "Holy shit," she whispered quietly to Aurora, "I had no idea that they had that much power."

Aurora smiled, "the vampires are an ancient and horribly persecuted people, there is a lot that no one but them knows about their culture." She smiled briefly, "I have known Ivanka for nearly fifteen years and there are still so many things I do not know about them."

"Can't she just bite her, make her a vampire?" Asked Oleander.

Muriel Fireskies shook her head. "That is a rather racist, deeply unpleasant human myth. The Vampires are a separate species who are unique to the Fae Realm. You cannot make a Fae into a Vampire."

"Pretty glad I didn't suggest that to them, I would hate to look like an insensitive bigot!" Said Oleander quietly.

"Now is not the time to worry about being insensitive." Hissed Mrs Nightsoul, "all ideas are welcome to save this special young woman, even the dark myths need to be questioned."

Oleander goggled at the old vampire woman. "I didn't know that you could hear so well."

Ivanka looked back and smiled, Aurora had never seen her full vampire heritage before and found that she was comforted by the change in the young woman's appearance, but Oleander was taken aback. The long black hair and the black holes in her face that were her eyes were creepy enough, but the thin lips and large fangs looked terrifying compared to the young blonde woman she had met only hours before. Ivanka grinned. "We have some mind reading abilities too!" She turned back to the dying woman in front of her, and joined hands with her mother who had begun chanting a repetitive and sonorous spell that sounded like it was coming from a demonic lifeform. An eerie glow of flickering purple light seemed to flow from her hands into Gladys.

Meanwhile the Doctor and the nurses were working

hard too. The Doctor called to the head nurse. "Right, let's get this thing out of her back."

"Yes Doctor. Ready." The Doctor tugged the ravaged wooden plank and with a horrible sucking sound it slid free of Gladys' body, which caused her to whimper very slightly. The King glared at the Doctor, his face white with fear. The Doctor gave him a grim smile. "If she can groan, she she's still alive."

Blood began to flow from the wound and the Doctor reaching into the wound and began repairing what he could, cleaning out splinters of wood and other debris from the bomb blast.

With the hall cleared of people and the injured given treatment, Thrashgood had returned to the barracks, he knew that less than a mile away from where he stood, his friends were fighting for the life of one of their number. He wanted to cry, he wanted to yell and he wanted to hit something very, very hard.

He sat at his desk and put his head in his hands, only looking up when he heard the near silent approach of Felicity. Her face was dusty, her pretty dress was tattered and torn in places and she was walking with more of a painful limp than usual. She approached him and without a word stood next to him and put her arms around his shoulders holding his head against her belly. She stood like that for a few minutes, until the pain in her back and legs started to become unbearable and she needed to sit down. Sensing her discomfort, Thrashgood stood up and helped her into his seat and sat on the edge of his desk, where she put her hands into his.

"We've lost good people before, but this hurts so much worse." He said, tears forming in his eyes.

"She's not gone yet." Said Felicity flatly. "She's a warrior, she will fight to the bitter end."

"It's not fair," said Thrashgood quietly. "They did this." He pointed to the files on his desk about the prisoners held in the detention block. A sudden dark thought occurred to him and he picked up the phone and dialled a number. It was answered quickly and he spoke. "It's Thrashgood. Check the status of prisoners. I'll wait." The phone went silent for a moment and then he could hear an alarm sounding and the phone was picked up again.

The voice on the other end was angry and harsh. "All present, one had tried to suicide, but we caught her in time. She was choking on torn clothing. One of the female officers is putting her in a paper suit for her own safety."

Thrashgood let out a sigh that he did not know he was holding in. "Keep me updated and I want them all on constant watch, I want to know when they sleep, move, piss, shit or fart!"

"Sir, yes Sir." Came the tight reply and the call was ended.

"Bad news?" Asked Felicity quietly.

"The woman tried to end herself. The troops got to her in time. Pulled a rag out of her throat."

Felicity blanched, her already grey face looking sickly pale. "Fuck, that's a nasty way to go." For a moment she was silent and then she spoke again, her voice going to a very dark place. "What the fuck are they so afraid of that they would do that?"

"That is what I want to know?"

The phone rang and Thrashgood snatched it up. "Speak!" He barked.

Felicity could not hear the voice on the other end, but she could see that it was not good news by the way Thrashgood sagged.

"We will be there in five, you tell her to fucking wait for us."

He put the phone down and could not hold back the tears. "Bobney wants us there, she's not looking good." Felicity climbed back to her feet, hissing in pain. She had been knocked about quite badly by the blast and the bruising was forming in thick dark patches on her already damaged body, arms and legs. "I can't walk there," she said. Her voice was sad, her face a picture of grief.

"Do you love me?" Said Thrashgood through his tears.

"Yes, with all of my soul." She replied gently.

He carefully picked her up, she had put on a little body fat since stopping her SFS training, as well as losing a fair bit of her muscle mass. However, she was still light and he walked to the door. "It's going to hurt and I'm so sorry for that," he said.

"I know," she said quietly. She kissed his forehead gently "Now run."

About the Authors

These lazy pair of bitches can't be arsed this year can they? It's another story about faerie folk, written by Jan and Jayne. I will admit, there were arguments about the final chapter and Jan is most insistent about what she wants to happen next.
Meanwhile, Jayne is already plotting more nastiness for you all to enjoy.

Anyway, the nice bits of the book were written by Jan and the nasty bits were written by Jayne. Jan is kind, helpful and nice, while Jayne is bitter, spiteful and vicious. They make a great writing pair and keep themselves occupied while poor long suffering Carol has to design the covers and take all of the photographs, as usual.

Also available by the authors

Rambles in Winscombe   &   Bleak Expectations

By Jan Housby and Jayne Hecate

By Jayne Hecate

The Vampyrica Saga

Leticia: Sunset Hunter   &   David Dark Walker

The Cast

King Bobney Wolfgang Jones	The King of the whole Faerie Realm
Queen Linda	Mother of King Bobney
Craig	Husband of Queen Linda
General Gladys Meuchelmorder	General of the entire Faerie Army
Colonel Thrashgood	Leader of the SFS, friend to King Bobney
Felicity Hopeforthebest	Scientist, former SFS operative. Now disabled
Deborah (Mother Nature)	The spiritual embodiment of Mother Nature
The Butler (Brian Butler)	Head Butler, advisor to the King's ear, Master of the household and organiser of Palace duties.
Mr Olajlámpás	Colonel with the SFS. Undercover operative
Professor Brianco Oxx	Master Magician, lives in the former Rusty Plough pub
Professor Sophie Daphodils	The Chancellor of Winscombe University
Wuffles (Prince Hatti)	Hellhound Mayor of Winscombe Prince of the Hellhounds
Princess Rupertina	Royal Dragon and SFS Operative
Major Chinara Adesina	The second in command of the SFS.
Mr Eli Klemp	Displaced Farmer & Royal Adviser
Florence Grim	Head Troll at the Dam building project
Muriel Grindingstone	Young troll apprentice at the Dam project
King Jong the 1st	King of Norfcorea and a master chef who has studied with Wuffles.
Sha Wren Ston	The Chief adviser to King Jong the 1st and his best friend.
Fred Bare Rug	Another of the King's advisers and friends.

Aurora Fireskies	University Student reading diplomacy. Friend of Ivanka, Girlfriend of Oleander

Ivanka Nightsoul	Daughter of Queen Nightsoul, reading science and engineering at university, friend of Aurora
Muriel Fireskies	Winscombe's ambassador to Norfcorea. Mother of Aurora
Oleander Thorntree	Student, Girlfriend of Aurora and future SFS operative
Queen Nightsoul	Queen of the Vampires, Mother of Ivanka
Queen Lupa of the Hellhounds	Queen of the Hellhounds, Mother of Wuffles
Bronwyn	Trans Girl from Hell, now a human metal fan who loves Slayer, friend of Wuffles
Abingdon Gentree	Political reporter with the Quotidian Hail
Reg Singingtrees	Editor Quotidian Hail
Commander X (Gregor the Gremlin)	Gremlin, technological genius and undercover operative with the SFS.
WPC Katie Flouers AKA Katie Flowers	friends with Herbert and Oliver and Deborah
Uncle Herbert	Elderly Uncle of Deborah. Widowed by Oliver
Piotre	Miner captured by the SFS. Translator
The Foreman AKA Otto	The man who ran the team of rogue miners.
Amanda Blutvine	CEO and interloper from the Miners realm
Simeon Whetwissle	CEO and interloper from the Miners realm
Grendal Halftoof	CEO and interloper from the Miners realm
Jeremiah Coldhart	CEO and interloper from the Miners realm

Bye then...

See you next year for more of the same... probably.

Printed in Great Britain
by Amazon

32492175R00195